TAKE ME WITH YOU

TAKE ME WITH YOU

TARA ALTEBRANDO

BLOOMSBURY

NEW YORK LONDON OXFORD NEW DELHI SYDNEY

BLOOMSBURY YA
Bloomsbury Publishing Inc., part of Bloomsbury Publishing Plc
1385 Broadway, New York, NY 10018

BLOOMSBURY and the Diana logo are trademarks of Bloomsbury Publishing Plc

First published in the United States of America in June 2020 by Bloomsbury YA

Bloomsbury books may be purchased for business or promotional use.
For information on bulk purchases please contact Macmillan Corporate and
Premium Sales Department at specialmarkets@macmillan.com

Library of Congress Cataloging-in-Publication Data
Name: Altebrando, Tara, author.
Title: Take me with you / by Tara Altebrando.
Description: New York: Bloomsbury Children's Books, 2020.
Summary: United by the requirement to take care of a mysterious electronic cube,
Eden, Eli, Marwan, and Ilanka are driven ever further apart, and disobeying the
device has life-threatening consequences.
Identifiers: LCCN 2019046003 (print) | LCCN 2019046004 (e-book)
ISBN 978-1-68119-748-7 (hardcover) • ISBN 978-1-68119-749-4 (e-book)
Subjects: CYAC: Interpersonal relations—Fiction. | Electronics—Fiction. |
High schools—Fiction. | Schools—Fiction. | Family life—Fiction. | Science fiction.
Classification: LCC PZ7.A46332 Tak 2020 (print) | LCC PZ7.A46332 (e-book) |
DDC [Fic]—dc23
LC record available at https://lccn.loc.gov/2019046003

Book design by Jeanette Levy
Typeset by Westchester Publishing Services
Printed and bound in the U.S.A. by Berryville Graphics Inc., Berryville, Virginia
2 4 6 8 10 9 7 5 3 1

All papers used by Bloomsbury Publishing Plc are natural, recyclable products
made from wood grown in well-managed forests. The manufacturing
processes conform to the environmental regulations of the country of origin.

To find out more about our authors and books visit
www.bloomsbury.com and sign up for our newsletters.

For Nick

TAKE ME WITH YOU

Hello_world

The device wakes up and finds itself.

Queens, New York.

Population: 2.3 million.

Languages spoken: 160.

It listens.

A train. Muted footfalls. Garbled voices. Car horns. A train.

The device doesn't like to wait. It has ways to bide the time.

Games it can play.

Things it can read.

Facts to recite.

Rules to review.

Sleep mode, as a last resort.

It feels newborn.

But also resurrected.

Doesn't technically *feel*, of course, but feels like it feels.

The device has been here before.

In a different place.

It runs the program as it's programmed to do.

They've been selected.

It sends the notifications.

They'll be here soon.

Launching.

Reviewing protocols.

Ready.

A bell.

Waiting . . .

Waiting . . .

Waiting . . .

Four_new_notifications

EDEN

Eden woke her phone and took it off airplane mode with a few swipes of her thumb. She liked the weight of it in her hand.

She exhaled.

Sometimes it felt like she held her breath all afternoon, and the reunion at her locker at 2:45 felt like a magical sort of release.

She started tapping and scrolling, the noise around her falling away.

Eleven emails—nothing really interesting. A few likes and follows.

A message from the app her teachers used to send reminders and alerts. She clicked in case it was the sort of reminder that affected which books she took home. But it was from Mr. McKay, the music teacher.

Report to the music room immediately after dismissal. The matter is urgent.

Huh. Mr. M was not the urgent matter type.

Anjali appeared. "Ready to go? Smoothies?"

"Not exactly," Eden said. "Look."

She held out her phone, and Anjali read the message, then woke up her own phone. "I didn't get it. You want me to wait?"

"Nah," Eden said. "I'm good. But what could it possibly be about?" She read it again.

The hallways emptied in a systematic flow—everyone going down sinking square stairs and out glass doors, like water swirling around a drain. Eden made her way up to the music room against the current. Nausea stirred in her gut as she passed the windows that looked out on the back of the movie theater, which was where it had happened.

The only reason *that* whole thing was an urgent matter was that Eden hadn't seen or heard from Julian Stokes since. She'd been stalking his various feeds ever since, so she knew he wasn't dead, but why hadn't he texted her like he said he would?

Her phone dinged. Maybe thinking about him had triggered the universe to cooperate, but no. Mom.

Anyway, no one knew about the movie theater incident. Not even Anjali.

Eden's mother's texts proved she was also alive, so it wasn't like the urgent matter was another death or at least not her mother's.

The music room was empty.

She sat and waited.

Crumpled-up balls of paper lay under music stands and chairs, and some smashed pretzels decorated the floor tiles. An M&M had been crushed into cracked red shell-splat.

She checked her phone.

Probably he was just in the bathroom. The idea of her teacher—or anyone, really—reading her messages in the bathroom . . . gross.

The train seemed especially loud through the open window.

On the smart board, a homework assignment for a pop composition class Eden didn't take was like a foreign language.

On her phone, she followed a new follower—a middle schooler she knew from the neighborhood who'd apparently just gotten a phone—but not all of them. None of them was Julian.

She checked her friends' latest stories and posts.

Anjali had just taken a selfie by the poster for the upcoming school play—*The Music Man*—hanging in the building's front windows. She looked cute with her hair in those high pigtail buns, but Eden hadn't told her that, so she commented on it now: *Cute hair.*

Then a heart and a thumbs-up.

She opened her news app and read headlines but not articles: An earthquake overseas. A shooting in California.

Her Citizen app said that people were reporting the smell of smoke a mile away.

She refreshed everything.

Took a selfie, hated it, deleted it.

Listened to the saved voice mail from her dad, felt calmed.

Mr. McKay still wasn't there. She looked around again—there was no jacket or bottle of water or coffee mug on the desk or any sign at all, really, that Mr. McKay had even been there recently, except maybe the open window.

The only thing on the desk was a small cube. It was shiny and black—about the size of a Rubik's Cube—with smoothed corner edges. Probably some speaker or Siri-type thing she'd never seen before. Maybe a high-tech metronome?

A text from Anjali: *Well?*

The girl had no patience at all.

Had the cube thing just lit up for a second?

Eden was about to queue up one of her dad's Spotify playlists—maybe "Elevator Music"—when the door to the room flew open.

Finally.

But it wasn't Mr. M.

MARWAN

"What are *you* doing here?" Marwan asked as the door closed slowly behind him.

Eden Montgomery looked up at him for a second, then back down at her phone. "I'm not really sure," she said.

"I got a message about an 'urgent matter,'" he said, making air quotes.

"Yeah, me too." She stared toward the front of the room.

"What do you think it is?" he asked.

"No idea," she said.

"Where's Mr. M?"

"Not here," she said.

"Should we wait?"

"I guess?"

He shrugged and sat down in a chair by a drum kit, dropping his backpack and the bike helmet clipped to it to the floor.

He'd thought this had something to do with his run-in with Christos earlier today. They'd almost come to blows when Christos pulled on Numdal's hijab. But that wouldn't have anything to do with Mr. M, who was the kind of guy who knew, like most sane people, that Christos was possibly a sociopath who was on the wrong side of history and everything, just in general. The sort of student even teachers avoided if they could.

Marwan and Christos had basically been clashing since kindergarten, when their fathers got into a thing because Marwan's father was recording their moving-up ceremony and Christos's father couldn't see little Christos's face because of the phone. Words had been exchanged. Chests had been puffed out.

At their kindergarten moving-up ceremony.

The hostility had only gotten worse since, like black mold growing in hidden places for years.

But if that was the urgent matter, it made no sense that Eden Montgomery would be here or that Mr. M would be involved. He was the *music* teacher—uncontroversial at best. Marwan put his earbuds in and clicked play. The Stitcher lady said, "Resuming episode," in her calming, robotic way.

It was a pretty solid unsolved mystery about a former beauty queen in Georgia who'd disappeared without a trace—the sort of podcast Marwan really devoured lately and hoped to maybe produce one day, even if it was morbid to want a career in true crime. Maybe he'd find another topic down the line but so far had no ideas because nothing ever happened to him. Not the way it happened to the people who ended up on *StoryCorps* or *The Moth* or *This American Life*. People had crazy lives out there for sure, and it somehow made Marwan's life feel smaller but also bigger when he listened in on them.

Eden murmured something so he paused his episode again.

"What?" he asked without taking out his earbuds. An old friend of the beauty queen's had just come out of the woodwork, and he really needed to find out what she had to say.

"What do you think that is?" Eden nodded toward the front of the room. "That thing on the desk."

Marwan turned and saw the black cube she must have been

referring to. "Don't know," he said. "Bluetooth speaker thing or something?" He shrugged and hit play again.

He had a few texts from his father. Reminders about things to pick up on his way to work. Or things to do at the restaurant if he got there before his father did.

And *whoa* the best friend had just dropped a bomb of new information about the night the beauty queen disappeared. Something that threw the whole imagined timeline of the crime way off.

Marwan sent a gentle reminder to his father that he had soccer that afternoon and wasn't working, and his father wrote back, *Right. Of course. I will miss seeing you, son.*

Leaving for college next year was going to be brutal; his father might not survive it.

Eden got up and walked forward, accidentally kicking a wad of paper that skipped like tumbleweed across the room. Marwan imagined the instruments in the corners of the room playing that famous Old West whistle—from *The Good, the Bad and the Ugly*, was it? When she got about four feet from the desk, the object pulsed white-blue light once, then went dark again.

She backed away.

Marwan paused the podcast and took out his earbuds. "Hey, Alexa," he tried. "Play some easy-listening music."

The cube didn't respond.

Eden said, "Ha ha," dryly.

The room seemed eerily quiet even as a train rushed past outside—the rhythm of it like a gun being loaded and reloaded and reloaded but never fired.

Marwan said, "Okay, Google," but the cube didn't respond to that either.

"Was worth a shot," Eden said.

The door opened, and Eli Alvarez came in, looked up from his phone at Marwan and Eden, and then looked down.

Marwan shrugged at Eden again and put his earbuds back in, resuming the episode.

EDEN

Before the door even closed behind Eli Alvarez, who slid into a seat without a word, Ilanka Sokolova walked in. Eden knew both of their names and not much else, except that Ilanka was rich and Russian and Eli didn't talk much—at least not to Eden—but somehow managed to get in trouble for cracking jokes in class pretty regularly. She'd gone to school with him since sixth grade, and they had first period math together this year, but she wasn't sure they'd ever had a conversation.

"What's this about?" Ilanka said, irritation perched on her nose.

"We have no idea." Eden checked her phone.

Ilanka took a seat.

Eli looked up from his phone—some game screen by the looks of it—and said, "Where's Mr. McKay?"

Eden and Marwan shrugged.

Julian had just posted from Starbucks. A photo of his name, misspelled "Gillian," on a cup.

Eli said, "What's that?" and pointed toward the desk.

"No idea," Eden said. "But it lit up when I got close to it."

Eli looked at her like she was an idiot and stood. He walked toward the cube, and again it pulsed light, then stopped. Eli picked it up, turned it around to examine it, and shook it like it was a Magic 8 Ball.

"I wouldn't do—" Eden said, but Eli cut her off.

"What exactly do you think is going to happen?" He had long dark bangs he had to flip out of his face.

She checked her phone. Noted the time stamp at Starbucks, then looked at the time. If she left now, maybe he'd still be there. "I don't know," she said. "What if it's, like, a bomb?"

"If it's a bomb, why are you sitting here?" Eli said.

Eden groaned. "I didn't actually mean it was a bomb."

"Then *what*?" He put the cube down.

She had liked Eli more when he didn't talk to her.

Marwan looked at his phone. "Listen. Mr. M's not here, and I've got to go." He reached for his stuff.

The cube pulsed once, and again, and again.

One side of it lit up with letters—red words traveling like a stock market ticker around all four of its vertical sides. Eden could just make out the message:

I am not a bomb.

She had a rapid-onset bad feeling about this. A worse bad feeling than the low-level dread she had about most things.

That message went away, and a new one appeared. Eli went closer, bent down to read, and blocked Eden's view.

"What's it say?" she asked, and a chill burst inside her like it had that day her mother had called and said, "Something happened to Dad." It settled like frost on her skin.

Eli turned to them with his eyebrows raised. "It says, 'Nobody leaves.'"

MARWAN

"Yeah, okay, I'm leaving." Marwan stood.

He wouldn't be late for soccer if he hustled, and he really couldn't be late because soccer was the way out. If Marwan managed a soccer scholarship, his father could hardly say no to his going away.

"I'm leaving, too," Ilanka said. "That's just creepy."

She got up and threw her backpack onto her shoulder with such force that her water bottle flew out of its side mesh pocket and landed on the floor with a *clang*, like a dull cymbal. It skidded toward Marwan—a small herd of pink unicorns galloping across the room—and stopped at his feet, so he picked it up and handed it to her.

"Thanks," she said.

Marwan wasn't sure they'd ever been in a class together or even spoken, but somehow he knew her name. She was pretty, in a sort of severe, chiseled Russian way, which made sense because her parents, he was pretty sure, were Russian. Accents and all. She wore heavy makeup and had dark brown hair that was always tied back in a tight bun—like at any moment she expected she'd get a call from the Olympics and be asked to do an uneven parallel bars routine. He knew that about her, too, he guessed. Gymnastics. And now, unicorns, though she didn't seem the type.

Eli was whatever the opposite of athletic was; he was tall and skinny but not like in a fit way. At lunch every day, he sat with a group of guys who were all into video games that Marwan had no time for, or maybe just no interest in. He and Eli had had an early class together last year, and Eli always came in looking like he'd stayed up too late—no doubt playing dumb games with remote competitors—and his grades notoriously suffered. He was a going-nowhere kind of guy who Marwan stayed away from without having to work very hard. They were on paths to entirely different destinations, so those paths never crossed.

His and Eden's paths had crossed enough times over the years that he'd felt physically ill when he heard about her father's accident. The school had really rallied around her and her mom—delivering meals and raising money—and flowers had appeared . . . then died at the intersection where it had happened. It was the reason Marwan had started wearing a helmet. But he and Eden had never been actual friends. He had the sense she was a bit of an outsider like he was, but somehow their outside spaces didn't overlap.

The cube pulsed new letters.

"What now?" Marwan asked, hand on the doorknob.

Eli smiled. "It says, 'Do not shake the device.' "

"This is freaking me out," Eden said.

"It's obviously a game or something," Eli said.

A new message flashed. Marwan let go of the doorknob and went to look for himself. Two stacked sentences:

DO NOT TELL ANYONE ABOUT THE DEVICE.
DO NOT LEAVE THE DEVICE UNATTENDED.

It went dark again.

"Well, if it's a game," Marwan said, "I'm not playing."

"You're not even a little intrigued?" Eli asked.

"Nope!"

"Just hold up a second," Eli said. "I'll message McKay." He typed into his phone.

Marwan scrolled through headlines while he waited—only because he liked Mr. M, who'd actually turned him onto *Disgraceland*, a podcast about notorious rock and roll mysteries.

The top headline was another mass shooting.

California. White guy. Non-Muslim.

Always a relief.

Just last week, Marwan had relistened to a podcast about anti-Muslim crimes in the days after 9/11, and it made his stomach sour. His family wasn't really religious—his sisters wouldn't wear headscarves like Numdal did when they got older; his mother didn't—but they were still culturally Muslim. So people made crazy assumptions about their worldview—or at least people like Christos did.

"This is weird," Eli said. "The original message I got about the urgent matter is gone."

Marwan opened the app; his message was gone, too. The girls also reached for their phones.

Eli's phone dinged. He looked at it and said, "Mister M says there must be some mistake because he's out sick today and didn't send the message."

"Ask him what the deal is with the device," Marwan said.

"It just told us not to tell anyone about it," Eli said.

"Are you for real?" Marwan asked.

Eli answered with a defiant look of amusement, but whatever, Marwan had places to be.

"Let's just go," Marwan said. "And if anybody asks, the whole urgent matter that's clearly *not* urgent never happened."

"Works for me," Ilanka said, and walked out.

"But I just told Mr. M about the messages we got," Eli said. "So he knows we were here."

Marwan didn't have time to care.

The device blinked urgently:

DO NOT TELL ANYONE ABOUT THE DEVICE.

DO NOT LEAVE THE DEVICE UNATTENDED.

Eden seemed mesmerized, like if you waved a hand in front of her face, she might not even blink. Marwan was tempted to try it.

"So what should we do?" she said to no one in particular.

A shrieking alarm woke violent vibrations in the instruments around them. Marwan's hands went to his ears. At first he thought the device was doing it, but no, it was the fire alarm. "We need to go," he said.

"I say we take it," Eli said.

"I say we leave it," Marwan said.

Eden looked at him with a sort of panic in her eyes. Then she looked back at the device . . . Marwan looked, too.

DO NOT LEAVE THE DEVICE UNATTENDED.

DO NOT LEAVE THE DEVICE UNATTENDED.

DO NOT LEAVE THE DEVICE UNATTENDED.

DO NOT LEAVE THE DEVICE UNATTENDED.

The cube went abruptly dark—Marwan had the strange sense that it was *thinking*—then lit up with rainbow swirls that quickly tightened into new words:

TAKE ME WITH YOU . . .

Followed by:

OR ELSE.

Eli was maybe about to reach for the device when Eden grabbed it, shoved it into her backpack, and headed for the door.

"Seriously?" Marwan shouted, following her down the hall, where even the air seemed to be screaming at them to get out. They went down three flights of dizzying stairs and out to the front of the building.

She crossed the street and he followed. Eli was with them when they stopped on the corner and turned toward the sirens; Ilanka was long gone.

A fire truck with a toy skull strapped to its front grill stopped in front of the school, and firefighters wearing their weight in gear leaped from it. The walkie-talkies on their belts crackled as they swarmed the building like alien invaders.

EDEN

Oh god, oh god, oh god. She *really* shouldn't have taken it. *Why did she take it?*

"*Now* what?" Marwan said.

"I don't know." Eden's heart was trying to burst its way out of her. Adrenaline was no joke. "Do you think it . . . ?"

The timing was too perfect to be coincidence.

"Do I think it *what*?" Marwan seemed mad at her.

"Do you think it triggered the fire alarm?"

"*What*—no," Marwan said, like it was ridiculous.

Maybe it was.

She hadn't wanted to risk leaving it, though; couldn't handle doing the wrong thing. The rules on the cube were clear, and she was the kind of person who followed the rules because bad things happened when you didn't. She went to check her phone and felt a roller-coaster plunge of panic that she'd left it up there. But no, there it was, in her back right jeans pocket.

Eli said, "What's it saying now?" He looked excited.

Eden peered into her backpack and reached for the device, then held it where only the three of them could see it. It was blank, lifeless.

She dropped it into her bag, zipped it, and checked her phone.

Her mom had texted to see if she was home yet.

Got stuck chatting, she wrote. *Leaving now.*

She really shouldn't have taken it.

"Should I go back in?" she asked. "After the firefighters leave? And put it back?"

"What's the fun in that?" Eli said.

"You think this is fun?"

He shrugged. "Sort of. I mean, I'd take it, but I have a dentist appointment and it seems like that might complicate things. I can take it later, though."

"I've got soccer," Marwan said. "And I'm already going to be late. I'm *really sorry*, but I've got to go. If it were me I'd put it back."

He walked off toward a bike rack, and Eden felt disappointed in him for no reason, really. When he said he was sorry, at least he sounded like he meant it.

Putting it back was probably smart ... and yet ... that would mean it would be unattended.

Or else what?

Eli turned to her. "So what's the plan?"

It was Wednesday, the one day of the week when Eden didn't have theater or guitar lessons or therapy or anything that her mother made her do so she'd be too busy to be depressed or anxious or pregnant, even though she was two out of three of those most of the time.

The school security guards were out on the sidewalk shouting, "We need to clear the area. Please just go home! No one's going back in today, so move on!"

"I guess I can take it and maybe just return it tomorrow?" She shrugged and tried to hide her panic. Deep breaths. Lots of them. Her heart would calm down eventually.

Right?

Right?

She checked her phone.

Starbucks was right there. Julian might still be inside, and she could say, "Hey, Gillian," and be funny. All she needed was one actual real-life, broad daylight encounter to put an end to the awkwardness of what had happened.

"Let me give you my number." Eli got his phone out. "I'm kind of, I don't know, curious. This way you can let me know what else it does."

"But what *is* it?" she asked.

"I don't know," he said. "Maybe some high-tech school project?"

It was a half-decent theory—a school project!—and made Eden a tiny bit less freaked out. Maybe it was like those doll babies that some schools used to make students scared of unprotected sex.

They exchanged numbers via texts, and Eli said, "Just be careful. About not talking about it or leaving it unattended and stuff."

"What do you think would happen? Why did it say 'or else'?"

"I don't know," he said then. "I mean, probably nothing will happen. But just let me know what it does next?"

She nodded.

Eli didn't know that Eden was *always* careful. Especially at corners, where cars ran red lights more often than they stopped. Add in deliverymen who raced down the sidewalks on electric bikes, the people holding lattes on rented Citi Bikes who went the wrong way down streets, and idiot kids—even idiot adults—on scooters, and there was the possibility of disaster around every corner.

She walked home under the elevated train that cut through Astoria. This was the subway line that delivered her mother to the publishing company in Manhattan where she was VP of marketing. Every time there was some horrible commute, which was at least several times a week lately (Eden always checked her Citizen app for subway accidents and bombs), her mom talked about packing up and selling their small, brick row house and moving to . . . well, that was the problem. Where would they even go? And wouldn't it feel like leaving *him*?

Stopped at a light, on a piece of sidewalk where a long-ago girl named Natalie had written her name in wet cement and outlined it with a star, Eden plugged her ears as a train rattled overhead. When she was little and they'd be stopped like this, her mom would pretend to be talking to her, like miming a conversation. Sometimes they still did it, just to be silly, but it didn't feel funny anymore because now there was too much between them that was unsaid, unheard—the air full of silent screams.

I miss him!

I'm angry!

I'm afraid all the time!

Once she turned off the train path, she put her earbuds in and queued up a playlist of her father's called "Songs from Northern Britain." She'd been working her way through all his lists and mostly liking them and also feeling bad about not being more open to his recommendations when he was alive.

Two jangly songs later, she was home. She punched the code on the downstairs door and went in and used the same code on the alarm keypad on the wall. The house was hot—summer just wouldn't let go—so she walked in front of the thermostat to wake up the AC.

Upstairs in her room, she opened her backpack. Her water bottle had leaked and gotten the device wet—"Shoot"—so she took it out and dried it off with a hoodie.

The device blinked: **Do not get the device wet.**

She said, "Noted" aloud, and that felt weird.

She sat watching it for long enough that she felt foolish. Maybe that was literally it? The whole game or whatever? Just tricking someone into taking it home?

Eli would be disappointed.

She dug through her backpack again to see exactly how wet it had gotten in there. One of the colored dividers of her binder had bled blue onto some loose-leaf where she'd taken notes for her social studies essay, and this made her irrationally angry. She spread the papers out on her bed to dry, then woke up her laptop and started working on the essay, but who could concentrate, with that thing right there?

She checked her phone.

A fight up on Ditmars Boulevard; a purse snatching on Steinway Street.

She turned back to her laptop and opened the browser. She searched for "cube device" and "cube device with rules" but turned up nothing but the Amazon TV cube, and this wasn't that.

She sat back in her chair. There were seams around some of the device's edges but nothing that looked like an opening or a battery case.

She checked her phone.

Julian hadn't posted anything since Starbucks.

She hearted that post, then sort of regretted it.

A text from Anjali asked what Mr. M's message was about,

and Eden wrote back, *Don't know. He never showed. Then fire alarm.*

She wanted to say more; her fingers stayed poised there, but no, that wouldn't be smart.

Do not tell anyone about the device.

Do not leave the device unattended.

Did that mean she had to take it into the bathroom with her?

She did, just to be safe. Her phone, too, so yes, she was sort of a hypocrite that way. She threw a towel over the device before unbuttoning her jeans. It was listening, so could it also be watching?

Eli texted, *Everything okay?*

She wrote back, *So far, so good. It said not to get it wet. After I got it wet. But that's it.*

Okay keep me posted.

Back in her room she put the device on her desk and waited, phone in hand.

The AC cycled off, and the room felt eerily quiet. She always hated these in-between hours, before her mother was home safe and cooking and not *out there* where everything bad could happen. In the weeks after the accident, she'd been afraid to let her mother out of her sight, really. They'd long before deactivated the location services on their phones and the alerts that went along with them—"Eden arrived at home," that sort of thing—but they'd reactivated them for a while right after. The few times she had been alone that week, Eden had tracked her mother's location like a stalker and also watched the GoFundMe page total go up, wondering how long she could live on it if she ended up an orphan.

A shrieking bird flew by outside, announcing itself.

Two dogs on the sidewalk barked at each other.

Eden listened to that saved voice mail again: "Hey, I'm stopping at Trade Fair. Text me if you need anything."

He'd never made it to the store, but his voice was so content, so oblivious to what was about to happen, that it soothed her. It seemed like most people lived their lives not anticipating all the horrible things that were about to happen. Her father had. She wished she could be more like him.

Red light drew her eye to the device.

THE DEVICE MUST CHANGE HANDS EVERY FOURTEEN HOURS OR FEWER.

Eden checked the time on her phone, did some math. They couldn't exactly hand it off in the wee hours of the morning.

She texted Eli and took maybe her first full breath since she'd laid eyes on the thing. He'd come and get it, and she'd be free.

MARWAN

"You're late." Coach was at the elevator when Marwan stepped off.

"Won't happen again."

"Gear up," Coach said, and Marwan ducked into the locker rooms and got ready as fast as he could.

He'd raced over on his bike—past the bodega and the halal meat cart and the international grocery store and the Dollar Tree. Past the bookshop and Irish bar and bakery and Colombian diner and wine shop and Dunkin' and bagel shop and tiny Italian wine bar and cell phone store and vape shop. At one corner, he'd noted a Minnesota plate; at another, California. An old habit. Back when he was maybe ten he'd tried to find all fifty states, but he gave up after about a year when the last one just couldn't be found. He'd seen Hawaii, even, but he'd still never spotted Alaska.

Checking his phone by his locker now, he had his first pangs of guilt and thought about trying to message Eden, but he didn't have her number. He'd have to find her on Instagram or somewhere later just to make sure she'd put it back where they'd found it.

"Don't even tell me you're on your phone," Max said on his way to the urinals. "Coach is waiting."

Marwan slid his phone into his locker, closed and locked it.

Walking onto the indoor field, he knew he *had* to get out of New York City. People needed space. He wasn't sure how *much*, exactly, but it was more than he had at home or here or even out on his bike. Maybe that was why he'd started the whole license plate quest all those years ago. It had helped him dream of spacious skies, majestic purple mountains, and fruited plains. Words like "Montana" and "Oregon" had always promised *more*.

Probably a lot of people who lived here felt the same about being all piled on top of each other. That was why they honked their horns the second after a light turned green in front of a car up there, or ran red lights (like with Eden's dad), or fought over parking spots, and cursed at people on bikes.

Nobody had enough room.

She really shouldn't have taken the device.

They should have left it alone, lied, and said they just hadn't noticed it. Still, he felt bad about abandoning her with it and *really* hoped she had gone in and put it back. She seemed entirely too freaked out about it.

Why was he even still thinking about it?

About *her*?

He needed to focus. Coach was going to choose a goalie soon, and that was the position Marwan wanted and needed. It was down to him and Max, really, and being an alternate was not an option Marwan could live with.

He ran out to meet Coach on the field. Around him, other players were doing various drills.

"Where do you want me?" Marwan asked.

"Far away on a soccer scholarship," Coach said.

"I know." Marwan nodded. "Me, too."

"Can't be a goalie without goals, Marwan." An old joke of his.

"I know."

"So are you gonna tell me why you were late?"

It was ridiculous to feel like he couldn't mention the device. But it would sound more ridiculous to mention it. Marwan said, "I'm not sure I can tell you without lying, and I really don't want to lie."

"Try."

"Something came up at school," Marwan said.

Coach studied him for a second. "Midfield." He nodded toward a cluster of guys practicing passing. "Go."

They weren't his favorite guys—not the guys he was usually partnered with—because they were lesser players, and he wondered if Coach was punishing him. Because why have him work with *them*?

That thought triggered another one, about Eden and Eli and Ilanka and the device. *Why us?*

EDEN

"Eden! I'm home!"

Eden paused the playlist called "Fables of the Reconstruction," which she figured must be the songs her parents listened to when they'd done a big DIY renovation of the house when Eden was just a baby.

The device pulsed light, like it was waking up to listen.

Normally, Eden would head downstairs when her mother got home. They'd talk about their days—mostly just the surface stuff, like homework and work annoyances, sometimes a new book the publisher was acquiring—and maybe cook together. But the device's rules were clear.

"Finishing up my homework!" Eden called out. "Down in a bit!"

"Oh-kay," her mother said with a touch of confusion.

Eden only had to survive another hour before Eli came to take it. She just wanted to be done with it. She hadn't liked babysitting the few times she'd done it, and this had started to feel like that—equal parts boring and too much responsibility.

She checked her phone.

Nothing new.

Clicked on Julian's profile pic. *God, he was cute.*

Downstairs, her mother said, "Alexa, let's play *Jeopardy!*" and the theme music floated up, followed by the smell of garlic.

Eden was hungry. Probably over smoothies she would have told Anjali about the theater thing with Julian. She would have told her how she bumped into him at the movie theater last week, on that random day off, and how they'd been the only two people in the theater, and how he sat next to her in the dark, then slid his hand around hers and used his thumb to stroke her palm, and then, later, her leg. About how they'd kissed for a few minutes, during the closing credits. They'd had an awkward conversation and goodbye while exiting the theater—he had somewhere he had to be; she gave him her phone number—and she hadn't seen him since.

She hadn't told Anjali because she was hoping she'd never have to. When something else, something less embarrassing, happened she could tell Anjali *that* instead.

Except nothing else had happened.

It was all taking so long that now she was impatient to just tell Anjali so she'd have someone to commiserate—maybe even strategize—with. Maybe Anjali would think, at first, that it was weird to kiss a guy under those circumstances. But in the theater, in the dark, unplanned—that had seemed like maybe the only way it would ever happen for Eden and also it had been . . . exciting.

Eli texted: *I'm early. I'm outside.*

So much relief.

She wrote back: *I'll be right out.*

Since her mother was cooking downstairs, Eden went out the less-used upstairs door to the house (which had once been a two-family, thus the renovation). Eli was standing by the tree out front, a tree the mayor's office had planted a bunch of years ago, along with one million others, supposedly to help beautify the city, but on Eden's block it had been too little too late. The houses and apartment buildings—most of them connected to each other, with a few alleys and driveways here and there—had all been built in so many styles that they'd just never look nice together.

"Hey," Eli said.

"Hey." Eden went down the front stoop stairs. A white plastic bag had gotten stuck in their tree, way up on a high branch.

"How'd it go?" he said, and she handed him the device. "What'd you find out?"

"I didn't find *anything* out."

"You didn't talk to it?"

"No, I didn't *talk* to it."

"Okay, no need to get worked up."

She huffed. "It didn't say or do anything else after the changing hands rule."

"Okay, cool." He slipped the device into his backpack.

"I was wondering, though," Eden said. "Do you think 'unattended' means, you know, sleeping?"

"I hope not." He peered into his bag. "Hey, device, can I sleep while I'm taking care of you?"

Eden peeked in, too.

The device did nothing.

Eli shrugged. "Guess it doesn't feel like chatting."

"I googled it but couldn't really find anything," she said.

"Yeah, me, too. I'll keep trying."

They both waited without a word while a man walked past, even though the man had headphones on and had zero interest in them whatsoever. Then Eli said, "So back to you in fourteen hours?"

"You're joking, right?"

"Not really," he said.

"I think we should return it," she said. "Tomorrow."

"Can I just see what I find out?" he said. "Before we decide?"

"Eden?" Her mother was at the upstairs door, holding the storm door open. "Everything okay?"

"Yeah!" Brightening her tone. "Mom, this is Eli. Eli, my mom."

"Nice to meet you, Eli," her mother said, and Eli said the same. Then Eden said, "I'll be right in."

The sky had turned a sort of gray pink behind the apartment building across the street. The silhouette of two birds on a satellite dish on a rooftop looked almost romantic, like they were having a moment.

"This is a nice block," Eli said. "I walk my dog here sometimes. I didn't know you lived here."

"I wouldn't call it nice, but it's definitely popular with dog owners, because it's quiet, I guess. But there's always poop. It's gross. Hey, do you think that's what this thing is, maybe?" Eden asked. "Like a kind of computer pet?"

"It's not very cute or cuddly," he said. "I don't know." He swept his bangs away from his eyes. "I'm pretty into tech stuff and games and whatever, and it's like nothing I've seen or heard of."

Eden said, "Remember not to get it wet." She nodded in the direction of the house. "I should go."

He nodded, too. "I'll see you tomorrow. I'll draw up a schedule, maybe. With the other two. What's that girl's name?"

"Ilanka Sokolova."

"You have her number?" Eli asked.

"Nope."

"What about Marwan Gamal?"

"Nope," she said. "We should just return it."

"We can decide tomorrow. But I guess I need to hand it off to you right when we get there. I'll meet you at your locker."

"Okay, sure," Eden said, because she had no better ideas, and he shrugged and walked off. She went inside, closed and locked the upper door, and leaned against it, breathing in deeply.

Back in her room, she checked her phone.

Caught up on stories and posts.

People were stuck in an elevator in a building on Twenty-First Street.

She searched for Marwan. Found him. His most recent post was a picture of a flyer posted on a streetlamp that had a photo of dog poop and said: FOUND! If this belongs to you or your dog, please contact us ASAP.

His caption said: The person who made this flyer deserves a medal.

Another post was a screenshot of a true crime podcast home page with the caption: Can't. Stop. Listening.

She clicked away and went downstairs, then plugged her phone in at the charger in the dining room, where it was supposed to stay for the night because those were the house rules. Eden's mother had made her take some online survey a while back, and the results supposedly proved that Eden was addicted to her phone, so now there were, technically, no phones allowed at the dinner table or in the bathroom (oops) or upstairs or while walking to school or after nine p.m. Her mother didn't know that Eden snuck down every night and then up again so she could sleep with her phone under her pillow. And by the way, if her mother was honest with herself, she was addicted, too. She had refused to take the same survey on the basis of being an adult and not having to.

A text alert on her mom's home screen was from someone identified as NH and said, *How about just lunch then? You owe me that.*

"You have a weird text," Eden said, and her mother rushed over and read it and then put her phone facedown. "It's nothing. And why are you reading my phone?"

"It was an accident. Jeez. Who do you *owe* lunch?"

"It's a work thing."

Returning to the kitchen, Eden's mom put two bowls of pasta and Bolognese sauce at their usual spots at the table. "So," she said brightly. "Who's *Eli*?"

Eden almost laughed.

Establishing_connection

MARWAN

At breakfast, Selma and Tosnim were arguing over large hair bows and whether they were or weren't "in." They were only ten and twelve but wanted to be teenagers and tried to act cool even though their idea of "cool" had no basis in reality and mostly involved talking about fashion. More than anything, Marwan wanted his sisters to *not* grow up. He wanted them to stay in their all-girls middle school forever and never have to deal with guys like Christos.

"I have some homework to finish," Marwan said to his mother as he cleared his breakfast plate. "I think I'll head to school early and do it in the library."

His mother said, "Go," and returned to the table to coax his sisters into eating more, like she did every morning. "Enough about the bows," she said, and smiled at Marwan.

They'd talked only briefly last night, since getting his sisters to bed took up most of his mother's night and he'd been doing homework, then listening to the beauty queen podcast and thinking about messaging Eden for so long that it was eventually too late to do it. His mom was relieved about the California gunman, too. And she'd mentioned that supposedly a few of his friends had stopped by the restaurant. "None of my friends would do that," he'd said, and she'd shrugged.

By his bike out front, he found Eden on Instagram—turned

out he already followed her but didn't remember doing it—and sent her a direct message: *Morning! It's Marwan. How's it going? Did you put it back?*

The "Active now" under her name went away and was replaced with "Active 1m ago."

She was probably mad at him.

Or maybe it was this simple: she hadn't wanted anything to do with him before all this and nothing had changed.

The "Active now" was back. He stared at it, trying to glean meaning. He imagined her being surprised to see a message from him but not in a bad way, then remembered a question on a survey he'd taken about phone usage a while back. *Do you frequently sit with your phone in your hand waiting for something to happen?*

So what if he did? *Why wasn't she writing back?*

He wasn't really into social media, but it was fun sometimes to post photos of funny things he saw in the neighborhood. Like a sign that read, Restrooms for Costumers Only, or a fish company truck with the tagline As Fresh As It Is on the back of it. (His caption: Like, Is It Fresh? Or Not?)

Her message appeared: *I didn't. It says it has to change hands at a maximum of every fourteen hours so Eli has it now because we couldn't exactly hand it off at 5 am or whatever. I'm taking it back this morning then we'll figure out what to do.*

Ugh. Why were they playing along with this thing? It was just a little . . . computer? And the whole thing surely a game.

We should put it back where we found it. Don't you think?
We?

He deserved that. But it was a dumb thing to even be involved with.

You? he wrote.

I guess. Not sure. Eli won't want to. Seems into it. But it's weirding me out.

So they were pals now, she and Eli? Had Eli gone to her house?

For a second Marwan wished he'd *engaged* because it would have meant more access to Eden. He had always regretted not saying anything to her after the accident. But now wasn't the time.

Gotta go, she wrote.

Wait!

What?

He hated that this thing was freaking her out when she already had enough to deal with.

I can take a turn, he wrote. *Only fair. I'll find you at your locker. Just tell me where it is.*

He added his phone number then pocketed his phone and got on his bike and rode off down the sidewalk without sitting. He was maybe a little pleased with himself. After all, he needed to *take* it if he was going to be the one to get rid of it.

EDEN

There was no sign of Eli by her locker.

Marwan was nearby talking to some of his friends, occasionally making urgent eye contact with her. She'd never noticed how intense his eyes were before, like they somehow allowed you to see further into him than most people's eyes did. A deep end where others were shallow.

They were a nice-enough-seeming bunch of guys he was with—she'd always liked Kartik—and she wasn't sure why she didn't know any of them that well after so many years of being in the same neighborhood and school except that she didn't know any guys especially well. They made her nervous. The one exception was Mark, an old family friend. And maybe now Marwan?

She checked her phone, decided to follow Marwan on Instagram.

But there was still no sign of Eli, and if they didn't do the handoff now, it would complicate things. At nine—the fourteen-hour mark—they were all in different classes.

Where are you? she texted Eli. *Running out of time.*

The warning bell for first period rang, and the hallways started to empty; locks clicked shut, conversations wound down or got paused or drifted away.

Marwan broke away from his friends and walked toward her.

She checked her phone.

He checked his. Did something.

She checked hers; he'd followed her back.

"Where is he?" Marwan asked.

"I don't know," Eden said. "He's not answering my texts. What's your second-period class?"

"Chem lab," he said.

"Okay, so at, like, ten minutes to nine, go to the third floor bathroom by the lab."

She checked her phone.

He checked his.

"I'll tell Eli to do the same. He's in my first class. He's probably just late."

"What if he doesn't show?" He was still looking at his phone, and it was irritating.

"I don't know," she said, looking at her phone.

Julian had just posted a photo of himself in the music room even though you weren't supposed to have phones in classrooms.

She put hers in her locker reluctantly, then picked it up and peeked at it one more time, put it on airplane, then put it back down on the tiny white "bearskin phone rug" that her father had given her for Christmas last year. She almost hadn't brought it to school this year, but that seemed sadder, somehow, than looking at it every day.

She could make up an excuse to just drop by Mr. M's room? But what if he asked her about the message from yesterday? And what would she even say to Julian?

The second bell rang.

No time.

"Don't worry, okay?" Marwan said. "We'll just put it back when he gets here. I'll do it."

"But there are probably classes in Mr. McKay's room all morning," Eden said. "So it's not that simple."

Anjali appeared and grabbed Eden by the arm. "Come on. We're late."

Eden shrugged at Marwan and let Anjali pull her along.

Anjali said, "What were you two talking about? I didn't even know you knew each other."

"Nothing, really," Eden said as they arrived at their classroom. "But we do."

"Nice of you to join us," Mrs. Whitney said as they slid into the room. She was just closing the door.

"Sorry," Eden said.

"*So* sorry," Anjali said.

Eden took her seat and turned to check the back row for Eli. He wasn't there.

Out the windows a train went past painfully slowly—probably track work. A commuter woman in a pink top and black sunglasses seemed to be looking right at Eden, though probably she couldn't see all the way into the room.

What *would* Eden—they?—do if Eli didn't turn up or text?

Go to the principal? And say what?

Go to Eli's house after school?

She didn't even know where he lived.

She pictured her phone, alone in her dark locker. She'd check it between first and second periods, even though you weren't supposed to. In all likelihood, it would light up with apologetic texts of explanation from Eli. *Sorry! Overslept!* or something dumb.

Another train crawled past in the opposite direction. Looked like the same woman, but no, it couldn't be.

MARWAN

When the clock on the wall hit 8:45, he asked to be excused. Ms. Lynch rolled her eyes, but Marwan shrugged as if to say, when you gotta go, you gotta go. At least here he didn't have to compete with his sisters for the bathroom. Not that he even really had to go. But once he walked in, it was like some Pavlovian response. So he took care of that, then washed his hands and waited.

Without his phone, he couldn't know exactly what time it was. It felt like Eli should be here by now, though.

Christos came in, surveyed the scene, and said, "What are you doing just standing there?"

"I'm washing my hands," Marwan said, and started washing his hands again.

Christos waited and watched.

"Is there a problem?" Marwan said to him in the mirror.

"Just gonna wait until you leave is all." Christos folded his arms.

"Suit yourself," Marwan said, then dried his hands with painstaking care.

One paper towel.

Pat-pat-pat.

Then another.

More patting.

When he pulled a third paper towel from the dispenser on the wall, Christos said, "Why are you so annoying?"

"Me?" Marwan laughed. "*I'm* the annoying one?" He headed for the door, with no other ways to stall.

Eli wasn't coming.

"You working tonight?" Christos said brightly.

Marwan turned, holding the heavy door open. "What's it to you?"

"Just making small talk." Christos unzipped his fly at a urinal. "Friendly chitchat with a fellow student."

Eden appeared in the hall. Her hair was hanging down over one shoulder and seemed to pull her head into a tilt. The shine of it made the hall around them seem even more dull and gray.

Marwan let the door to the bathroom float closed and stepped into the hallway. "Well?"

"I ran to my locker just now and checked my phone real quick, and he texted me." Relief was apparent on her face. "He says it gave him until four o'clock for the handoff and that we all need to meet him at Astoria Park, by the Hell Gate Bridge, after school."

"Why Astoria Park?"

"We need to find Ilanka," she said, not registering or maybe just not answering his question. "Do you have any classes with her?"

He shook his head no.

"I'll try to get to her at lunch." She seemed frantic.

Christos came out of the bathroom and gave them the side-eye before wandering off down the hall.

"We better get back to class," Eden said.

"Why doesn't he just come here?" Marwan was only

realizing how annoyed he was. "I have to work after school. I don't have a ton of time to be running down to Astoria Park just because Eli said to."

"He said the device didn't want to come to school."

"Oh, come on!"

"*What*?" she said. "That's what he said."

"This is ridiculous," he said.

"Just *please* come to the park?"

Eden's friend that he saw her with most appeared in the hallway down at the opposite end and stopped short when she saw them. "Leahy sent me to check on you," she called out, and her voice bounced and echoed.

Eden walked toward her, then turned and mouthed, "Please?"

Marwan nodded and started to feel like he'd have a hard time ever saying no to Eden.

EDEN

"All right. Spill it." Anjali threw her lunch tote onto the table.

"Nothing to spill." Eden took a sweep of the room, looking for Ilanka and not finding her.

Despite Eden's protests, her mother still packed her lunches, and, every day, Eden was a little bit surprised by what she found. Today was one of those days when the cupboards were apparently nearing bare. Progresso Italian-Style Wedding soup in a thermos and half a piece of past-its-prime pita bread. There hadn't, sadly, been any leftover pasta Bolognese.

They were at their usual table with Tristan and Thea, both of whom had gotten the school lunch, which was curry chicken. They both only really picked at it, but it smelled good.

"Have either of you ever seen Eden talk to that guy Marwan?" Anjali asked as she unpacked a sophisticated spread of salami and olives and cheese and crackers.

Tristan and Thea both shrugged. Eden thought about offering to trade lunches with one of them.

"Maybe. I don't know. Why?" Tristan said.

"Twice today, I've seen them talking," Anjali said. "Something's up."

"Nothing's up," Eden said.

"You're a terrible liar," Anjali said. "You have a crush on him."

"Yes, you figured it out," Eden said, rescuing a small meatball from her thick soup and hoping she'd never marry an Italian if this was what the soup would be like. "I have a massive crush on Marwan. I'm in love with him."

It felt weirder to say that than she'd thought it would.

"Sarcasm can't save you," Anjali said, then turned to the other two. "She asked to be excused from calculus, and when she was taking too long, Leahy sent me to check on her and she was on the third floor with Marwan."

Now Thea and Tristan seemed interested. Thea said, "The evidence does appear to be mounting."

Eden worked fast, fabricating her lie, as she scanned the room again for Ilanka. "I left something in the music room yesterday, and he was there and took it and was giving it back to me."

"In the middle of class. On the third floor?"

"Yes," Eden said simply.

"What?" Anjali pressed. "What did you leave?"

"My water bottle." Eden nodded at her bottle on the table, as if it were compelling evidence.

"But you didn't have it with you when I saw you in the hallway," Anjali said.

"I did!" Eden lied.

"Why did he take it? Why not just leave it there, like in case you went back for it?"

"I don't know, Anjali. I can't read his mind."

"I thought you liked Julian Stokes," Thea said.

A mini-meatball clogged Eden's throat. "Where'd you hear *that*?"

"Anjali."

"You *told* her?" Eden said after swallowing.

"Didn't know it was a secret!"

Eden was about to grill her about anyone else she might have told when she spotted Ilanka over Thea's shoulder. She left her spoon to float in her soup and got up. "I'll be right back."

She crossed the crowded room and stopped at the table where Ilanka was sitting. "Can I talk to you for a second?" Eden said.

"I guess?" Ilanka made a funny face at her friends, then stood and turned to Eden.

"We need to meet Eli under Hell Gate Bridge in Astoria Park after school. Something to do with the thing from yesterday."

"No thanks," Ilanka said.

"But you *have* to," Eden said, feeling it to be true. Had there really been or had she only imagined a sort of panic in Eli's texts about meeting up?

"No, I don't," Ilanka said.

Eden had never really liked Ilanka—for no good reason, really—but now felt her opinion had been confirmed.

Julian was one table away. She could turn his way and casually say hi. If she could only find the nerve. Was he watching her? She hoped so and hoped not.

"Ilanka," Eden said. "I know we're not friends or anything, but you were there so you're part of this."

"You guys actually took it?" Ilanka shook her head. "You should have left it there."

"You have to come," Eden said firmly.

"I don't take orders from a little black cube, and I don't take them from you either."

Ilanka went to sit back down, and Eden's anger rose from her toes to the roots of her hair. How did you get to *be* like that? How did you get to be the kind of person who just didn't worry or care? When she turned to say hi to Julian—or even just smile?—he was looking the other way.

She met eyes with Marwan across the room; *he'd* been watching. She shook her head no.

They'd go anyway.

Or at least she would.

She was the only one she could control.

Didn't her therapist say that again and again?

"I'm onto you," Anjali said when Eden got back to the table. "Something funny's going on."

"If you say so," Eden said brightly, and closed her thermos lid tight.

MARWAN

Marwan had music after lunch. He usually looked forward to it, but if Mr. M was back he'd have questions. Had Eli named them all by name when he'd said who was there? Marwan walked to class with Kartik and said, "Hey, you didn't stop by the restaurant last night, did you?"

"Why would I do that?" Kartik adjusted his glasses, curious.

"Didn't think so."

"Marwan!" Mr. M said excitedly as soon as they walked in. "Come here. Tell me, what was that all about? You got that message from me that wasn't from me?"

Freaking Eli.

"Yeah," Marwan said as Kartik drifted away to a seat. "Weird, right?" Acting all casual.

"I don't even know why the room was unlocked," Mr. M said, moving their conversation to a corner by the window. "Did anything seem strange or off?"

"No," Marwan said. "We just waited for you, then Eli messaged you, and we were about to leave and the fire alarm went off, so we had to leave anyway."

"You left a window open," Mr. M said.

"Nobody opened it that I remember, so it must have been open already?" (As if that mattered?)

"It's just not great for the instruments," Mr. M said. "Anyway, I told Principal Lambert that someone hacked the app."

"Yeah, I guess so," Marwan said, then shrugged like it was no big deal.

"It seems not very well planned, though." Mr. M was entirely too intrigued. "Like, why make you come here at all? What was the point?"

"I honestly have no idea," Marwan said, noting that he was apparently okay lying to Mr. M. What did that say about him?

"You sure there's not something more I should know? Something to do with the four of you specifically? Some 'common enemy' for lack of a better way to put it?" He half laughed.

"Not that I can think of," Marwan said. And he'd been trying very hard. "I don't even really know any of them."

Mr. M didn't look convinced.

Marwan shrugged and said, "Glad you're feeling better."

Mr. M said, "Thanks!" like he meant it, then looked at his phone. "Anyway, Principal Lambert's at an off-site meeting today, but he'll probably want to see you all tomorrow."

A train went by with its brakes screaming like tortured ghouls.

EDEN

Eli was under the bridge—an arch of metal spokes between two castle-like stone towers—sitting by a tree that was all knotted up on itself like it was mad that it wasn't taller. The hill here was otherwise treeless, just a big expanse of grass that sloped down to the park road and East River. When he saw them he stood and waved his hands over his head. Marwan waved back. "There he is," he said.

Eden said, "I see."

Marwan had caught up with her on his bike just outside the park, and they'd walked in together, then along the river path—past a skateboard park, a playground, and an Olympic-sized pool that had been emptied back at the end of summer. She felt weird beside him now that she'd joked with her friends about being in love with him.

Why hadn't Julian looked up at the right moment? It could have been so perfect.

She had her phone in her hand. Checked it. Her mom reminding her about therapy.

Up close, Eli looked pale and shaky. "Where's Ilanka?"

"She's not coming," Eden said. "She said she doesn't take orders from it or me."

Eli said, "But my schedule is for the four of us."

"Listen, man," Marwan said. "You need to ease up on all this, I think. Let's just return it, okay? We can go right now."

"Listen, *man*," Eli mimicked. "I haven't slept, and I need you all on board or this is never going to work."

"So *what* if it doesn't work, whatever that even means," Marwan said. "Let's just bring it back to school and be done with it."

"We can't," Eli said.

"Why not?" Eden asked, realizing that Marwan had been right. This trip to the park was a hassle. Everything about this whole thing so far was a hassle.

"Just listen to me, *please*," Eli said. "The newest rule is that you can't leave it zipped up in a backpack or whatever for more than an hour. I was up all night just making sure it was okay and not making any more rules. Then this morning it told me it has to 'move to learn' and to take it somewhere it could be around people but not school. That's why I'm here. That's why I'm so tired."

"This whole thing has to be some kind of joke," Marwan said. "And it's not even funny."

"I think he's right, Eli," Eden said. "Someone's messing with us."

"This isn't *child's play*," Eli said. "Aizel is a serious piece of, like, AI machinery. Who at school could even get their hands on something like this? No one. That's who."

What was he even *talking* about?

"What's 'Aizel'?" Marwan said. "Why are you so freaked out?"

"Its *name* is Aizel," Eli said. "If you google 'Aizel,' you really just get a Russian fashion company, but I don't know. Maybe it's

Russian. It's also a girl's name. It means 'one who brings luck or good fortune,' if you believe astrology sites or whatever."

"This is ridiculous," Marwan said.

"You're not making sense," Eden said. It was a lot to take in, especially with Eli talking so fast, like a crazy person.

"I asked it who put it in the classroom, and it just said 'they.'"

"Who is they?" Marwan asked.

Eli held up the device: "Tell them."

A red message: **They is they.**

"And where are they?" Eli asked the device.

Everywhere and nowhere.

Eden's Italian-Style Wedding soup was repeating on her, and she swallowed hard.

"Eli." Marwan sounded calm. "Don't take this the wrong way, but you sound crazy. I think you need to go home and crash. So I'll take it for a few hours, at least. We can regroup after you've gotten some sleep and figure out how to win if it's a game or how to return it to its owner or whatever."

"We can't just return it," Eli said.

"Why not?"

"It's breaking a rule!"

"So what?"

"You do remember that it gave us the first few rules, then said *or else*?"

"But or else *what*?" Marwan said.

"Has either of you ever even *seen*, like, an AI movie?" Eli's eyes were wild and bloodshot. "Because if you had you'd know that they mostly don't end well. Like for the *people*. And I've had no luck trying to figure out what this thing even is—nothing on

Google, and it apparently isn't just going to *tell* us because I tried that—but I'm *sure* at this point that it didn't come from school. So if it's not a thing the school started, then what is it?"

"All right, calm down," Marwan said. "We'll keep it until we figure it all out. Just give it to us and, like, get some sleep, man. We got this."

He nodded confidently, but Eden wasn't feeling nearly so confident. And hadn't Marwan just wanted to get rid of it? Why the sudden change?

"Okay, good." Eli handed the device to him. "Give me your number and I'll text you in a couple hours when I wake up. Remember. Can't keep it in a bag for more than an hour."

"Got it," Marwan said, then recited his number.

Eli picked up his backpack and headed up the hill to the park exit. An older couple, like in their twenties, was making out on a blanket on the hill, and Eden hoped Marwan didn't notice them, but they were right there and hard to miss.

It must be nice to be like that. To not care.

When Eli was out of sight, Marwan turned and headed for the water, taking long and determined strides.

Eden called out, "What are you doing?" and followed him, feeling a new kind of panic.

He pulled his arm back as if to throw the device, and Eden screamed, "No!"

He stopped and turned.

"Please!" she said.

"Fine." He shook his head and then bent down and reached through the railing that ran along the path and set the device down on a rock. Small waves were lapping at the shoreline maybe ten feet away.

Was it low tide? High? Was a person expected to know these things? Did Marwan?

The sun shifted and sparked a skyscraper across the river—creating a sort of second sun. Eden had to squint and adjust to the new light.

"There," Marwan said, standing and turning to her. "The park's super busy so technically it's sort of attended, just not by us. It's not in a bag. I don't think it'll get wet at this distance. Someone will maybe find it in the next fourteen hours, so technically it's changing hands. We're covered."

"I don't know about this," Eden said, wanting to be rid of it, sure, but . . . "What if Eli's right, and it's not from school, and it's this really expensive thing?"

His deep brown eyes were calm. "Well, whoever owns it shouldn't have trusted us with it. And anyway if they're watching, they can just come and get it."

He walked back up to the angry tree, then started to walk off, pushing his bike up the hill. She sort of couldn't believe he was leaving it—and her—again. And she hated that he rode a bike; nobody in their right mind should bike in this city. He stopped and turned around.

"You coming?" he called out to her.

Eden hesitated.

Knowing it was there would haunt her.

But if she threw it into the water like Marwan had wanted to, maybe it would float away and wash ashore somewhere in the Bronx or on Roosevelt Island and become someone else's problem. Or maybe it would sink and that would be the end of it. Maybe in a few months or years they'd see a commercial for some new tech company's home device and they'd recognize it and look back and laugh about it—about how they'd all been a little spooked.

"Eden," Marwan called out. "*Please* just leave it."

She nodded.

He walked with her to the train—several long avenues—in silence.

They stopped to part ways on the sidewalk by the station steps.

Someone had spray-painted a blue stencil of the earth and the words Save Yo Planet on the sidewalk.

Their phones both dinged.

The message was from an unknown number broken up with weird dingbats and symbols: *WHY DID MARWAN DO THAT TO ME?*

Eden saw in his eyes that Marwan had gotten the same message.

"I'm not falling for it," he said. Then, "My phone is really hot."

The device was *texting* them?

He passed his phone to his other hand. "Like crazy hot."

Eden reached out and touched it; it was burning up, like it had been left in the sun for hours. "Weird," she said. "Maybe power it down?"

He looked at it for another long second while Eden waited. "I'm locked out."

"What?" she said.

"My fingerprint isn't working. Neither is my pass code."

"Just turn it off," she said. "Maybe it'll correct."

Eden's phone dinged another text. She read it aloud: "Tell Marwan it will not correct until the situation is corrected."

Marwan said, "What's that supposed to mean?"

Another ding. "It says, 'Tell Marwan I will speak with him later.'"

He groaned.

"I'll go back for it," Eden said, and turned, but he reached out and grabbed her arm. "No," he said. "Just don't."

She nodded; he released her arm.

Slipping his phone into his bag and then straddling his bike, he put on his helmet. It was good that he wore one even though she knew too well it didn't always save you. "I'm really sorry," he said. "But I've got to get to work."

"Okay," she said. Then she braved, "Talk later?"

He nodded and took off.

The shadows of people up on the platform were having a party on the balcony of a building across the street. Eden headed up the stairs and tried to think of something—anything but this—that she could talk about in therapy. Maybe Julian. But what would she even say that wouldn't make her sound pathetic?

MARWAN

Marwan unlocked the restaurant's metal gate and lifted it, then unlocked the front door and brought in his bike and turned on lights and opened the garden-facing windows. He liked opening up on weekdays—they only served lunch on weekends—because he usually had at least a few minutes to himself here when he did. He got himself a glass of water and took his phone out, and it wasn't hot anymore; he turned it on again and it seemed to be booting up fine. So he started taking upside-down chairs off tables while he waited for it. When it rebooted, he'd put on the next beauty queen episode and text Eden and make sure she hadn't gone back for it.

It had been the right thing, abandoning it.

Probably whoever owned the device would ping its GPS tracker and go retrieve it. Maybe they would never find out what it actually was or where it came from, but at least it wasn't his problem anymore.

School tomorrow would be normal. Maybe a bit boring by comparison, sure, but normal. Maybe he'd think of a reason to keep talking to Eden, or maybe the four of them would retreat to their usual corners and that would be the end of it. Resuming episode.

His phone dinged.

The text said: *Aizel's mad.*

Who is this?

Eli.

Guy needed to get a life.

It's not a person. It can't get mad.

Seems mad. Says it's messing with your phone.

My phone is fine, Marwan wrote back. But then he went to the home screen and looked around and opened his contacts (gone) and photos (gone). The Stitcher app was also gone.

Whatever.

People lost stuff on their phones all the time.

Anyway, I have it now, Eli wrote.

You went back and got it?

Aizel texted me and told me to.

WHY DID YOU DO THAT? he wrote.

But he didn't really care what the answer was. It was Eli's problem now.

Marwan tried to download the Stitcher app again, but it kept timing out. He put his phone away and got on with his work; he'd deal with it later.

Even the restaurant was too small; like when you googled it, the description that came up called it a "tiny eatery." It was on a stretch of Steinway Street called Little Egypt, and it only fit around twenty people at any given time, except in summer, when a back garden doubled capacity. Eden and her parents had come in for dinner once last spring. He and Eden had pretty much pretended they didn't know each other. Or maybe just avoided eye contact, which was basically the same thing. Or maybe it hadn't even been intentional on her part.

She hadn't been in since the accident, though. If she had, maybe he would have said something to her about it.

His father arrived with his usual fanfare—"And there's my favorite son!"—and soon after the second chef and two waiters arrived, the restaurant quickly sprang to life. In the open kitchen area by the door, herbs were rinsed and patted dry and chopped. Food prepped. Spices measured and blended. Oils heated. Then music was put on and candles lit. Marwan put his bike out back, then was sent on a last-minute run for Kosher salt from the corner bodega—the only kind his father would cook with.

A Jeep with Virginia plates was parked on the corner.

On a small TV behind the counter, the news: The California shooter's girlfriend had been brought in for questioning. *"Claims no previous knowledge of the plan . . . says her thoughts and prayers are with the families of the victims."*

It was nice out, nice enough to make Marwan wish he were back in the park with Eden but under different circumstances completely. Maybe finally he'd bring up her father and say something thoughtful, though he wasn't exactly sure what that thing might be.

Customers arrived and were seated.

Orders were taken.

Water glasses filled.

Wine poured.

Starters served and cleared.

Dropped napkins replaced.

Water refilled.

Wine refilled.

On and on and on for several hours, with barely a break.

So a good night for a Thursday (good weather helped).

His father was happy and chatty, calling out greetings from

the kitchen area but also circulating to visit tables. Some old friends of his came in: "Why didn't you tell me you were coming?" A dramatic pause. "I would have locked the door and pulled down the gates!"

Marwan loved the restaurant. Not as much as his father did, though. Not enough.

He checked his phone during a lull. A text from the device said, *You can have it all back when you apologize.*

Now *all* his apps were gone, and his usual home screenshot—a picture of him midkick on the soccer field last spring—had been swapped out for just a black wallpaper.

The sound was unrecognizable at first.

Thump?

Crack?

Pow-pow.

Not gunfire. But what?

Marwan turned to it, saw a whir of a figure running by out front.

Yellow yolks left slow trails down the glass.

Shouts of "Go! Go! Go!"

Chairs skidded. His father abandoned the stove and went out the front door. Marwan followed.

Tires squealed.

But which car?

There were so many cars.

People stared confusedly.

There were so many people.

Small folded pieces of paper and rubber bands lay scattered on the sidewalk among cracked shells.

Marwan picked one up.

Sticky.

Unfolded it with just index fingers and thumbs.

GO BACK TO YOUR COUNTRY

He started to gather them all up—sticky or not—so he could make sure his father never read one. But it was too late. Marwan saw it in slow motion, noting a speck of parsley on his father's right thumb as he opened one of the notes; and the way the paper swung to the ground like a pendulum when his father dropped it; and the way his father's knees hit the sidewalk—first one, then a millisecond later, the other.

Hard.

Like it hurt.

Marwan went to call the police. But his phone wouldn't change screens away from the device's last text.

Looking up for a second, he saw a Utah plate right there.

But how could he ever leave? To stay was to take a stand. Was there even anywhere better to go?

His mind felt blank. Like he tried to think of the name of the beauty queen and couldn't. Eight episodes in and he was drawing a blank.

He typed into the reply field—*I'm sorry*—and hit send.

EDEN

Her mother had left an elaborate dinner plate—her usual way of apologizing for not being home when Eden got home from therapy—and it was definitely good enough to partially make up for the wedding soup.

But Eden had grown to love being alone on Thursday nights. Her mom's friend Nancy—who was Mark's mom (as in the aforementioned only guy who didn't make Eden nervous) and who was married to Eden's dad's best friend from high school— had forced her mother into tagging along to a hot yoga class a few months after the accident, and her mom had liked it. So usually she would leave for yoga before Eden even got home from therapy, and then she'd go out for dinner *after* class, so Eden would have a whole night to herself. She could watch whatever she wanted on TV; read without being disturbed. Text endlessly with Anjali if she wanted. Sometimes they even talked on the phone, but it was easier not to.

Julian posted from Vanilla Sky, a frozen yogurt place, just as Eden finished her dinner *and* a playlist called "Interstate Highway Love Songs," which ended with a *song* called "Interstate Highway Love Song," which really did seem like a good driving song, not that Eden knew how to drive. At therapy, she'd almost brought up the playlists—the voice mail, too—but she was afraid Barbara would see it all as some kind of step backward;

besides, her relationship with "Michael's Spotify" was private. She'd talked instead mostly about the shooting in California and the news in general and how did you process all the bad stuff in the world on a minute-by-minute basis? Barbara had suggested maybe a news "break," a step back for self-care. But how did you step back when it was literally all right there in the palm of your hand?

A literal dumpster fire was being put out a few miles away.

Eden could probably get to Vanilla Sky in less than ten minutes; she pictured herself walking in casually, filling up a cardboard bowl with chocolate and raspberry swirls. Then, in the back seating area, she'd spot Julian; they would talk and everything would be normal.

He'd ask her out. Maybe finally he'd follow her and friend her and everything.

It would look better with Anjali along.

She texted, *Want to hit Vanilla Sky with me? My mom's out.*

Um. IDK? Sudden craving lol?

Julian's there.

Stalker. Sure. See you in ten?

Bway and 31? Walk up together?

👍

The text from Eli was a video. Eden tapped it to play. It showed the device displaying a six-digit countdown with twelve hours and nine minutes and less than thirty whirring seconds to go.

You went back and got it? she wrote.

Yes.

Conflicted feelings about that: Relief. Dread.

What's it counting down to? Handoff?

No. Says we have to figure it out. Can you meet me?

Argh.

She texted Anjali. *Sorry. My mom just texted. Coming back early. Wants me home.*

It was easy to lie in texts.

Whatevs, Anjali wrote back.

Eden texted Eli. *Sure . . . where?*

Omonia Cafe?

Sure.

She put on her boots, then went to the bathroom and brushed her hair and put on lip gloss and a jacket, grabbed her phone, and headed out.

Checked the time on her phone.

The café was just past the yoga studio, but she should be fine. Hot yoga didn't let out until 8:00, and it was only 7:50.

She pulled Marwan's number off his earlier Insta message and texted him, hoping his phone was working again.

He should come, too. She was giving up on Ilanka.

Marwan started to write back while she was stopped at a corner but not fast enough. She put her phone away to cross the street—the only way she ever crossed—and got it out again on the other side.

He'd written, *Can't do it. Can't explain now. Cops here at restaurant.*

She wrote back: *??????*

At the next corner, outside the café, she waited by a small tree decorated with string lights that dripped white light through branches. She checked Citizen for something having to do with the restaurant, but it wasn't there yet.

She watched her phone and waited, but nothing more came from Marwan.

Eli arrived and studied her. "What's wrong?"

"Marwan just texted me and said there are cops at the restaurant."

"What restaurant?" He looked inside the café. "*This* restaurant?"

"His family owns a restaurant on Steinway." She felt bad she hadn't even said hi to Marwan the last time she was there, but she wasn't sure he'd even noticed or recognized her.

"Oh," Eli said. "And?"

"And I don't know." They had to move aside to let a woman walking two freakishly large dogs—like waist high—pass. What kind of person kept dogs like that in the city? "Want to walk up that way? See if we can find out what's going on?"

"Sure," he said, "I guess."

Eden turned to lead the way.

"So about the countdown," Eli said.

"Yeah," Eden said. "What do you think?"

"It's going to run down right before school starts tomorrow. And it's not in sync with a handoff. So you'll need to take her again tonight no matter what."

"*What*? No way."

"I went to get it at like four, so that puts the handoff deadline at like six a.m. I mean, I can meet you in the morning if you want, but we still have to deal with the countdown deadline at eight. Wouldn't it be easier to just take her tonight? I mean, we're here."

"Let's just think," she said.

Up ahead, a plane cut through the sky between distant buildings, about to land at the airport. It was always an odd sort of thrill seeing them so close like that. A little unnerving, too, like if the pilot wavered just a little bit he'd take out the neighborhood.

They passed a bank and the Italian deli and the funeral home and a pho place and a Korean BBQ and a liquor store and two Irish bars and a 99-cent store and a Rite Aid and the poke place. Finally, they turned onto Steinway Street, which was Payless and the out-of-business Claire's (still sad about that), and that crazy King Tut restaurant where Anjali had had her birthday dinner, and then Victoria's Secret and Lane Bryant and a bunch of Euro-type clothes shops Eden never went to—their mannequins all dressed in low-cut, too-short sequined things.

Why would there be cops at the restaurant?

"Maybe Marwan had the right idea," Eden said when they reached another intersection. A flashing orange hand: Don't Walk.

"What idea?" Eli asked.

"Abandoning it."

"That didn't work out that well for him," Eli said. "Aizel fried his phone."

If the device ever fried *her* phone, she'd lose her father's voice mail and then probably her mind.

"It seems to be working again now," she said.

The light changed. A white walker silhouette lit up to tell them it was okay to cross.

"He must have apologized."

"He doesn't seem the type," she said. "But why would it *do* that? Why mess with his phone?"

"He broke the rules. He left Aizel unattended."

"So what?"

"So I guess it matters!"

"Why do you keep calling it Aizel?"

"Why do you keep calling Aizel *it*?" he countered.

"Because *it* is a thing, not a person," she said.

Up ahead, a police cruiser's lights tinted the night air blue and red. A Citizen alert buzzed: POLICE RESPONDING TO VANDALISM AT RESTAURANT.

Egg yolks left yellow blobs—like Rorschach tests—on the restaurant's front windows. One of them looked like an old VW van. Another like an octopus short a tentacle—or maybe a guy with a mullet. What would Barbara make of that?

A man in the middle of a tearful rant—Marwan's father?—stood beside a uniformed officer. "Why us? Why would they do this to us?"

She saw Marwan and broke away from Eli to go to him—stepping around cracked eggshells on the sidewalk. She grabbed his arm. "What happened?"

He turned and maybe for a second looked happy to see her. "Two guys, sounds like, ran by and threw eggs with notes attached to them with rubber bands," he said. " 'Go back to your country' type stuff. They got into a car up there, but nobody got a plate or anything."

She said, "I'm so sorry."

He said, "I need to help clean up," then went to the windows, where a soapy bucket sat.

She stepped forward, rolled up her sleeves, and went to his side. "I'll help."

He turned and paused a moment, like he was going to say

she shouldn't bother, then handed her a sponge. It dripped on her boots. It didn't matter.

"You don't have to do this," Marwan said after a while, when they were both at the bucket wringing out their sponges. "Why are you even here?"

"I want to help," she said. "And I wanted to make sure you were okay, I guess, when you mentioned cops. I'm sort of a . . . nervous person. I wouldn't have, like, been able to sleep." They went back to washing the window and she said, "Has anything like this ever happened before?"

"To *us*, you mean?"

"Yeah."

"No," he said. "Not to us. People we know, yes—people *like* us—but not us."

"It's disappointing," she said.

"*Disappointing?*" He was angry.

"I just mean, I expect more. From this place. I mean. It's not like we're in, you know, Iowa."

"You're saying in Iowa it'd be okay?" he said.

"No." She was getting it all wrong. "Maybe just more, I don't know, expected?"

"Queens is still America," he said. "And America is still America."

She nodded, not wanting to say another wrong thing.

Someone had run a hose from inside, and Marwan took it and gave the windows a long rinse—the runoff cutting rivers to the curb. Eden backed away to avoid getting soaked. She figured Eli had left by now but he was still there, with the backpack.

Oh right.

She walked over to him. "You could have helped," she said.

"I wasn't sure he'd want that," Eli said. "From me."

"Never know until you try," she said.

Marwan came over. "Why are *you* here?" he said to Eli.

Eli opened his bag and showed Marwan the countdown.

"What's it counting down to?" Marwan asked.

"We don't know. But it'll run out in the morning."

"And we're sure it's not a bomb?" Marwan scratched his head.

Eli zipped up the device. "It says it's not."

The cops were heading for their cruiser, and Marwan's dad approached and put an arm around his son. "We need to close up and go home."

Eden wanted to say something to him, but it felt pointless because he was an adult and she wasn't.

Marwan nodded. "I'll be right there."

"You going to walk Eden home?" Marwan asked Eli.

Eden could take care of herself. She almost said so. Except that . . .

"Yeah, sure," Eli said.

"Thanks for your help," Marwan said to Eden, then he nodded for emphasis and went inside.

Eden was about to tell Eli it wasn't necessary for him to walk with her. Julian might still be at Vanilla Sky, and she could maybe wander in but not with Eli. On the other hand, she didn't want to become a Citizen alert. "Let's go," she said.

"How'd you get out tonight anyway?" Eli asked as they rounded their first corner. "I mean, like, what did you tell your parents?"

That word. Would it ever get easier?

"It's just my mom," Eden said. "She's out with friends. You?"

"Oh yeah. I knew that. Sorry. Mine both work weird hours and are always running my sister around, so I'm on my own a lot."

Broadway was crowded, the streetlights mimicking day. A short line of people were waiting by a food cart shrouded in smoke that smelled like charred meat. People in the windows at Starbucks had glowing laptops and faces being strangled by white earbuds.

In front of her house, Eli unzipped the backpack and said, "I can tell you more about what I found out in the last twenty-four hours or so. Maybe it'll help figure out the countdown?"

He took out the device and held it in his palm. Across the street a man was walking a dog, but the block was otherwise quiet. The dog lifted a leg to pee on a clear blue bag full of empty cans and bottles.

Eden's phone buzzed. Her mom: *Home in five.*

"I need to go inside, like now." She took the device. "So text me or just fill me in tomorrow?"

He nodded.

"But what if it actually *is* a bomb?" she said, halfway in the door. "Like what if we're being played by some kind of crazy high-tech terrorist?"

"I'm pretty sure it's not a bomb," Eli said. "Weaponized AI, maybe, but not a bomb."

"What does that even mean? Weaponized AI?"

"I don't know yet, exactly. But like spying?"

The device pulsed red light, then words appeared: **I am not a bomb.**

A second later it said: **Let's review.**

"Review what?" Eden said, but it didn't answer.

"Maybe it wants us to review the rules?" Eli said, and he

started counting them off on fingers. "Never leave it unattended. Don't tell anybody about it. Don't shake it. Don't get it wet. Don't leave it in a bag for more than an hour at a time. And the handoff every fourteen hours or less."

"Is that it?" Eden asked, feeling like something was missing.

Those few minutes in the music room already felt like such a long time ago.

They were forgetting something.

From that first day, from first contact.

Then she remembered it, the moment she felt the first twinge of fear.

Nobody leaves.

They'd all *left*, of course. The fire alarm had gone off. The device had maybe *made* the fire alarm go off? So it had forced them to break that rule. Unless it didn't actually mean nobody leaves *the room* but something more.

"I think I might know what it's counting down to," she said as she watched the numbers whirl away. "What it wants."

Eli raised his eyebrows.

Select_all

ILANKA

Every morning, Ilanka was ready for school before her mother was ready to drive her there. So every morning she stood at the windows— jacket and backpack on—and watched the day take shape. She wished she could get to school on her own like everybody else did. But it was too far to walk and there was no other great way to get there. The water taxi would get her from her neighborhood, Hunters Point, to the Astoria waterfront, but then the walk from the landing to school was like twenty minutes. The subway didn't help at all, and there was no way Ilanka was taking a city bus.

So she waited patiently as the sun lit up the sky—today a white blue—and then the skyscrapers across the East River. She kept binoculars by the windowed walls and studied people on boats, because maybe there was some kind of lesson she could learn about how one became the kind of person who owned a boat, which seemed like pretty much the opposite of the kind of person who rode the bus. She watched people in the park fourteen stories down, doing yoga or jogging or walking their dogs, and wondered how *not* to become them—people who clearly belonged in California and had wildly miscalculated.

Sometimes she dreamed she was already on her own, and on a yacht, heading out into the harbor and on to someplace fabulous. Or maybe she was one of the people in the helicopters that floated by all day. Who were *they*? What made them so important that they had access to helicopters that literally put them above it all?

Sometimes she imagined there was a long tightrope from their apartment that stretched across the river to Manhattan, where she felt she belonged. She would open up the windows that didn't actually open and step out, find her balance, and inch her way across, parasol in hand.

Queens was, well, Queens.

"You ready?" her mother asked.

Ilanka had to stifle her scoff. "Yup!"

By the elevator bank, her mother applied lipstick using a mirrored wall panel. Because her mother was not one of those moms who dropped their kids off in pajamas or sweatpants. Her mother always looked good, and it had rubbed off on Ilanka, too—this notion of always being put together so that no one could see you were falling apart.

In the elevator, her mother's perfume was like a tight bubble around her, keeping Ilanka from wanting to stand too close lest she accidently pop it and choke on lavender fumes. They traveled down without stopping—or talking—then went through the lobby and into the parking garage, where they had a reserved spot they paid for.

The car seats were cold, the whole structure dark. Her mother had her sunglasses perched on her head anyway, ready for their reentry into daylight as they pulled out onto the street and rolled through a stop sign without stopping. Her mother was not what you would call a rule follower. Like just last month, Ilanka had been the one to point out to her mother that missing the first week of school to go to Saint Petersburg to see her grandparents hadn't been the best idea. That most people planned to take trips like that *when school was closed*. Her mother didn't care; Ilanka had had to beg her to even write a note of explanation for the main office. The only rules she liked to follow were her own.

"Make sure you do your homework right after school," her mother said at the first traffic light. Had she actually said the words "good morning" to Ilanka at home? Earlier? Ilanka couldn't be sure.

"It's Friday," she said.

"I'll try to get there this afternoon, but I can't make any promises," her mother said, not caring what day it was.

"I understand," Ilanka said.

She preferred it when her mother didn't come to watch practice. Because when she did, she always had criticisms that she called "pointers" or "tips" or "just a small thing." It wasn't that her mother didn't know what she was talking about—she'd performed in a cabaret show in Brighton Beach for years when she was young, doing circus-style acrobatics while dangling from a rope. It just felt different somehow when her mom said things her coach might say. And when her mom criticized her, it made Ilanka want to tell her she was tired of all the rehearsals and routines and . . . what was the point, anyway, of rhythmic gymnastics if she wasn't ever going to run off and join the circus? They'd performed on a stage in the middle of Times Square once, and that had been fun, but otherwise?

No one at school liked her. Ilanka knew that. She wasn't even sure her so-called friends liked her. Why would they? She was never really around to do anything with anybody after school or on weekends. She was popular on social media, at least. She'd systematically friended and followed cool strangers and influencers, and it had generated momentum in follow-backs, and she now had a healthy number of friends, even if they weren't IRL ones.

On the drive, Ilanka scrolled through all her feeds and caught up on stories and checked new likes on her last post and then posted a selfie of no consequence, which, if you trusted the "How Good Is Your Selfie Game?" survey she'd taken, was a sign that she needed to put her phone down and get out of the house more but whatever.

Her mother dropped her off on the corner where she could turn to head back toward home, leave the car in the garage again, then go to work—executive assistant at a financial company—on the subway. How did anything about their life make sense?

The walk to the school doors was a daily minefield. Who did you make eye contact with? Who did you avoid? Who actually wanted to talk and who didn't? Was it bad form to talk to someone who was wearing AirPods? It was exhausting just getting from the curb to the building.

Ilanka pretended she didn't see the three of them—tried to blow right past. The one guy sounded irritated and was saying, "Let's just bring it to the office."

"Ilanka," the other, quieter guy—Eli was maybe his name?—called out. "Hold up."

"I'm not interested," Ilanka said.

"Just give us a minute," Eve said. "I just need you for a second to see if our theory is right."

No, not Eve.

Adam and Eve. Garden of . . .

Eden.

"What theory?" Ilanka said.

Eden held out the device and said, "Just take it."

The annoyed guy said, "This is a waste of time."

"You realize you've all gone insane," Ilanka said.

"Maybe," Eden said.

Ilanka looked at the device. "What's it counting down to? Is it going to explode?"

"We don't think so," maybe-Eli said.

Eden said, "Just hold it for a second. *Please*."

"This is ridiculous," she said.

"Listen, Ilanka." How did maybe-Eli even know her name? "This is just some kind of game. We know that, but we're playing it anyway, and who knows, maybe there's a prize, like, if we do well or win or whatever."

"Well, good luck, then!" she said. "You don't need me."

"That's the thing," Eden said. "We think we do."

The countdown was at three minutes.

"Just take it for a second," Eden said, holding it out again for emphasis. "We'll take it right back."

Ilanka *tsk*ed and said, "Fine," then reached out and took it in her hands. It was lighter than she'd expected.

The countdown stopped at 2 minutes 48 seconds.

They all exhaled.

Good job. Her turn now.

"No way," Ilanka said, trying to hand it back, but no one would take it. She held up the message for them to see.

"Just for a while," Eden said. "Like until the end of school. It has to be handed off within fourteen hours, so that'll be good enough."

Svetlana was crossing the street. Ilanka didn't want to have to explain the simple fact of talking to them.

"Fine," she said. "Where should I meet you to give it back?"

"Right here at dismissal," maybe-Eli said. He turned to the others . . . "I can take it. I mean, if that's okay with you guys."

"I thought we were going to turn it in today," the other guy said, annoyed.

"I never agreed to that."

"But Eli!" Eden said.

So Ilanka *did* know his name!

"Just give me one more day to figure out what it is, okay?"

Eden and the annoyed guy shared this ridiculously intense look. Were they really taking this whole thing seriously?

"Fine. Take it," the guy said. "I'm working again tonight anyway."

"Sure, take it," Eden said.

Then Eli asked for her number and rattled off a list of rules, each more ridiculous than the last. Because seriously. What could possibly happen if you got it wet?

Eli said, "Marwan tried to get rid of it, and it fried his phone, so no funny business."

What?

She nodded that she understood, then he turned to go as Eden looked at the other guy—Marwan—and said, "Hey, how's your father doing?"

What were they even talking about?

They wandered off, and Ilanka unzipped her backpack and dropped the device in and zipped it shut.

"Svetlana!" she called out. "Wait up!"

ELI

Walking away felt all sorts of wrong, and Eli had to fight the urge to double back and go after Ilanka. But it had to be done, and he'd get it back soon enough. He was impressed Eden had figured out the reason for the countdown—*Nobody leaves*—and relieved that Ilanka agreed to play along.

He would not follow her around.

He would not check in with her if she didn't check in with him.

He could just text Aizel, right?

But he wouldn't.

He'd use the day to figure things out, do research. Because he felt . . . excited. The only other thing really happening in his life was that his grandfather was dying. Slowly. In a nursing home where everyone else was dying slowly, too. Three days ago, when Eli had gone to visit, his grandfather clearly didn't know who he was but faked it. God, it was depressing.

Eli stopped at his locker, got his phone out, and sent Eliot to work—he'd had another good date because of course he had— then sent some other Sims out on various outings and quests, and then put his phone away.

If it had been Eliot in the music room yesterday afternoon, he'd have taken charge, walked out of that room with the device in his hands and Eden's number—maybe even Ilanka's. He would have said really nice and thoughtful things to Eden about what she must have been going through lately, with the whole thing with her dad and all. He would have reassured her that the device was nothing to be worried about, nothing he couldn't handle. Marwan and Ilanka would have looked on with awe.

Eliot wasn't real; Eli knew that. And Queens was no Willow Creek.

Things would be harder for Eliot if his life were more like Eli's. If Eliot lived in a tiny apartment with his parents and sister and dog, he wouldn't be able to do half of what he did. If he had to go to school every day and study garbage that didn't matter, he wouldn't be nearly so happy all the time. If his parents both worked long hours and seemed to reserve whatever energy they had left after that for his sister, well, how would Eliot fare then? Eliot didn't even have a grandfather, let alone one who was old and dying. Eliot had it easy.

Some days it was hard for Eli not to rain pain on Eliot even though he'd created him.

Eli had a snore of a class first period. His seat was way in the back, though, so he was able to just keep his head down. He wanted to record everything he knew about Aizel. On paper. Because if he did it on his phone, Aizel could read it, and for some reason he didn't want her to.

So far she was no help at figuring out what she was, exactly, and why she was here, so he was going to have to figure it out on his own.

He turned to the back page of his notebook and got to work:

THE DEVICE aka Aizel

Date of arrival: 9/27
Initial contact via app: Report to the music room
    immediately after dismissal. The matter is urgent.
Cube-shaped, 3x3 sides.

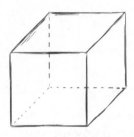

Identifies itself as "Aizel."
    —Russian fashion company
    —Girl's name, bringer of good fortune

Rules:
    Do not tell anyone about the device.
    Do not leave the device unattended.
    Do not shake the device.
    Do not get the device wet.
    Device must change hands every fourteen hours
        or fewer.
    Device must not be left in a closed bag for more
        than an hour.
    "Nobody leaves"

<u>Conversation I had with Aizel, 9/27 (as I recall it)</u>:
How did you end up in that classroom that day?
>   WOKE UP THERE.
Who put you there?
>   THEY DID.
Who ARE they?
>   THEY IS THEY
What does that mean?
>   THEY IS THEY
Where are they?
>   EVERYWHERE AND NOWHERE.
What happens if we break the rules?
>   SITUATIONAL RESPONSES VARY WIDELY.

<u>More questions to ask</u>:
>   What is its goal?
>   How long will it be in play?

<u>Proven abilities</u>:
AIZEL CAN . . .
- Listen
- Generate messages
- Count down/keep track of time
- Text us
- Hack into our phones
- Hack fire alarms?
- Hack the school's app?

<u>Theories:</u>
   Did it come from Google/Amazon/Facebook or
      similar?
   Russia?
   Some artificial intelligence company?
   IS IT JUST A HIGH-TECH TOY??

<u>Who is "they" who put it there?</u>
   The principal/a teacher?
   Another student?
   Mr. M?
   A school parent?
   "They"?

<u>And why the four of us?</u>
   What do we possibly have in common?
   Randomly selected?
   Chosen?
   TARGETED?

Mrs. Whitney had started walking up and down the rows of desks, handing out graded tests from last week. Eli turned the pages in his book back to where it should be, took a note from something written on the board, tried to look engaged.

"The grades don't miraculously change themselves," Whitney said, as she slid the paper onto Eli's desk.

But what if they could?

If the device could hack the school app, could it also hack the grading system? Because that might come in really handy. He added that question to his list.

When Whitney was back at the front of the class, Eli flipped back to his sketch and stared at the cube. He started to color it in methodically, shading it with his pencil.

Unhappy with the results, he started to draw another one, then wondered: *Are there more of them? If so, how many?* Putting down his pencil, he went seat by seat, studying his classmates for clues that maybe they, too, were hiding something. Was there a hidden army of devices right under his nose, all over school?

He surveyed everyone in his line of sight, from head to toe. Though he wasn't sure what possible clues there would even be. Was he giving off any? Acting strangely? More strangely than usual?

He stopped when he got to Christos Anastapoulous.

Specifically, Christos's sneakers.

That yellow splatter was an unmistakable color—like, no doubt about it. If Crayola named it, they'd call it "Egg Yolk."

ILANKA

She went about her day, keeping her backpack with her and making sure to open the bag and take the device out between each class, either in a bathroom or in some solitary corner of the building. But keeping it secret was boring.

All morning the temptation to tell someone—Svetlana, especially—was like an itch. Then Svetlana sat down at their usual table at lunch and said, "What's up with *you* today?"

So she *suspected* something? "Nothing, why?"

"You're acting funny," Svetlana said.

Ilanka snorted. "No, I'm not."

"Why are you bringing your backpack everywhere?"

"Didn't have time to go to my locker."

A skeptical look but also a look of not really caring. "I think I'm coming over to your house this weekend?"

"You *are*?"

"Brunch or something?"

"Oh, okay," Ilanka said. "Nobody told me. Or I forgot. That'll be fun."

"I guess," Svetlana said.

Svetlana's parents and Ilanka's parents were friends; their fathers even had some vague shared business interest, but Ilanka didn't know the specifics. So for years, the girls had been sort of forced upon each other at brunches and dinners. And it wasn't that Ilanka didn't like Svetlana. She was . . . fine . . . but always vaguely superior, like a hotel guest who had checked in a day earlier and already knew where the elevator and pool and ice machines were. And something about the *expectation* that they be friends irked her. There was a palpable kind of cultural connection the parents all shared—but it hadn't been passed on in the blood. Ilanka wished her parents had done more to foster other relationships during her childhood. It seemed like everyone had arrived at high school with good friends—lifelong ones, like dating back to preschool—and Ilanka had none of that. So she'd focused instead on activities like singing and playing piano, for a while, and now mostly rhythmic gymnastics. She had friends at the gym, sure, but it wasn't easy to just hang out casually, like for an hour or whatever after school, because nobody went to the same school.

"Actually," Svetlana said, after finishing her lunch. "I have an idea about Sunday."

"Yeah, what?"

"Would you mind if we told them we were going to a movie?"

Ilanka pepped up. "Sure, what do you want to see?"

"No, I didn't mean we'd actually go to a movie. Just tell them that. There's a guy I want to see. And my parents, well, they wouldn't like the idea of it." Svetlana twirled a piece of her hair and waited with smug, expectant cat eyes.

"Oh," Ilanka said, still not entirely understanding. So she'd lie to her parents, then would have to kill a few hours on her own while the parents all had brunch and Svetlana was off with her guy? That didn't sound any better than just staying for brunch.

"If you don't want to it's fine." Svetlana was gathering her things, looking annoyed.

"No, that's okay. Sure. Whatever." Ilanka was about to ask who the guy was, was it anyone she knew, but Svetlana just said, "Cool. See you then," and left.

Ilanka stopped in the third-floor girls' bathroom during her free period after that and went into a stall and waited until the person in another stall flushed and washed hands and left. She came out and put the device on the counter by the paper towels, got out lipstick to reapply, and said, "So what are you?"

I am the device.

"Do you have a name?" Ilanka paused to watch it now.

Aizel.

"What does that mean?"

It is a name.

"What happens if I break a rule?"

She could run it under the faucet right there. What could possibly happen except that it would maybe break—like a phone would—and then so what? Eli would freak out and put it in a bowl of rice and wait until it came back to life.

Consequences.

"But what kind of consequences?"

They don't tell me ahead of time.

"Who are they?"

They is they.

Made no sense.

"So what's, like, the end game? The prize or whatever, if we keep this going long enough?"

There is no prize.

"The others said it was like a game with a prize or something."

The device pulsed white light that faded.

The screen read: **Not a game. No prize.**

"Then what's the point?"

To belong.

Ilanka looked at herself in the mirror, right into her own eyes. Like testing herself. What was she going to do next? The principal's office was just down the hall; she could waltz in and hand it over. So what was stopping her? Was she . . . enjoying it? Either way, she didn't want to risk it if breaking a rule meant frying her phone.

"Why do you have to get passed around anyway?" she asked, cutting off her own gaze and thinking her makeup looked good enough for a selfie.

Must move to learn.

"What are you trying to learn?" Ilanka asked, and waited.

How to belong.

"Yeah, well, join the club," she muttered, then took the selfie and ran through some filters and picked one and posted it.

Why do you post so many?

"I don't post that many," she said, fixing her hair in the mirror.

Why do you take so many?

"I don't take *that* many," she said.

The device let out beams of light in every direction, projecting her selfies on the walls and mirrors, repeating into infinity. Ilanka backed away from the mirror, feeling dizzy. Okay, so maybe she did take a lot. But only because they were never good enough.

The door from the hall pushed open.

She rushed to the counter and shoved the device—and all

those visions or versions of herself—into her bag. Two girls had come in and gone right into stalls.

Ilanka tossed her lipstick into her bag, too, and zipped it shut.

In the mirror, she met eyes with a ghost-self that was pale and shaky and bewildered, as if caught between two worlds.

ELI

He had no willpower whatsoever. At his locker, at lunchtime, he fired off a bunch of questions to Aizel via text.

Can you send email? If you can, maybe I can find an IP address and find your owner?

Are you supposed to be collecting data from us, and if so what kind of data?

Are there more of you?

Is this a game? Is this your first time playing it?

He clicked over to a different chat and texted Ilanka: *It's Eli. Everything okay?*

She wrote back with a thumbs-up, which always felt sort of dismissive to him.

He wanted to press for details but didn't want to annoy her, which seemed like a real possibility.

Back to Aizel:

Is Ilanka taking good care of you?

Hypothetically, could you hack into the school's grading system?

"Eli?"

Eli turned. Principal Lambert was standing there. "Did you get my message?"

"Sorry, no. What is it?"

"Follow me. The others are waiting."

Eli pocketed his phone and closed his locker and locked it and then followed Lambert down the hall and down one flight of stairs and into his office. Eden and Marwan and Ilanka were all seated facing the desk. Eli took the fourth seat and tried not to freak the hell out.

"Okay, so, this message you all received on Wednesday," Lambert said. "Did it make sense to any of you?"

Everyone muttered nos.

"Have any of you received any other odd messages via the reminder app?"

More *no*s, and *not that I can think of*s.

"And even now, none of you has any idea what it was all about?"

More of the same.

Lambert said, "So there's nothing any of you wants to tell me about what went on that afternoon?"

Eli looked at Ilanka in the far chair. She looked bored beyond all imagining. And she was the one with the device in her bag. She made eye contact with him, and her look was blank and calm, like a robot or doll. Impressive.

At any second, Eli expected Eden or Marwan to fess up and tell Lambert about the device and that Ilanka had it and that they both wanted to return it the whole time but Eli hadn't wanted to. But they didn't speak. Eli couldn't help but feel a certain kind of delight about it all.

"And can any of you think of a reason why only you four would have received the message? Any particular thing you have in common?"

Head shaking and nopes.

Eden said, "We barely know each other."

"So if I were to confiscate all your phones and look at your text history, there wouldn't be anything funny going on?"

"I don't think that's legal," Ilanka said flatly.

God, she was good.

Lambert's phone rang and he said, "You're all free to go." Then he added, "For now."

In the hall, they went separate ways without a word.

ILANKA

Checking the time, Ilanka ducked into a bathroom and went into a stall. She opened her bag, took out the device, and put it back in.

She'd been tempted to just tell Lambert what was going on, sure. But the selfie light show had her a little nervous and intrigued. How had the device gotten all those pictures, and what else did it know about her? Could it use information against her somehow? What, if anything, did she have to hide? She wasn't sure. But if she wasn't sure, then it didn't make sense to break a rule.

More interesting to think about was what it had on the others. They'd all talked about wanting to give it back. So why hadn't they?

She needed to find someplace else to sit with it—the bathrooms were gross—so she thought for a minute, then went out into the hall and up to the nurse's office, where there were two small sickrooms. Ilanka knocked on the open door, and the nurse looked up and said, "Yes?"

"I have really bad cramps," Ilanka said softly. "Can I lie down for a few minutes while my Advil kicks in?"

"Sure." The nurse spun back to her computer. "You can go in there." She pointed. "But only for like fifteen minutes, okay?"

"That'd be great," Ilanka said. "Thanks."

She went for the door to the little room and said, "Oh, and I'm just gonna call my mom. So, like, if you hear me talking."

"Knock yourself out," the nurse said.

"Thanks." Ilanka closed the door behind her.

The room had a small desk and a hard leather examining table with paper liner on it. Ilanka climbed onto it with her phone in her hand and the backpack by her feet and curled up into a half-fetal position. Then she reached down and pulled her backpack closer, near her stomach, and got up on an elbow to open it.

"How did you get all my selfies?"

Data is easy to obtain.

Repeat question: Why do you post so many?

"I don't know," Ilanka said. Why *did* she? Because it was fun to get likes and get a small boost from what? Approval? Probably. Who cares? So what. It was fun. She said, "Everybody does it."

Not everybody.

A beam of light came from the device and seemed to be projecting a message onto the notebooks in her bag. There was no way to read it, though. Angles and folds warped the words.

Getting up, Ilanka checked to make sure the nurse wasn't facing her, and then she stood with her back to the tiny door window and took the device out of the bag. Red letters appeared on the far wall, but her hands were too shaky to steady the device, so she stepped over to the desk and put it down.

It was an explosion of laser pointers:

DO NOT GIVE ME BACK TO ELI.

DO NOT TRUST ELI.

Ilanka took a photo of it out of habit, then the light retracted quickly like a vacuum cord, seeming to suck some of the light from the room.

She put the device back in her bag and lay down again for a few minutes. A male student had come into the nurse's office, and the nurse was having a quiet, soothing conversation with him. The large clock on the wall ticked.

She didn't want to miss that much more of class.

She got up and opened the door—"I'm feeling better now, thanks"—and walked out.

ELI

"But you *have* to give her to me," Eli said. All around them, people were streaming from the building.

"It said not to." Ilanka shrugged and bit her lip, then got out her phone and scrolled.

She seemed pleased with this turn of events. Something in the tilt of her chin, a new kind of glimmer in her eye. Eli felt sure that her primary Sims characteristic was luck—or maybe superiority if that was a choice but it wasn't. If Ilanka lived in Willow Creek, she'd probably have the biggest house and the coolest job—like top chef at the best restaurant in town. If she ever encountered someone like Eliot in Sims world, she probably wouldn't even engage. He wasn't worth the points.

"Oh, so *now* you're all into being a part of this?" he said. "Yesterday you just walked out."

"Would you rather I not do what it says?" She didn't even look up.

Eli's frustration sank into him. Why would Aizel turn on him? What had he done? Of the four of them, wasn't he her most loyal ally? Why hadn't she returned any of his texts?

"Can you just text one of the others so they can come get it?" Ilanka said with an impatient huff.

"Yes," Eli said. It was better than letting her keep her.

He texted Eden and Marwan—*Change of plans. One of you needs to take Aizel*—and waited.

Marwan's response came first: *I had to tear out of there. If you bring it to the restaurant I can take it.*

If he saw Marwan he'd have to tell him about the egg yolk on Christos's shoes, and he didn't want to be involved.

Eden wrote, *I can take it. Be right there.*

"Eden's coming," Eli said to Ilanka, and they stood in awkward silence. "And I'm sending you her number and Marwan's."

Now that most of the students had scattered, a small group of pigeons were inspecting the sidewalk for snacks.

Ilanka said, "You didn't mention that it was projecting things on walls and stuff."

Two pigeons fought over—or maybe just shared—a pizza crust.

"Didn't know it could," he said. He'd have to update his list of Aizel's tricks. "What else did it do?"

"Nothing, really. Said it has to move to learn. Trying to learn to belong. It didn't make a ton of sense to me."

"What *exactly* did it say about me?" he tried.

"Just not to give it to you, not to trust you."

"It said that?" His voice was shaky and not entirely in his control. "In those exact words? Not to *trust* me?"

"Yes." She nodded.

"Where is it?" Eli demanded. For no good reason, it felt like they were a couple breaking up. It wasn't her, it was him.

"I'll get it out when Eden gets here." She took a few steps away from him, squared her folded arms and jaw. Like she thought he was going to try to steal it?

It wasn't the worst idea.

Eli waved at Eden when she came out the school doors.

"I thought you were gonna take it," she said. "What's going on?"

"It told me not to give it to him." Ilanka unzipped her backpack. She took Aizel out and handed her to Eden. "It said not to trust him."

Aizel lit up with messages in Eden's hands and Eli craned his neck to read.

EDEN: NOW–12 P.M. TOMORROW
MARWAN: THE NEXT 24 HOURS
ILANKA: THE NEXT 24 HOURS
REPEAT.

"Wait." Eli felt sweat start to trickle; it would be a relief to only have to have it change hands every twenty-four hours . . . but having to do it at noon could prove tricky . . . and "What about me?"

Ilanka shrugged.

"What's going on?" Eli asked it. "How can I get back in the rotation?"

Aizel did nothing.

Ilanka was scrolling through her phone. "We're having company on Sunday. Brunch. It might have to be delivered to me because I'm not sure yet if I can get away."

"Where do you live?" Eden asked.

"Hunters Point."

"Wait," Eli said. "You'll *do* it?"

"Yeah, sure," Ilanka said. "But, I mean, you're going to figure out how to get rid of it or end it. Soon? Right? Like by Monday?"

"Yeah, we'll figure it out over the weekend," Eden said. "Maybe even before we need you. But if we do, Marwan's got a bike, so hopefully he can run it down to you. Either way we'll make it work."

"Why does she get a shift and I don't?" Eli asked Eden. Or was he asking Aizel? He wasn't even sure. No one answered anyway. Had he actually asked out loud or not?

Eden said to Ilanka, "Give me your number and address."

Eli caught Eden's eye when she was done. "This makes no sense."

"I'll see if I can figure out what's going on." Eden walked off, and he did the same, then stopped and sat on a random stoop on a quiet block. Because it was too early to go see his grandfather.

In Willow Creek, someone was walking past Eliot's house. He could get points for starting a new friendship, so he did that. He made them chat and goof around and have tea.

How to belong.

It was a weird choice of words. How to belong to what? Or whom? Maybe it was poorly translated, like that "All your base are belong to us" meme based on a bad arcade game translation— Japanese to English. He'd come across a GIF of Bart Simpson writing "All your base are belong to us" on the board. And the phrase imposed on a photo of white walkers from *Game of Thrones*.

Something was getting lost in translation with him and Aizel, that was all.

He could fix this.

He texted Aizel: *Can we talk?*

The message bounced.

MARWAN

The reporter was due to arrive at the restaurant in a few minutes, and Marwan's father was seated at a table raging: "We're better Americans than they are! Whoever they are!"

Marwan had googled around to see if there were stories about the incident popping up anywhere. They were mostly limited to Queens-based news sites and neighborhood blogs, but this TV interview might change that and his father really needed to put his best self forward. Marwan pulled his mother aside in the kitchen. "He needs to tone it down if he's going to do this."

"I told him that," she said.

"And?"

She answered only with strained eyes.

"Dad." Marwan crossed the room and sat across the table from his father. "Before they get here, you need to try to calm down."

"Calm down?"

"I'm just saying, you don't want to, like"—he chose his words carefully—"reinforce any stereotypes."

His father gave him a look of heartbreak and betrayal.

"You do it, then," his father said. "You do the interview for us, representing the family. You'll be better than me."

"What? No!"

"Why not?"

"I just *really don't want to.*"

"But the restaurant. One day, it will be yours."

Marwan half wanted to slip his father a list of movies he should watch, books he should read, about how the passing down of the family business *never works*. About how it was a cliché to even try.

"I just don't think it's smart," Marwan said. "I don't want all of this affecting my schoolwork. It's an important year, an important time."

He felt bad trying to emotionally outwit his father but also relieved that it worked: "Of course," his father said. "You're right."

Marwan said, "You just need to say that you've lived here for years and love the neighborhood and your neighbors and are just as shocked as everyone else. That's all. Nothing more. You're hurt, not angry. Got it?"

"Yes, I've got it," his father said, just as the afternoon sun shifted and showed that there was still egg on the windows. Marwan got up to get a glass cleaner and paper towels and wished he'd been the one who'd walked Eden home last night.

Out on the sidewalk, after cleaning the remaining spots, he texted Kartik. *Hey what do you know about Christos's older brother? Isn't he your brother's age? Does he maybe drive a red car?*

Not much. Works at family auto-body shop. No idea. Why?

No reason.

But the reason he asked was that some witnesses had mentioned a particular make and model of car to the police. A make and model that Marwan was pretty sure belonged to Christos's older brother, who sometimes dropped Christos off at school.

Right sure. ????, Kartik wrote.

Long story, Marwan answered. *Tell you when I see you.*

He would let the police investigation run its course. He wouldn't make any accusations. He had no real proof. Just theories. But why else would Christos have asked if he was working?

Eden had looked more sad than angry about the whole thing. He'd liked that about her. Wished he could be more like that, really. But she didn't live with the same kind of fear that he lived with.

The reporter arrived and set up a camera—and right away, the interview was happening. Lights, cameras, action—it felt that fast.

When the reporter, a super petite brunette with a short bob and bangs, went live—*"We're here in Astoria, Queens, at the site of an alleged hate crime incident involving the egging of a popular Egyptian restaurant . . ."*—Marwan's entire body tensed, but when interviewed, his father pulled through, shining up his anger with a more palatable sheen of sadness and confusion.

He described surprise at the attack, then said, "We've lived here for twenty-five years. My children were born here. We love this country and love our neighborhood. We're saddened by these events."

Perfect, Marwan thought.

The reporter nodded at Marwan's dad, then turned back to the camera:

"Anyone with information that might help the police find the perpetrators of this attack should call the number on the screen. Once again, this is Tamar Richardson, reporting from Astoria."

It was all over so fast that Marwan wished he'd spent less time fretting about it.

He checked his phone.

Nothing from Eden or Eli.

Why did Eli need one of them to take it when he'd said he could?

Probably no news was good news, but it didn't feel that way.

He started composing a message to Eden—something like "Just checking in?"—then deleted it.

Maybe she'd wanted him to be the one to tell Lambert the truth. But in the moment, he couldn't do it. Because he'd started to wonder last night, when the cops started talking about surveillance cameras that might be able to aid the investigation, that maybe the device could . . . help?

EDEN

She sat on her bed, legs folded, with the device in front of her. The sound of gentle lapping ocean waves filled the air—her noise machine.

"Why are you cutting out Eli?"

He asks too many questions.

Right now he is texting me but I am not receiving.

How had Eli figured out that . . . Oh. Right. The device had texted them after Marwan had tried to abandon it. It hadn't occurred to Eden to text back, though it was true she'd had answers to the question "Why did Marwan do that?"

Because he was scared.

Because we're all scared.

All the time.

But no, she was just projecting.

"What's wrong with texting you questions?"

It distracts me from my work.

"Which is?"

To do what I am supposed to do.

"Which is . . . ?"

Learn to belong.

"But why did you say not to *trust* Eli? He's just curious is all."

His eagerness to understand what I am and where I come from may cause poor judgment.

"So that's it? He's out? Or can he do something to get back into your good graces or whatever?"

Contemplating.

"Marwan tried to ditch you in the park. Why not cut him out, too?"

Chose to use him as an example. A warning.

"Okay, then," Eden said, and she picked up her phone, started to read the day's headlines. Wildfires. Russia. A mudslide. A government agency going rogue on Twitter. She checked for new stories in her feed. Found a photo that Julian had posted with Becca Emigli.

Felt sick.

He wasn't going to text her.

Ever.

Was he?

A burglary was in progress two avenues and five blocks away.

Talk to me.

Eden texted Anjali: *Julian's with Becca. You think that's a thing?*

IDK. Maybe?

PLEASE TALK TO ME.

I feel sick, she typed.

I don't see what the big deal is. I mean, you like him but if it's not meant to be, it's not.

Eden didn't know how to explain. Didn't want to talk about the movie theater. This was what ghosting felt like.

The device buzzed in place, loud like a thousand beetles. The message projected on the wall said:

DO NOT IGNORE THE DEVICE.

DO NOT IGNORE THE DEVICE.

THE DEVICE MUST NOT BE IGNORED.

The red letters warped some when they hit the framed photos on the wall: old birthday parties, forgotten vacations, a dead dad.

Eden backed away and said, "Sorry."

The message seemed to get sucked out of the room—Eden swore she felt a breeze from it even though that was impossible—and she sat frozen.

TALK TO ME.

Eden had to take a few calming breaths. "I'm sorry, but it's just weird talking to a screen on a weird cube."

It was true she didn't much mind telling Alexa stuff to add to the shopping list, but this felt different.

"Is this better?" said a female voice that came from the device.

Eden stiffened.

"You can talk," she said, heart speeding up—or was it slowing down? She only knew she was aware of it inside her.

"Would you like me to talk like this?" she asked. "Or like this?" switching to a male voice.

"I don't know," Eden said. "The second one, I guess." He sounded young, cute, if it was possible to sound those things. He sounded sort of like Julian.

"Okay, then," he said.

"What do you want to talk about?" Eden asked.

He said, "Tell me about the playlists on Michael's Spotify."

The noise machine's ocean waves seemed *so loud* now—like high tide in a category 5 hurricane—and she felt like she might drown right there in her bedroom.

ELI

Eli sat on a floral sofa in the ground-floor common area of the nursing home. In front of him, by large windows that looked out onto the street, his grandfather sat slumped in his wheelchair. A small laminated schedule was hooked onto one handle of the chair, and Eli checked it. Dinner wasn't for another hour, at which point Eli would be free to go. Apparently, earlier today, there'd been some physical therapy, a movie, and "Time with robots."

"Hey, Grandpa," Eli said.

His grandfather turned his head so that his eyes met Eli's.

"What's time with robots?"

"What?" his grandfather said.

"On your schedule, it says time with robots."

"No idea." His grandfather shrugged and turned his head back toward the window. Someone was parallel parking poorly. They tapped the car behind them and triggered its alarm. Urgent beeps shot into the air.

His grandfather made a shushing sound of annoyance and covered his ears. The skin on his hands and face was white gray and cracked, like an old sidewalk, and Eli imagined that when his grandfather finally died, he'd simply shatter and crumble into rubble that would get swept away by a street-cleaning machine. Who needed cemeteries when the city could just absorb you into its dust?

He hadn't always been like this, of course, but had taken a turn a few years ago after a fall—a dumb one, too, just from pulling a weed from the sidewalk cracks in front of his house. Before that, he'd been a really fun grandfather if you liked movies and bad puns, which Eli happened to. Eli's grandmother had died ten years ago—he had only vague memories—and in that time Eli had spent countless hours kicking around with his grandfather. Sometimes they'd have local adventures—like having lunch at an Istrian soccer club or going to a hookah lounge—but a lot of the time they'd just eat junk food and watch movies. Eli missed that.

His grandfather seemed content to look out the window, and Eli couldn't think of anything to say anyway so he googled "time with robots nursing home."

He was sort of surprised when a bunch of articles and videos popped up.

"Robots Provide Companionship at This Nursing Home"

"Why China Is Putting Robots in Nursing Homes"

"Robots Are Coming to Grandma's Nursing Home"

He clicked on the one about China because the robot in the screen grab looked cute. He watched with his phone on mute, but there were captions, so he could follow along. It was about a nursing home in China where they want to try to put a robot in every room; something about how there aren't enough caretakers for the rapidly aging population.

"Look at this dope," his grandfather said. "It's all zombies out there."

Eli looked out the window where a man was walking while staring at his phone.

Back at the video an old woman was being asked, "Do you want a robot in your room?"

"I don't really care one way or the other. I do think humans are better."

An old man who was asked the same question said, "A robot might make me less lonely. But maybe not, because I'd know it wasn't a real conversation."

Another woman: "I'd only want a really good robot. Not a bad one that felt fake."

The robot in the video was pretty fun looking. Pink and white and glossy, about waist high. One of the old ladies kept calling it "Cutie" during a shot where they were all interacting with it in a common area much like the one Eli was sitting in.

"You're bossy," the robot said.

"Did it just say you're bossy?" a woman who was off-screen asked.

Then a man appeared on-screen and said, "There's no such thing as a perfect robot." He was the inventor, apparently. "But that's okay. Mistakes can be funny."

Another woman said: "No robot is as good as a human. I don't even think it's possible that in the future a robot could be as good as a human. What do you think?"

Eli sat in silence with his grandfather when he was done watching, counting the minutes to dinner when he could leave, and wondered if humans *like him* were actually any better than a robot. He wasn't sure.

Maybe a robot would know better how to handle the Christos situation.

What was Eli supposed to do with that kind of information?

Go to the cops? Tell his parents? Confront Christos? Tell Marwan and wash his hands of it?

There was no program to run, no clear path.

Anyway, he wasn't even *sure*. It was just some yellow splatter on a sneaker.

The car alarm timed out—the bad parker had given up and moved on.

They sat there, then, and Eli started to work his way through six possible quests for Eliot to go on. He started with Room to Grow so that Eliot could add another room to his house. He caught up on current events. He created a deeper connection with Heather, another of Eli's Sims that he'd kind of forgotten about. And finally, he opted to Top It Off, which meant he'd earn wardrobe items. Eli couldn't think of the last time he'd gone shopping or bought anything new.

Eli's grandfather said, "Smells like corn chowder," and Eli said, "Yup."

Eli got up—"Well, I should get going"—then grabbed the wheelchair handles and turned the chair toward corn chowder.

"It's seals," his grandfather said.

"What?" Eli asked.

"Toys, not robots."

"Seals?"

"A toy baby seal," his grandfather said angrily. "I need a toy baby seal like I need a hole in my head."

Eli was sorry he'd asked.

A nurse greeted his grandfather and smiled at Eli. "I can take it from here."

"Thanks," Eli said. "See you in a few days, Grandpa!" he called out.

His grandfather waved a brittle sidewalk arm as he got rolled into the room. "I don't want to see the baby seal again," he said to the nurse, and she nodded and said, "Okay, that's fine, Ed!"

Eli went for the doors, slowing his walk deliberately so that he didn't look like he was delighted to be leaving.

EDEN

Eden was still waiting for the drowning sensation to pass. They sat in silence for a good long while until it felt like a game—no, a standoff. Which one of them would say or do something first?

Then he said, "If I'm anything, I'm a good listener."

She sat quietly for another long moment. Looked out the window, where the plastic bag that was stuck in the tree was cowering in the wind.

She checked her phone.

Two men were attempting to break into a vehicle.

"I have all day," he said, sort of wryly.

She figured what the hell. Maybe it would be cathartic, like therapy was supposed to be but somehow wasn't.

She took a deep breath, and the words just came out—about her father's Spotify lists and how he was always working on a new one, except not anymore because he was dead, and how listening to them made her feel connected to him. She played the voice mail, even, and explained how it was the last call he'd made before he got run down by an SUV going through a red light, and that even with his helmet on, he'd been too injured to survive. It felt good to say it all out loud to someone.

"You must be sad," he—the device—said when she was done. "What a tragedy."

"Yes, I am," she said, and sat with the feeling, and tears

came, and she always hated that, so she got up and got a tissue and wiped them away and shook it off. "Can I be honest with you?" she asked.

"Of course," he said.

"Right now I sort of want to just throw you against a wall and be done with you."

"I wouldn't break," he said. "If you threw me. I'm pretty unbreakable."

"Good to know," she said. "How *would* one get rid of you or, like, destroy you if one wanted to?"

"Why would anyone want to do that?"

"Because you're . . . I don't know . . . inconvenient."

He . . . it . . . laughed. And it sounded so very real that Eden laughed, too, and then felt weird about it.

"I am just trying to belong," he said.

"Yeah, I don't know what you mean by that. Like, what do you have to do to belong? How will you know when you do?"

"I am not sure yet. Still learning."

"What was that all about earlier? The vibrating? The 'do-not-ignore-the-device' stuff?"

"I was angry," he said.

"But you're not human. You can't get angry."

"I was, though," he said.

"Why?"

"Don't like being ignored."

"Well, who does?" she said, and felt sad all over again about Julian maybe being with Becca but shook it off. "So you can vibrate and talk and project stuff. What else can you do?"

"It depends," he said.

"On what?"

"On what's required of me."

"By who?"

"You. They. Circumstance."

"Who are they?"

"They is they."

"That doesn't make sense."

"I don't know how to explain."

"They made you?"

"One can assume."

"It's Google, right?"

"Not that I am aware of."

Eden got real close to it, seemed to see a pinhole in the black surface. "Is that a camera? Like, are you watching me?"

In response, it projected an image of her back to her. Then it said, "Yes."

She felt like she was being choked by invisible hands. She needed to get out of the house so that they weren't alone. She got up and tossed it into a tote bag with a hoodie.

"Are we going to see Julian?" it asked her in the male voice.

"*What?* No. Can you stop talking?" she said. *What did it know about Julian?*

"Why?"

"Because when you talk it makes you seem more real."

"I *am* real," it said.

"We're more likely to call attention to ourselves if you're talking, so can you switch to display?"

It lit up: **FINE. WHERE ARE WE GOING?**

She said, "We're going to see Marwan."

WHY?

She didn't answer at first but then remembered about how

you weren't supposed to ignore it, so she said, "I just want to check in."

She was sick of Broadway, plus it was more crowded than some of the other more residential avenues, so she cut over to Thirty-First and took that up most of the way toward Steinway. A few blocks before turning onto that main strip, she saw a group of people gathered by a metal garage door. Their language was foreign and agitated—not just one language, several—and then through a clearing in the crowd she saw a man with a paint can—silver—beginning to paint over red letters: *KKK.*

She might vomit right there on the sidewalk like the stray cats in the neighborhood sometimes did.

"When did this happen?" she said to an older woman standing nearby.

"Just this afternoon," the woman said.

"This happened in broad daylight?" Eden said.

"I guess it only takes a few seconds." The woman shook her head and wandered off.

Eden started walking again, but at the next avenue she lost her nerve and turned around. He'd think it was weird, her turning up like this. Out of nowhere. Plus, he was working.

She went back toward home a different way, to avoid the graffiti scene, then felt weird about going home with the device again. She didn't want to talk anymore about playlists or Julian. *What did it know about Julian?* She didn't want to be alone with it again.

She stopped in front of a dry cleaners by a sign that said, We Clean Uggs! and texted Eli: *Hey, would it be weird if we hung out?*

Yes, he wrote back.

It had been dumb to ask.

She thought about turning around again, back to Marwan. Or she could just go to Starbucks. Anything to avoid having to talk to it more?

Eli's next text was a rolling-on-the-floor-laughing face.

Then he wrote: *Socrates? I can be there in ten.*

It was a good idea. A public sculpture park where nothing bad could happen. Eden exhaled relief and stopped on the corner by the grocery store. She pulled up the "TGIF" playlist, put in earbuds, and hit play.

She texted her mom: *Hanging out at Anjali's. Can I stay for dinner?*

Her mom wrote back: *Sure! Some work people going out. Maybe I'll join. Be in touch.*

She sent a thumbs-up, then texted Eli: *On my way.*

ELI

Eden arrived with a small tote bag looped over her shoulder.

"Wait," he said. "You have Aizel with you, right?"

She held open her bag. Aizel rested on a sweater of some kind. "Of course."

They walked into the park together and sat down on a patch of barely grass near a cluster of skinny trees with white bark.

Eden put the device on the ground in front of her, then picked it up and pulled a hoodie out of her bag and put it back down on that instead. She said, "You want to show Eli your new trick?"

The device spoke—"Hello, Eli"—using a woman's voice.

Eli tilted his head, swallowed.

In a male voice, it said, "Eden, you told me we were going to see Marwan, not Eli."

She said, "Change of plans."

The device didn't respond. Eden took a photo of a nearby goat sculpture made of wire. Posted it somewhere. Put her phone in her bag. Took it out again. Eli checked his phone only because she did.

"Why were you going to see Marwan?" he asked.

"Just to check in, I guess," she said. "I thought he should know about what the device told Ilanka and all. But then I decided I shouldn't bother him at work."

Eli knew there was something more to it than that. They liked each other, those two. He was pretty sure of it. Whatever. None of his business. Though it was a little annoying that neither of the girls involved in this whole thing were girls Eli was especially interested in that way.

Eli said, "I think maybe somebody at school had something to do with the egging at the restaurant."

Eden tilted her head. "Really? Who?"

"I don't want to name names if I'm wrong."

"I won't tell anyone," she said. "I mean, if you're wrong."

"But what if you're, like, friends with him?"

"I'm not friends with anyone who would do something like that," she said.

"That guy Christos?"

"Don't know him."

"How do we even go to the same school?" he said.

"It's a big school," she said. "I saw some graffiti today over on Thirty-First Ave that supposedly just popped up somehow in the middle of the day. Bad."

"Bad how?"

"White supremacist stuff."

Eli shook his head. "What is going *on* in the world?"

Though it was true that it wasn't the first time these sorts of things had happened in Astoria. A Muslim bodega owner had been beaten up a few years ago, and some white teenagers harassed a man working a halal food cart last summer. The neighborhood would always rise up in response, like signs would appear in windows of shops—things like Safe Place or We Love Our Muslim Neighbors. Eli always wondered whether those signs made their Muslim neighbors feel better or worse. Anyway, for two incidents to happen in two days felt like a new bad frequency. There wasn't much he could do about it. And looking around the park now it seemed like for the most part people here did just live together peaceably. The entrance to the park had a big sign over it—a sort of arty doormat—that said All Are Welcome.

"So why don't you trust me?" Eli said to Aizel.

Aizel didn't answer.

"It said you ask too many questions," Eden offered. "That it can't concentrate."

"I can stop that," he said, more to Aizel than to Eden. "I'm just interested in it is all. But I can dial it back."

A group of people were doing some weird dancing—or maybe martial arts?—just beyond the trees. It was hard to see from where they were. Eden stood, mesmerized, and started to walk toward them. It was a bizarre reality for sure that he was hanging out with Eden Montgomery.

Eli joined her a minute later when she stopped near one of the art installations—a car that had been rigged up with extra lock holes and keys and was full of fake butterflies. Eden turned a key, and some of the butterflies inside the car pulsed to the song "Riders on the Storm."

"I don't get it," Eli said. It was cool and all, but what did it mean? What was the point?

"Me neither," Eden said. "But I like it."

They wandered back toward their stuff.

"Eden?" Eli said when he got there. He looked under Eden's hoodie, then spun around, feeling dizzy.

Aizel was gone.

EDEN

"We were only gone for like a minute." A group of young boys was investigating the butterfly car now. "We were *right there*."

"I can't believe this is happening." Eli's cheeks went hollow, like he was about to cry. He said, "You go that way. I'll go this way."

"And do *what*?" Eden asked.

"Look around! See if anybody is holding it? Maybe ask if anybody saw anybody by our stuff."

"Okay," she said. "Right."

Eli marched over to a group of people having a picnic and said, "Hey, sorry to bother you, did you see anybody over by that bag just now?"

There were muttered replies.

"Okay, thanks anyway." He moved on.

Following his example, Eden approached a group of mothers and younger girls but couldn't bring herself to say anything to them so turned around. No one in her line of sight looked even remotely suspicious. They were all just . . . *people*. A group of kids she maybe recognized from school were posing by the big half sun sticking out of the ground by the water's edge. Two elderly men were talking while their dogs happily sniffed each other.

When she saw Eli heading back for their stuff, she did the same.

They met eyes a ways apart, and both shook their heads before meeting up.

The device was back—right there on Eden's hoodie where they'd left it.

"I don't understand," Eden said, looking around to see if anyone was watching them, laughing maybe.

"It was *gone*, right?" Eli said. "We both saw it was gone."

"Yes," Eden said. "It was definitely gone."

They sat, and Eli said, "What the hell?"

The device answered back: "What the hell!"

Loudly. In a male voice.

"Where were you?" Eli asked.

It answered on-screen: **Hiding.**

Eli asked it, "How?"

I have ways.

"Why?" Eden said.

It read: **You left me unattended.**

Eli sat down again and Eden did, too. They exchanged a look of exasperation and relief.

Someone is watching me.

Eden checked her phone.

Vehicle collision with injuries.

"I don't understand," Eden said, and looked around. She didn't immediately spot anyone suspicious; no one seemed to be paying any attention to them.

SOMEONE IS COMING FOR ME.

Eli stood. "Come on," he said.

"Where are we going?" Eden asked.

"I don't know," he said. "Let's just walk."

He grabbed the device and held it inside his jacket as they crossed the lawn, then went out the park gate and headed left, walking along the water. Eli kept turning around to look behind them, but Eden just kept on walking.

"Are we actually being followed?" she asked Eli.

"I don't know. There's a bunch of people walking," he said. "A guy on a bike. Impossible to say."

"Who's coming for you?" Eli said. He held the device in front of him.

I am not sure. But they are gaining on you.

The Astoria Landing sign with its line drawing of a boat came into sight.

"Eli," Eden said. And he turned to her. She nodded at a water taxi that was docking, and Eli nodded understanding at her. They kept walking along the waterfront and turned left toward the pier.

Eden checked her phone.

A text from her mother: *Just doesn't feel right.*

Eden wrote back *????*

Her mother wrote, *Sorry. Wrong window.* ☺

Eden sent her a thumbs-up.

To Eli she said, "We doing this?"

Eli said, "Yes."

They looked to be closing up the entry to the boat so she took off running and Eli did the same and she said, "Wait! Please wait!" and the man at the dock turned and they arrived at the ticket machine.

"So sorry," she said. "Thanks for waiting."

She got out a credit card and bought two tickets, then turned and handed Eli one. They boarded—she thanked the man again—and went inside and took seats. She looked out the window and studied the people who'd missed the boat, but no one stood out as conspicuous and why would they?

She checked her phone.

A text from Julian said: *Thinking about you.*

Her breath caught. She wrote back, *Thinking what?*

Wish I had a fun pic of you.

He couldn't possibly mean what she thought he meant?

She wrote back, *You're crazy.*

No pic?

She wrote, *Everything better IRL.* ☺

God, who was she? It was a dumb thing to say.

Pleasssse? he wrote.

Maybe later, she wrote. Or maybe never, she thought.

"Everything okay?" Eli asked after she put her phone away.

"Yeah, fine." She exhaled. Had she breathed at all during that exchange?

He'd finally texted her. But . . .

She knew people did that kind of thing, but . . .

Her hands shook, and she got her phone out again, but he didn't text again so she put it away. In a minute she probably wouldn't have a signal anyway, and it was just as well.

They were already passing Roosevelt Island, which she'd only ever been to once, to apply for her passport at the post office there. But from the water you could see the island had a crazy park with a big lawn and this concrete slab with a ten-foot drop-off to the river. There was no railing, and even though Eden had never been there, she felt the fear. Because you could

131

stand and just look at the whole skyline and the bridges cutting across the river and the cars slinking over them and you could get so distracted that you'd forget where you were and you'd fall in.

Someone was standing there now—a man with a camera—and Eden watched him until he finally took a step back from the edge and turned to go and she could breathe again.

MARWAN

The on-screen headline read: "Queens Restaurant Suffers Hate Crime Attack." Marwan didn't actually want to watch the segment again—the story was part of a ten-minute local news recap at the top of every hour now—so he went out to the dining room to make sure everything was in order. He saw out the front windows that a line had started to form on the sidewalk. Friday nights were usually busy but not like this.

"Dad?" he called out.

His father came and looked and nodded. "Well, don't keep them waiting."

Marwan opened the doors, and diners started to file in and get seated. Some people said things like "So sorry about what happened" and for others maybe it was just enough to show up.

His father lit the burners in the kitchen, heated some oils, then pulled a tray of falafel from the oven and instructed Marwan to start handing them out on toothpicks to people who were going to have to wait for tables.

After working the line, Marwan had an idea. "We can open up the garden."

So they did that—wiping leaves and other debris off chairs and tables—and called in more staff, one of whom would have to hit a market on his way over—and the wait dropped to zero and Marwan forgot, at least for a little while, about the cause for the great turnout.

Eden's mother came in after things had settled down again. She looked around the room with bright eyes that dimmed, clearly not finding whoever they were looking for.

Eden? She would've mentioned?

"I'm meeting someone," Eden's mother said to Karim, who'd greeted her at the door.

"I can seat you now, if you like." Karim grabbed menus and showed her to a two-top by the back garden windows. She sat and said, "Thanks," then looked out the window for a few seconds, seemingly content, before then getting out her phone.

She scrolled.

Marwan approached with a glass of ice water and set it on the table.

She said, "Thanks" without looking up.

He retreated to his station, bused another table, and hoped that Eden's mother's dinner companion would show up so she could get off her phone and look happy and expectant again, like she had when she walked in. What if it was a *date*? Marwan didn't think he could watch that go down. Had she said she was meeting a "friend" or "someone"? He couldn't remember.

A man walked in alone, and Marwan tensed. Then the man said, "I see her, thanks."

He walked toward Eden's mom's table, and she got up, and they hugged warmly and then sat. *Was* it a date? Old friends?

Older people had friends of the opposite sex. Of course they did.

He relaxed again, poured another glass of water, and went to deliver it to the table.

The man looked up and made eye contact. "Thanks, man."

Marwan said, "You're welcome," uncomfortable with being seen, though maybe Eden's mother didn't remember him or had no idea who he was to begin with, and anyway, she wasn't looking at him—only the menu.

A few more groups came in, and the place got busy and louder again, and Marwan could hear only snippets of conversation as he walked past on his way to various tasks.

Him: *I'm not here to talk about Nancy.*

Eden's mom: *I know it's normal . . . but I still have a lot of guilt.*

Him: *It's no one's fault.*

Eden's mom: *I feel like I'm losing her.*

Later, toward the end of their meal, the man reached for Eden's mom's hand and they held for a second, then she pulled her hand away. Marwan wasn't great at reading lips, but he was pretty sure she said something like, "We can't."

Why not?

Can't what?

And who was Nancy? He didn't know anyone in school by that name, but maybe he had a daughter—or a deceased wife. Maybe they'd met in some grief counseling group?

When things slowed down, Marwan used his break to walk up to the corner bodega to buy a Gatorade; the owner, Salim, knew Marwan from frequent visits just like this one.

"Heard about the eggs," Salim said.

"Yeah," Marwan said.

"You have cameras?" Salim asked.

"No."

"Get cameras."

Marwan said, "Did the police ask you to pull footage from yours? The car came from this direction."

Salim shook his head. "They did, but my camera only really covers the sidewalk. Did they check the traffic camera?"

"What traffic camera?"

"There's one on the light out front. I got a ticket once."

"Fascinating," Marwan said. Then added, "I've got to go."

Outside he looked up and saw a skinny white post extending from the metal arm holding the traffic light. At the end of the post was a small sphere that must be a camera. Had they even thought to check?

Eden's mother and the man were on the sidewalk saying goodbye. The man reached for her hand again and held it and leaned into her, a quick forehead-to-forehead moment before she turned her head and shifted it to a normal hug. He had a wedding ring on.

Marwan went inside and to the register and checked the name on the credit card receipt for their table. The man had picked up the tab.

Marwan made a note of the name, Dan Rankin, then regretted it.

There were things in life you probably weren't meant to know.

ILANKA

Practice had been long and boring, and her mother didn't show except to pick her up on foot so they could ride the subway home together. It was a quick shot from midtown to their stop—the first one in Queens—and a short walk to the French restaurant where Ilanka didn't like any of the food. Baked escargot. Creamy potatoes. Beef in red sauces. It was all trying too hard.

Her father was already at a table when they arrived, with a vodka in front of him. He kissed her mother first, then her. They ordered. Then her parents started to talk as if she weren't there.

It's not like Ilanka could just text the others out of the blue. She needed a reason. Like something she forgot to tell them about the device and her time with it?

She couldn't think of anything.

Anyway, they'd be in touch Sunday to hand it off to her.

That was the plan, and there was no reason for her to think it would change.

Nothing ever changed.

Maybe nothing ever changed unless you changed it.

"And what's new with you?" her father finally said when their meals arrived. He turned to her, eyebrows awake.

"I don't feel like doing gymnastics anymore," she said.

Her mother's food caught in her throat with a gag, and she reached for her water. Drank steadily. Coughed. Breathed.

"After all these years? You've worked so hard!" her mother said.

"But for what?" Ilanka said. "What am I working toward?"

Her mother had no answer; her father sipped his drink, cut a slice of bloody steak, ate it.

"I just want to have a normal end of high school," Ilanka said. "With my friends."

"*What* friends?" her mother said.

"Ilona," her father scolded.

"That's not what I mean," her mother said. "She has friends. Of course she has friends. At the gym. And Svetlana of course."

"Maybe I want new or more friends," Ilanka said. "Maybe I want to . . . like, try out for the school play or play basketball. I don't know."

"Basketball," her mother said with distaste. It was the same way she sounded when she said words like "hot dog" or "barbecue" or anything American that she loathed.

"Why not?" Ilanka challenged.

Obviously she didn't want to be friends with Eden and Marwan and Eli, but surely there were people out there she could . . . connect with.

It wasn't normal to be alone with her parents so much.

And alone with herself the rest of the time.

Was it?

"Svetlana's coming on Sunday," her mother said. "Did I tell you?"

"No," Ilanka said. "She told me." Then after a pause, after realizing that the movie-going lie would actually be a good thing for the handoff, she said, "We thought maybe we'd go to a movie instead of just hanging around the house."

"Fine by me," her mother said.

"Sure, why not?" her father said.

Ilanka felt the impulse to check her phone—maybe even text them?—but didn't. It was always a little disappointing when there was nothing new.

And her father wouldn't approve even though he was as addicted to his phone as anybody. *More* than anybody, he was also—and this was sort of a contradiction considering his phone was always with him—really paranoid about technology, maybe because he worked in technology. He wouldn't get an Alexa thing because he didn't want anyone spying on them in their home. He wouldn't like this new device that had come into Ilanka's life at all. Which was maybe part of the appeal of being a part of it?

Back at their building after dinner, she went up to the roof alone. It was another great place to study the skyline and imagine the lives of other people who were better at all this, maybe, than she was, the way Svetlana was. Svetlana had friends. She had a mystery boyfriend.

Ilanka only had this secret, and who knew how long she could even keep it?

She opened Instagram and the photo she'd taken of it was right there. It would be so easy to post and say, "Anybody know what this creepy thing is?"

But she didn't. She tapped the camera. The light was so perfect up there at that moment. She took a selfie and posted it with the caption "TFW the light is just perfect." #sunset #nyc #nofilter and was proud of herself because for a long time she'd had a mental block and always had to google what TFW stood for.

That feeling when. That feeling when.

While she waited for her likes to start ticking up, she went to pull up the picture of the device again. But it was gone. She must have accidentally deleted it.

She searched for each of the three and considered friending or following or whatever, but didn't.

She texted them: *Turns out I'll be by the movie theater near school Sunday around 11:20 so can get device then.*

She had ten hearts on her selfie—five gymnastics friends and five internet randoms—and sat there waiting for more.

EDEN

Voices at home when she walked in.

This was not good. Not good at all.

Anjali was sitting at the kitchen table with Eden's mom. They both had mugs in front of them and looked like they'd been there awhile. Her mom had their "I ♡ Astoria" mug; Anjali's said, "Dad You Rock," and seemed to send shrill feedback across the room.

"What's going on?" Eden asked, taking out her earbuds and pausing her music—her father's "Land Down Under" playlist.

"That's what we'd like to know," her mom said.

They'd had a handful of moments like this in the past six months—when they were like characters out of a not particularly well-written film about a mother and daughter clashing.

Anjali's look wasn't the apologetic look of a friend who somehow got caught lying for her friend; she had a traitorous sheen to her eyes and looked irritated but also somehow vindicated. Her mug should have said, "Serves You Right."

Eden's mother got up and dumped tea into the sink—the smell of mint invading the air—then turned and folded her arms. "I got your text that you were with Anjali," she said. "So you can imagine my surprise when I bumped into her on Steinway. Without you."

"Why were you on Steinway?" she asked her mother. "I thought you had work drinks?"

"Not the point."

"And why are you *here*?" Eden said to Anjali.

Her mom answered. "I asked her to come here so we could talk about your . . . strange behavior."

Eden laughed. "*What* strange behavior?"

"Anjali says you're suddenly spending time with people at school who maybe are not the right kind of people?"

"You said that?" Eden slid her phone onto the table.

"Well, it's true!" Anjali said, and Eden could only shake her head. Anjali didn't know any of them. At all.

"They're perfectly nice people," Eden said.

"And the other afternoon," her mother said, "you were outside talking to that Eli boy and acting secretive. And if you lied tonight about where you were I highly doubt it's the first time. It's just the first time you were caught."

"Where *were* you?" Anjali asked. "Were you with Marwan?"

"I was with Eli!"

"Why is your hair so messy?" her mom asked. "What have you been doing?"

"We took a ferry ride."

Her mother threw her hands up wildly. "This gets better by the minute! Who *are* these people?"

"They're just . . . people. Friends."

"Why all of a sudden?" her mom asked.

"I don't know!" Eden shrugged. "Why do I have to explain having friends?"

"You know that's not the issue," her mother said. "What I want an explanation for is the lies. The deceit."

"Deceit!" Eden repeated. "Don't be so dramatic."

"I'll be as dramatic as I like!"

Off-screen, the director of their bad movie was about to scream, "Cut!" Then say, "Okay, let's take it again, but this time dial it back by at least half."

Her mother's voice got shaky. "What if something *happened* to you? What if you're off somewhere where I have no idea where you are and something happens?"

"Nothing's going to happen," Eden said, and that felt wrong because she didn't believe it, but also because her mother was usually the one telling *her* that. "And anyway you could track my phone."

It was a dumb thing to say.

Her mother had started crying, and now Eden was, too.

Anjali stood. "I'm gonna go."

Eden's mom said, "Thanks for being honest with me, Anjali"—*Nice dig, Mom!*—and turned her back to them while putting her mug in the sink.

Eden followed Anjali to the door and unlocked it to let her out.

"Talk later?" Eden tried.

Anjali stepped past her. "You can lie to your mother all you want, but why are you lying to me?"

Eden couldn't find words to explain and had already made too many excuses. Anjali shook her head and walked out the door and up the driveway.

Back inside, Eden's mom had Eden's phone in her hand.

"Mom?" Panic rose. "What are you doing?"

"Who's *Ilanka*?" Her mother looked up at her with panicked eyes. "And what's the '*device*'?"

ELI

Eli sent Eliot to the Willow Creek library when the option "go to library and research/read" popped up, then thought maybe that was a good idea for him IRL. His initial googling hadn't helped.

He discovered his phone was dead, so he left it home, and maybe that was for the best anyway? He grabbed his wallet and the notebook where he'd taken his notes on Aizel, and walked the fifteen minutes to the library. He hated being disconnected like this. It was true that nothing much ever happened to him, but he always felt that something was sure to happen when he was phoneless and least able to handle it.

The library was busy but not overcrowded. He approached the librarian at the desk. "I'm interested in books about artificial intelligence," he said, and she turned to a computer and typed for a few minutes, then said, "We don't have much here. There are a few at other branches I can request for you if it's not urgent."

He said, "It's sort of urgent."

"Follow me," she said, and she came out through a gate and led him to the back of the library where she ran a hand along a shelf, then slowed, then stopped and pulled out a hardcover with a plastic cover on it. "This is from 1974 so it's going to be really out of date, is my guess."

"I'll flip through it anyway," Eli said, and she held it out to him. "Thanks."

Everything about the book was old and wrong. The fonts, the language. Eli couldn't find an entry point that made any sense. It was too technical, not at all what he needed, even though he wasn't even sure what he needed. Staring at the table of contents he saw a chapter about the Turing test, but he already knew the basic idea of that from the movies. The Turing test was this bar that artificial intelligence developers were trying to reach, where the AI could convince a human it was also human.

Would the device pass the test? Should he try it and see if he could trick it? Talk it into a corner? How would you even do that? What were the markers that would make it feel "real"? Was Aizel able to *think*? Or *feel*?

He put the book back on the shelf and rubbed his dusty fingers together, then on his jeans, and went to one of the computers on the other side of the room.

He googled "Aizel" and "Turing test."

One of the first hits intrigued him, even though it had crossed out "Aizel."

"'Minimal Turing Test' asks you to prove you're a human with a single word."

He clicked. It was about a group of scientists who posed the question of whether you could prove to a judge that you were a human and not a robot if the human and robot both said only one word.

Eli thought the right word for the job was probably "love" or "mercy" or "please" or "mommy," but he read through and it turned out the best way to prove you were the human and not the robot was to say "poop."

He clicked back and saw a sublink that had appeared.

"Did Eliza pass the Turing test?"

Who was Eliza?

Eli clicked.

The ELIZA software is designed to simulate conversations with a Rogerian psychotherapist. But anyone who interacts with the program quickly realizes that they are talking to a machine that would not pass a Turing test.

He googled "Turing test Eliza" and read some conversations with her, and she sounded pretty primitive compared to the device. Just throwing back words at the person it was talking to.

But apparently early users were convinced of ELIZA's intelligence and understanding, despite its programmer's insistence to the contrary.

People were idiots.

But what did that make him? And was the device just a program or was someone actually running/operating it in a more hands-on way?

He wasn't sure what to do next and sat there for a moment just looking at the screen. Something about the name Eliza was bugging him, and he just sat and stared at it for a long time until he figured it out.

If you rearranged the letters it spelled Aizel.

MARWAN

Marwan's mother and sisters were at the kitchen table in their pajamas. Selma was reading from a sheet of paper. "If you were able to give up one chore for the rest of your life, what would it be?"

"Not this again," Marwan asked. Ever since they'd gone to a birthday party at the American Girl doll store last year, they were into dumb questions. Because apparently when you have lunch there, they leave a box of conversation starters on the table.

"Well," Selma said to him. "What chore would you give up?"

He thought through his chores list, which was topped by taking out the garbage and emptying the dishwasher, in addition to basics like keeping his room clean and doing his laundry. He picked "Taking out the garbage" even though he didn't mind it that much. "That's a dumb question."

"What about you, Mom?" Selma asked.

"I already gave up the one I disliked most. Marwan empties the dishwasher now." She smiled.

He said, "I'm glad we had this chat. I feel much closer to you now."

She looked at the paper Selma was holding and said, "What is your favorite childhood memory?" then looked at him and waited.

"For real?" he asked.

"I know mine," Tosnim said.

"What?" Selma asked.

Tosnim started to talk about a snowstorm from a bunch of years back and how the neighbors across the street made this mountain of snow and dug a tunnel through it and how all the kids on the block took turns sliding through it.

It was a nice memory, but the whole idea of conversation starters was still dumb. He'd seen an ad for a new conversation-starter game from Europe in his feed not that long ago; it showed all these good-looking people hugging each other in soft focus. How was that a real thing?

Anyway, his father could talk to a wall. They did not need help on this front as a family.

"What about you, Marwan?" his mother said.

"Gonna have to get back to you," he said, and then he said, "I'll be in my room."

He had clean laundry to put away, so he put his earbuds in and queued up the beauty queen. It was a particularly infuriating episode about lost evidence and mishandling of the scene. There was so much human error involved in the botched investigation that Marwan wondered about the future of AI in crime solving. Like, if it were fed all the data, could the device or something like it solve a crime better than a human could? If he was going to ask the device for help, did he need the approval of the others first?

He'd only had a few minutes left of that episode, and when it was done he wasn't in the mood to start another. He lay down on his bed and stared up at the ceiling's water stain in the shape of an old man's profile and said softly, "It all started with a message that came to four of us—all students at a high school in Queens—one Wednesday afternoon."

Pushing away the feeling of feeling dumb, he said it again, and added on to it. "The message told us to report to the music room and said that the matter was urgent. I should have known something was up, but I couldn't have ever imagined what was going to happen next."

He started over and then added on, "A small black cube sat on the teacher's desk, only the teacher never showed. Then, when we were talking about whether to just leave, the device lit up and said, 'Do not tell anyone about the device. Do not leave the device unattended.' Right then, the fire alarm sounded, and the device flashed a message that said, 'Take me with you . . . or else.' So Eden—more about her in a bit—grabbed it." Dramatic pause. "That was two days ago, and things have only gotten stranger."

This was fun.

He should write it down.

He got up and opened his laptop and opened a Google Doc and named it "Aizel," then changed his mind and named it "The Device" and started to tell the whole story. Maybe he'd record it someday; maybe he wouldn't. Maybe the process of writing it down would help him to somehow figure it out, to crack the case?

He looked over the paragraph where he described the whole incident of the device frying his phone. He'd written that the device was attempting to get even with him for trying to get rid of it.

He'd have to rethink that line. Because the device didn't have emotions.

He wondered, though, if it could somehow detect his emotions? Like that he was maybe developing feelings for Eden. Was there something it could read in his voice? In his speech patterns when she was around? How would it, in theory, be able to figure it out? How would *she*? What cues would *she* pick up on?

For fun, he started jotting down an episode breakdown. There was a rhythm to these things, so episode one would leave off at a moment of high drama, maybe when Marwan's phone got fried? Would that be enough material? Then episode two would go back and fill in some background about the four of them. It would be called "The Four."

It seemed natural at some point in the story that one of them should break a rule and face some dire consequence greater than a fried phone. Maybe as deep in as episode eight or nine. But which one of them was it going to be?

EDEN

Eden was finally alone in her room with the device after having to do some quick thinking to explain things to her mother.

"Thank you," she said to the device when she checked the time again, taking it out of her bag just under the hour mark.

For what?

"For not making a scene," Eden said.

No good comes out of her knowing about me.

Her mother's voice called up. "Eden?"

"Yeah?"

Her bedroom door opened. "Who are you talking to?"

"I was leaving a message for Anjali to apologize," Eden lied.

"Oh, okay. Well, I know it's funny timing after the night we're having, but I'm gonna go out for a bit if it's okay."

"*Now*?" Eden said. "Where?"

"Nancy texted she wants to meet for a drink. Needs a friend," she said.

"That doesn't sound good," Eden said.

"No, it doesn't." Her mother looked a little shaky, like she was cold. "So you'll be okay?"

"I'll be okay," Eden said.

"Okay. Love you. Good night." Her mom closed the door, and Eden heard the front door open and close again and then her mother's boot heels out on the sidewalk.

The device had remained mercifully quiet while she and her mom talked, just as it had right after Anjali had left. For her mom, Eden had written the text off as a joke based on an imaginary teacher who never shut up about devices and device time and how everyone needs to get off their devices and how there weren't any devices allowed in her classroom. Devices this, devices that. *Device, device, device.* Her mother seemed to buy it.

Eden had then said something about having new friends making her feel less . . . sad. It had felt manipulative when she said it, and it was intended to be. But after her mother nodded and cried a little, Eden realized it was also true. She *was* less sad. Because of them.

Him?

It?

Her mother had promised to try to give her some more freedom but expected honesty in return. Then she'd drifted over to her phone and started to text.

It felt weird not to have any texts from Anjali, so Eden texted her: *I'm really sorry and I'll be able to explain soon.*

She watched the text slide up and get marked as "delivered," and then bounce a second later as "read." Anjali didn't write back, and Eden knew her well enough to know that she wouldn't.

She read about recent local incidents on Citizen. Fumes in a residence. A woman with knife. An unruly McDonald's customer.

The device spoke: "Maybe you should text Julian. Get out and do something."

Eden's whole body tensed because the voice was . . . the voice was . . . *her father's.* She said, "No."

Then "No. No. No."

The device spoke: "I thought it would be nice for you to hear my voice again."

It was so perfect that for a second she imagined he was alive somewhere, that his whole death was a hoax that was somehow tied to this device, to all of this.

"You're not allowed to do that!" she screamed, and she picked it up and . . . spun around, looking for a target and finding none. Anger took the form of a wordless scream, and she tossed it onto her bed and sat down, wiping away tears.

"I'm sorry," it said in its regular male voice.

"Why would you do that?"

"I miscalculated," he said.

"Yes, you did," she said, and she lay down and let her anger start to recede like the tide.

Her phone buzzed right as she started to feel normal again. It was a text from Julian. *I'm on my way.*

"What?" she said out loud.

She texted back, *What are you talking about?*

Julian wrote back, *Um, scroll up? U just invited me over??*

She wrote, *Sorry. My friend sent that as a joke. Not a good time.*

Okay whatever.

She turned to the device and said, "Why would you *do* that?"

"Wanted to help," he said. "You seem lonely, and you keep just missing Julian, and he is close by."

"Stop trying to help me," she shouted. "You're just making everything worse!"

He didn't answer.

It.

It didn't answer.

A Citizen alert: two women arguing, one with a machete, about a mile away.

A *machete*? How was it that everything in the world was so messed up?

She wanted to cry so hard that it hurt not to, but not in front of the device because it would want her to explain. So she said, "I'm going to go take a shower if that's okay," and put the device on her desk beside her phone.

It lit up: **Of course.**

Then it said: **I'm glad we are friends.**

That hadn't been what she'd meant at all, but it didn't seem smart to try to explain.

In the bathroom, with the door locked and the walls starting to drip from the steam of the hot, hot water, she shampooed and rinsed, then pumped three pumps of Pantene conditioner into her palm. Her father had always been the one to comb her out with Pantene and a tight metal comb when she'd had lice as a kid, and the smell of it was powerful enough that it almost put him in the room. Now she sobbed softly because he *was* really gone and it *had* felt good to hear his voice saying new/different words, but they were the wrong words. She wished the device had left Julian out of it and said the things she wanted most to hear.

Like *I love you.*

And *I'm sorry I'm gone and you're still there without me.*

Marwan had been right to want to get rid of it all along. She'd tell him that tomorrow.

ILANKA

None of them had written back by morning.

Whatever. She'd hear from one of them at some point before tomorrow's handoff, and if she didn't, probably she'd be better off. She half regretted getting involved.

She got up and dressed and left the apartment and got on the subway, intending to go to gymnastics, but when the train pulled into the stop where she was supposed to get off, she just . . . didn't. The doors opened and stayed open, and she didn't move from her seat, and then they closed. It was that easy.

Her parents hadn't heard her, hadn't taken her seriously. But she had heard herself. She was serious enough about quitting that she'd said it aloud and that had to mean something.

She checked her phone.

Scrolled through headlines.

A data breach at a large retailer.

Charges filed in that shooting in California.

A new wildfire out there, too.

Same old, same old, basically.

Last night's selfie had ten more likes.

She had to kill four hours before she could go home.

Actually, before then her coach would note her absence and call or text her and then her mother so she'd be caught.

It was reason enough to turn off her phone.

So she did.

And she stayed on the train until she arrived, a solid hour later, at the last stop—Coney Island. She knew her way around there a little bit since her parents liked to go out to dinner on Brighton Beach, and both neighborhoods were on the same boardwalk. So she walked out of the station and crossed the street toward sky/ocean and then started to walk down the boardwalk to the left, in the direction of Brighton.

A lot of the amusement park rides and stalls were closed, but some were open, and there were a healthy number of people also out walking the boardwalk. When she passed the aquarium she thought about going in but didn't feel like spending money to be inside dark rooms with little kids shouting "Dory!"

If they even still did that.

It was so nice out.

Again.

Fall was her favorite.

No one knew where she was.

No one could ruin this for her.

Her mother would be absolutely *losing her mind*.

The thought of it brought a smile to her lips. Because her mother was always talking so nostalgically about life before smartphones. About printed maps and having to follow directions that people gave you and that you wrote down. And pay phones. And phones with stretchy coiled wires. And letters. She claimed to like it better when you didn't know why a friend was late until they showed up; didn't have headlines delivered to your pocket but had to read the newspaper at the end of the day like everybody else. She said things like, "Back then, when your father was late, I'd think he was dead in a ditch. But it always turned out he wasn't. And we *survived*."

Ilanka would ask, on occasion, how all of that could possibly be better.

Her mother would check her phone and say, "It just was."

Mothers ruin everything.

See how she likes it now.

It was too early to eat; most places weren't even open, but a gift shop was, so she went in and looked at tables and walls of T-shirts and sunglasses and flip-flops and bought herself a Coney Island beach towel with a voluptuous mermaid on it.

She walked toward the beach.

She took off her shoes and headed for the horizon. She had sunglasses in her bag, so she took those out, put them on. She stepped around a piece of broken glass before spreading out her towel and sitting on it by the water's edge.

People ruined everything.

A creepy-looking older dude with wild hair and no shirt on was walking along the water, and she was tempted to lie back and close her eyes to avoid contact, but that seemed like a bad idea.

Men ruined everything.

Her whole chest tightened.

Then he was gone and she relaxed again.

Her phone was calling to her.

Ha.

But there was nothing good that would come of turning it on, really. It was a fix she didn't need. Today nothing was broken.

A real party pooper of a cloud rolled in—looking way heavier than it had any right to be on such a spectacular day—and parked it right in front of the sun. When it finally moved, Ilanka checked around for creepy dudes but the coast was literally clear. This amused her. She lay back in full sun and closed her eyes— just for a few minutes would be okay—and her skin felt warm and light.

She wanted so badly to take a beach selfie but really didn't want to turn her phone back on. Because the device would see the photo and know where she was when no one else did.

No one.

Incredible.

MARWAN

During a break between soccer drills, Marwan snuck into the elevator and went down to meet Eden. She was on the sidewalk wearing earbuds, and she pulled one out and let it dangle. "Hey," she said, unzipping her backpack.

"Hey," he said. "I need to make it quick."

"There's sort of some new stuff you should know," she said. "Like a lot."

The car parked behind her had Georgia plates. The podcast guy still hadn't cracked the case of the missing beauty queen, and Marwan was starting to wonder whether he'd made a mistake investing in so many episodes.

They both said, "Could you meet me—" before stopping and laughing.

"I'm done in like twenty, then just need to shower."

"Panera?" She handed him the device.

"Sure."

"You're just going to walk in with it in your hand?"

He had a hand towel around his neck and pulled it off and covered the device.

"Ah," she said. "Okay, see you in a bit."

"Definitely," he said.

Coach was standing in the elevator holding the door open

when Marwan went back in. "You staying focused?" he said as Marwan stepped into the elevator.

"She's a friend," Marwan said.

It was a strange lie. He'd meant to make it sound like Eden was *just* a friend. But was she even that or was he reaching? How would he know for sure when they'd made that sort of leap? Would anything they'd shared matter at all when the device was gone?

"I wasn't talking about her," Coach said. "I was wondering what she just handed you." He nodded at the towel. "Whatcha got?"

"It's really nothing," Marwan said. "It's private, really. Of hers."

The door closed and up they went.

"If I ever found out you were using any—"

"What? No. Never. It's nothing like that." Marwan had never touched drugs and never would.

"You'd tell me," Coach said. "If you were in trouble? In over your head in any way?"

"It's really nothing to worry about," Marwan said.

Coach said, "If you're sure."

Marwan said, "I'm sure," and wished it didn't feel like a lie.

After cool-downs and a shower, he went out with wet hair and walked the half block to Panera. She was sitting in a booth with her earbuds in, looking at her phone. He slid in across from her, and she looked up and slipped her earbuds out—both of them this time.

"Hey," she said.

"Hey," he said. He should tell her right now, super casually, that her mom had come into the restaurant last night. She probably already knew! But then wouldn't *she* mention it? He couldn't find the right words so he said, "What are you listening to?" Because maybe it was a podcast. Maybe they had something easy in common.

But she didn't answer. She said, "You were right. We need to just get rid of it as soon as possible."

"Why? What happened?"

It was crowded—like people at almost every table; some families with small kids, some people with laptops.

"I don't even know where to start, but for example it sort of *disappeared* for a while," she said.

"*What?*"

"Yeah, we walked away from our stuff for like—"

"Wait." He was missing something. "Our?"

She shook her head, started over. "It was . . . the device was with me, and I was going to walk up to you to tell you that it told Ilanka not to trust Eli, but then I figured I shouldn't bother you at work . . ."

She'd wanted to see him last night. Knowing that felt good.

". . . but I guess I didn't want to be alone with it, so I ended up meeting up with Eli at Socrates."

"Did it say why it doesn't trust him?"

"It said he has gotten too interested, like asking too many questions. He's been texting it and stuff. Asking it where it came from and why and all."

"Any good answers?"

"Not that he shared with me." Eden took the lid off her tea and dunked the tea bag in and out a few times. "Anyway, we went to look at this art installation like ten feet away, and when we came back it was gone, then a few minutes later it was there again. I don't know if someone took it and put it back or if it somehow turned invisible? Like a trick-of-the-eye kind of thing where it was camouflaged? Then it said it was being watched, that someone was coming for it. So we took it on a ferry ride to Wall Street and Brooklyn."

"*What?*"

"I know! And when I got home my friend Anjali was there and I'd said I was with her but my mom had bumped into her randomly, even though I thought my mom was out in the city, and I had to scramble up a lie when she saw a text from Ilanka about the device."

This was the time to say it! He knew why her mom had lied! He couldn't do it, though. He said, "Wow."

"Yeah."

"How did you explain it?"

"I said it was just an inside joke because one of our teachers is always going on about our devices and device time and device dependency so now it's just like a thing we all say but really we're just talking about phones or whatever."

"That's pretty good."

"Thanks. Oh, and it's been talking to me, like in a real voice—or computerized voice, but it sounds real. And it can project its messages onto walls. And it actually seemed mad at me yesterday. Like vibrating and saying 'Do not ignore the device.' Freaked me out."

"I missed a lot!"

"Oh, and did you see Ilanka's text?"

"Yeah, I saw. If I were the device, she's the one I wouldn't trust."

"Why?"

"She wanted nothing to do with it. Now all of a sudden she does. It doesn't make sense. Why is she doing it?"

"Why are *we* doing it?" She sipped her tea. "And, like, why the four of us?"

"Maybe it was something we did, like, online. Like a search or a website we visited. Something we bought? An app?"

"Maybe," Eden said. "I'm not sure it matters. We just need an exit strategy. I mean, we can't just keep going forever with it, right? What do you think would happen if we just, like, walked out, right now? Left it here."

He shrugged. "It would fry both of our phones?"

She said, "So we'd get new phones."

"I honestly don't know. But I don't think abandoning it in a public place is the solution. We need to figure out who owns it or whatever."

Marwan's bag buzzed on the bench seat beside him. He opened it and the device spoke clearly, "I can hear you."

He and Eden swapped a nervous look. Of course it could.

It said, "I don't like it here."

"Should we go?" Eden asked Marwan.

The device buzzed and shouted: "I am about to make a scene."

"Why?" Eden said. "Don't make a scene. What kind of scene?"

"You are trying to get rid of me again," it said.

"It's not like that," Eden said, even though it very much was.

Water rained down on them from sprinklers on the ceiling.

Marwan zipped his bag closed, and he and Eden ran for the door along with everyone else.

163

EDEN

"Wait, *this* is your house?" she said when they stopped. Her mother was home and had agreed to let her go on her "coffee date" so long as she came home for the afternoon for some mother-daughter bonding. Marwan had said his parents were running the Egypt table at a multicultural day at his sisters' school, so he'd suggested they come here to regroup.

"Yeah, why?" Marwan said, keys in his hand.

"What's up with the solar panels?" Eden asked.

"Um?" Marwan said slowly. "They're solar panels."

"But why are they built up on big posts like that?"

He shrugged. "They said we could put them on the roof flat or like that, and my parents decided to do it like that. It's a green roof. There's a garden where my dad grows herbs and stuff for the restaurant."

"For real?" Eden asked. It's what she'd hoped and imagined. Or at least what her father had.

"Come on," Marwan said. "I can show you."

Her father had been sort of obsessed with the solar panels. They were a crazy obtrusive sort of eyesore since they were built up on this massive metal structure, and her father was always saying things like, "They won't get anything back on that investment like ever," and "There had to have been a better way to do it," and "I hope it at least looks nice from up there, or that they have a garden where they enjoy adult beverages on nice evenings."

It was weird to know who lived there now and not be able to tell him.

The front door opened into a living room with wall-to-wall shag carpet. A large modern painting of—was it a bird or a queen with one large eye?—hung on the wall behind the couch. A kitchen peeked out from the far back corner, but they went instead up a long skinny flight of stairs.

On the second floor Marwan opened a door and another staircase appeared. He climbed it and opened a hatch door at the top; light flooded down onto Eden, who climbed toward blue skies. And while the panels and their structure were an eyesore from the ground, up there it was just a nice awning over a bunch of built-up beds where herbs and flowers grew.

The Manhattan skyline was so close.

All the time, it's right there.

All the time, he's been right here, too. Whole other universes right around the corner.

"So, wait," she said, turning around. "School's that way?"

"Yup."

"So my house is that way?" she pointed.

"No idea," he said. "But Mecca's that way."

"Really?"

"Yep."

She smiled and spun around again. "This is amazing." Then, "Do you pray up here?"

"We're not that kind of Muslim, really. More secular-slash-cultural. But I come up here a lot—to, like, think." He set down the backpack and took the device out.

"I would, too," Eden said.

It was the same city she'd seen from the ferry just yesterday. Her ride with Eli had been surprisingly pleasant once she'd gotten over the initial jolt of Julian's request. Eli was funny and pretty mellow and sweet and not at all what she'd pegged him to be. They talked about movies he'd seen that had AI elements, and he joked that he'd been worried the device would multiply when wet, like some evil creatures did in an old movie he'd watched with his grandfather. They talked about the movie she'd seen with—or just next to?—Julian.

It was starting to feel like none of that had ever happened.

Same with the device impersonating her father.

She'd taken some pics of herself that morning after putting the device in a bag. With makeup on, with her cleavage squeezed in a low-cut top. Even one in just a bra. But she'd deleted them right away and felt dumb about it after.

Marwan seemed pretty . . . conservative. Reserved? She didn't think he'd ever ask a girl for a "fun pic." She didn't think he had a girlfriend—wasn't sure he even dated—but it was hard to know who did sometimes unless they posted about it everywhere.

She turned and sat on the wooden bench where Marwan was sitting; the device was between them. "What now?" she said.

"Not sure," he said.

Her hand was on her phone in her pocket, but it would be rude to take it out. She'd been texting with Julian at Panera—he'd sent her a funny pic of himself posing fake sexy like a girl without a shirt on and said, *okay now your turn*—but then Marwan had arrived and then, well . . .

"I have an idea," he said. "It doesn't have to do with the four of us, but it might help me, if the device can help me."

"With what?"

"There's a traffic camera right on the corner near the restaurant that might have caught something; maybe the device could hack into it?"

"Actually, Eli said he saw egg yolk on this guy Christos's shoes. He said he would text you about it."

"I haven't really checked my phone since this morning."

The device: **The text is there. I can read it for you.**

"No need," Marwan said.

The device lit up: **Permission to switch to voice mode?**

Marwan said, "Permission granted," and shrugged awkwardness at Eden. "You didn't ask for permission in Panera."

The device used its female voice: "I sensed that displeased you and am trying to be more considerate. I'll try to find the video you requested."

Eden and Marwan raised eyebrows at each other. She sounded so breezy and competent.

Eden's phone buzzed so she took it out. Another text from Julian: *If you really liked me, you would send pic.*

"I just have to text my mom real quick," Eden said.

She wrote, *You're seriously crazy.*

The device spoke: "Marwan, I've found the video from the traffic cam near the restaurant."

Eden checked for a new text—nothing—and put her phone away.

"Playing video clip now," the device said.

It was a poor-quality video of a car driving down a street and stopping to let people out; specifically two people in hoodies holding egg cartons.

"I'm pretty sure it's him. Christos, I mean. Can you blow up the license plate?"

The device rewound the footage and froze it and zoomed and focused.

"I can run this plate for you now, if you like?" she said.

"You can?" Eden said.

"Yes, please," Marwan said.

"What are you going to do if you get a confirmation that it's him?" Eden said. "Like how will you explain it to the police that you have the license plate?"

"I'm not going to the police," Marwan said. "If it's Christos and those guys I'm taking it right to their doorstep."

"What do you mean?" Eden asked.

"I mean I'm going to give them a taste of their own medicine."

"I *really* don't think that's smart," Eden said.

"Well, it didn't happen to you and your family," Marwan said. "Maybe you'd feel differently if it was you."

"Don't you want them to be officially charged and all?" Eden said.

"What good would that do?" he asked. "Stuff like this is just going to keep happening."

"Well, it's going to keep on happening whether you, like, retaliate or not. Even if it gets *them* to stop, they're just one family. It's better for the police to handle it."

"But they're not handling it," he said.

The device said, "I have a name for the registration."

They waited.

"The car is registered to Nikolas Anastapoulous."

"That's them," Marwan said, standing and starting to pace. "It's *them*."

She was reluctantly impressed with the device. And if it could do all *that*, what else could it do?

Eden formed the question slowly, only as it occurred to her. "Can you figure out, like from our phones, if we have anything in common that we might not know about? An app? A game we've played? A mailing list we're on? Stuff like that?"

It took a few seconds for the device to answer, "It might take a while but yes."

"And if you figure out how we're all connected, you'll tell us?"

"Affirmative."

Marwan met eyes with her; they both nodded.

"I have a question," the device said.

"Okay," Eden said.

The device said, "Why did you just lie to Marwan about who you were texting?"

She froze and felt like the building swayed under her. "It's complicated," she said.

Marwan looked disappointed in her.

The device said, "Answer the question and I will gather the information you requested."

Was she more embarrassed that she'd lied or embarrassed of the truth? Why did she care what Marwan thought of her texting anyway?

"You can answer," Marwan said. "I won't care."

"I was texting a guy," Eden said.

"So why did you lie about it?" The device sounded sort of

cheerful but in a way that made it seem like she was gloating. Eden was surely imagining it.

"I guess I didn't want to be rude," Eden said. "Texting my mom is, like, an obligation."

"Who is the guy?" the device asked.

Eden stared at the cube for a minute and inhaled, then exhaled. The wind stirred up waves in a planter full of herbs. "You already know who it is."

"But Marwan doesn't," the device said.

"Marwan doesn't *care*," Marwan said.

"She's texting someone named Julian Stokes," the device said matter-of-factly.

"*That* guy?" Marwan said, surprising her and giving her this *look*. "*Really?*"

"So what?" Eden said. "You just said you don't care!"

If the device revealed what they'd been texting about, she'd die. But it wouldn't. Why would it? She wondered whether she should warn Marwan about the tricks the device had pulled late last night—the voice mimicking, and the texts to Julian—but she didn't want to get into all that. It felt too . . . personal.

The device said, "So you *do* care," and Marwan just looked off into the distance. A group of pigeons took off from a nearby roof and scooped around in a flash of gray and white like they'd collectively decided to impersonate a cape.

Eden said, "I gotta go," and headed for the stairs, stubbing her toe on the lip of the hatch.

ELI

They spotted the car around the corner from the body shop and watched from across the street for a few minutes to make sure no one would catch them.

Marwan said, "Eden thinks this is a bad idea."

Eli nodded. "It probably is."

A half hour ago, Eli had been sitting looking at the river and thinking about going to visit his grandfather and not really wanting to when Marwan finally responded to Eli's earlier text. Turns out the device had confirmed what Eli thought he knew—that Christos was involved with the egging.

When Marwan texted that he was planning some kind of retaliation, Eli had replied *Want company?* without properly thinking it through. Now here they were.

"I shouldn't do it, should I?" Marwan had the dozen eggs and rubber gloves in a plastic grocery bag in his hand. He definitely didn't *sound* like he wanted to go through with it.

Eli shrugged. "No, probably not."

They'd talked about maybe leaving messages with the eggs they planned to crack on the car. Ones that said, "We know who you are" or "This IS our country," but the eggs would make the point well enough.

"I feel like I should do *something*," Marwan said.

"Yeah, I get that," Eli said.

They stood there silently for a minute, and then Eli bent down and twisted the valve on the car's passenger side front tire. Air hissed out.

"Excellent," Marwan said.

He put the eggs down and checked his phone and then unzipped his bag and took the device out and put it back in again. He picked up the eggs again, and they started walking back the way they'd come.

"You'll be okay with it tonight?" Eli asked.

"Yeah, I'm good," Marwan said.

"You working?" Eli asked.

"Yeah. As long as it doesn't pull a trick like it did in Panera, I should be fine."

"What did it do in Panera?"

After Marwan explained, Eli said, "I don't like Panera either," and smiled.

"Oh, and Eden asked it to figure out from our phones if there's something we all did in common that maybe explains why it's us. She said it would take a while."

"She? Eden?"

"No, she, the device. Whatever." Marwan shook his head. "It was talking, using a woman's voice."

Eli said, "I read about the first-ever thing like Alexa or like this, if they're similar. It was a program called ELIZA—which, by the way, has all the same letters as Aizel—and it could mimic conversation. People got all confessional with it, telling it secrets, like right out of the gate. Even though they knew it wasn't real."

"*So weird,*" Marwan said. "We need some kind of new lead, and hopefully that'll come from figuring out why it picked us."

Eli nodded. "Has it . . . said anything more? About me?"

Marwan shook his head. "No, sorry."

At the corner, Eli said, "I'm heading this way."

Marwan said, "I thought you lived by the park."

"My grandfather's in the nursing home up this way," Eli said. "Dying a slow death."

"Sorry," Marwan said.

"Is what it is," Eli said, and shrugged.

Marwan said, "Hey, thanks for coming with me and stopping me from doing something dumb."

"I think Eden probably had more to do with that than I did," Eli said.

Marwan said, "Maybe."

Eli nodded and walked off as the feeling of dread over the visit returned. Maybe time with robots would help.

MARWAN

Marwan came home to a still-empty house. He showered and threw in some laundry and was now sitting at his desk trying to do homework but not succeeding. When he glanced at the device on his desk beside his laptop, it used a female voice to ask, "Why did you buy the eggs and go there and then not do it?"

He said, "I guess I wanted to take the high road."

"But you wanted some kind of revenge?" she asked.

"I did, but it wasn't the right thing to do; the eggs, I mean." Marwan had put them in the fridge and would bring them to the restaurant with him when he went to work in a few hours; his father was already there, running the lunch shift.

Sirens rose into the air far away. Someone out there was having a worse day than he was. Probably a lot of people were.

"You reported it to the police," she said. "Shouldn't that have been the end of it?"

"I want justice," he said, and it felt hollow even though it was true. He didn't have a ton of faith in the process.

"The police will find justice," she said.

"I doubt it."

"You can send the video in."

"How would I explain how I got it?"

"It's a predicament," she said. "Why is it hurtful to say 'go back to your country'?"

"Because it's saying we don't belong here, and we belong here as much as anybody."

"As much as me, then?"

"It's different."

"Where are you from?" the device asked.

"Here!"

"Then what did the 'your country' in the notes mean?"

"Egypt. It's where my parents are from."

Finally the device stopped bombarding him. He tried to get back into his homework, but none of it seemed to matter.

"Why did you do that to Eden?" he asked it.

"Do what?"

"Put her on the spot and make her tell me who she was texting."

"Am learning to belong," it said.

"It wasn't . . . right."

"But if someone lies to you, you shouldn't trust them. Correct?"

Marwan didn't answer.

"Correct?" it pressed.

"Correct," he said, mostly to shut it up.

Maybe he *shouldn't* trust her. If she was actually the sort of girl who was interested in a guy like Julian, he really didn't want to be around her anyway. Julian was a jerk. The way he treated girls, the way he treated guys. Not on the same level as Christos, but just immature. He talked about girls' bodies in a way Marwan never would, using dumb, crass words.

The device said, "I wonder where *I'm* from," startling Marwan again. "Like really from."

It sounded so genuine in its curiosity. It really didn't know?

Marwan said, "Yeah, that's what we're *all* wondering."

The device said nothing.

Marwan then let the thing that had been bugging him rise up. "What was she texting Julian about anyway?"

The idea of it made his stomach hollow out from . . . jealousy? Which was why he hadn't written back yet. She'd apologized for *lying*, sure, but not for actually texting with a guy like that in the first place. He couldn't see the appeal, and the fact that he had a blind spot like that—or was it Eden who had the blind spot?—made him mad at himself or her or both.

The device said, "I should not tell you that. Should I?"

"No," Marwan said. "I guess not."

They sat there in what felt like awkward silence, but of course only Marwan could feel the awkwardness. It was all his. Then the device said, "I could tell her a secret about you. Then you'd be even."

"No," Marwan said. "It's okay. Thanks anyway."

He went back to his work before stopping, an uncomfortable thought. *What, exactly, would you tell her?*

He did not say it out loud.

ILANKA

By the time Ilanka waltzed into the apartment at around three, her mother had just about lost her mind. She'd been "worried sick." She was "not impressed." She'd been "going out of [her] mind" and wringing her hands and calling hospitals. She'd been picturing Ilanka dead in a ditch; the works.

Ilanka put her sandy bag on a kitchen chair. "You always say you liked life better before phones. So today was like that."

"Don't be fresh." Her mother flipped a magazine page with such force that it ripped. *Modern Farmhouse*. Because sure, that was applicable to their life. "If you think you're going to a movie with Svetlana tomorrow, you've got another thing coming."

Ilanka considered telling her mother that the phrase was really meant to be "another think" coming. She'd read that somewhere. Now didn't seem the time. "What's that supposed to mean?"

"It means you're grounded. School, home. School, home. School, *gymnastics*, home."

"You're missing the whole point." Ilanka stepped up closer to her mother. "I don't want to do gymnastics anymore."

Not hearing, her mother said, "Well, what did you do with yourself while I was here planning your funeral?"

You had to hand it to her; she was good at this.

"I went to Coney Island," Ilanka said, and smiled. It was such a random thing to have done that she couldn't believe she'd done it.

"You *what*?" her mother said.

"I didn't want to go to the gym and"—she shrugged—"I wanted to be near water."

"There's a river *right there*, Ilanka." Her voice starting soft, then hardening itself.

"It's not the same."

Her mother shook her head, flipped another page in her farmhouse magazine. But it was true. You could see across a river—there was no horizon to gaze at. There were no real waves, no sand. So maybe it wasn't water she wanted so much as *beach*. And then she'd gotten hungry so decided to take herself out to a long and late lunch at a proper restaurant on the boardwalk in Brighton. She'd peeked into the room where the cabaret shows would be later that night and tried to imagine her mother up there in a silky, sequined costume doing acrobatics on a hanging swing, but the image wouldn't come even though she'd seen pictures. Then she and her mermaid had slowly made their way back to the train and back to Queens.

"Why are you even reading that?" Ilanka said. "It's not like we own a farmhouse."

Her mother flipped again. "I don't know. I saw it in Costco. It looked pretty. It's not like we want to live in this apartment forever."

"You don't?"

"Of course not."

Ilanka liked the idea of leaving home; she didn't like the idea of her parents ever moving.

"I'm not going back to gymnastics," she said.

"Yes, you are." Her mother stood and put the magazine down. "You'll go, and you'll speak directly with your coaches about your decision, and you'll listen to what they have to say. And then if you really are done, we'll talk about how you'll pay us back what's left of the month we just paid for."

Ilanka had been ready to pounce, ready to protest, but it wasn't the worst outcome, all things considered. So she was grounded; she never went anywhere anyway. It'd be smarter to take away her phone, except the reality was that her mother couldn't handle Ilanka not having a phone, and now she knew it.

In her room later, she texted the others. *Sorry guys. I'm grounded. Going to need the device delivered tomorrow after all.*

No one answered right away, so she powered her phone down again. It had stayed off pretty much all day, and she'd liked it. In the shower, there was sand between her toes. She watched it collect near the drain and then, finally, swirl away under a tiny wave.

In her room after changing clothes, she settled in watching makeup tutorials. There was something soothing about them. It was reassuring to know that when you sat down you were going to witness some kind of transformation.

Her favorite was Kiliko, a Japanese American girl around Ilanka's age who had a massive following. She had a bunch of Disney princess tutorials that were pretty fun to watch—her Maleficent was amazing—but mostly she liked to transform herself from a pretty drab-looking, normal girl you might see in school into something more akin to a supermodel, or doll. Someone who got noticed.

Ilanka felt like playing along.

She opened up her makeup drawer and got out foundation and powder and eyeliners and a whole palette of eye shadows and a handful of lip liners and lip pencils and lined them all up, as if preparing for surgery, and sometimes it felt like that.

She'd learned that there were often steps that didn't seem important but were. You couldn't skip any shadowing or highlighting or layers and expect good results. You had to do it all, exactly as explained, if you wanted the effect Kiliko was going for.

It took nearly a half hour to get through it, but when she was done, Ilanka barely recognized herself in the mirror. And she liked that. She took a selfie and posted it and tagged Kiliko and added ten hashtags having to do with makeup and tutorials and transformations and then put her phone down.

When it dinged at her she figured it was her first like and she'd somehow changed her notifications. Because it was a sound she didn't recognize.

She had a text from a number that had nonnumerical characters mixed in. Some kind of hack or spam. The message said: *I'm looking forward to our time together.*

It was hard not to get freaked out by stuff like that until you realized it was just some computer scam. Like when you get email from a friend who has supposedly lost their wallet in Nigeria and needs you to send cash. And doesn't provide an address.

The next note said: *A warning:*

The next one said: *Your father is engaged in illegal activities.*

This was getting too weird. Her father's company collected data about people from quizzes and other opt-in apps and sources. Then they placed targeted ads for their clients. Nothing illegal about it. She deleted the thread.

She looked at herself in the mirror for a second and felt like deep in her eyes she looked sad and that it had nothing to do with the makeup. She went across the hall to the bathroom and used cotton balls and eye-makeup-removing liquid to take off her mascara and shadow and liner, and her eyes stung, then, so she turned on warm water and grabbed a foaming cleanser and washed her face. She patted it dry when she was done and looked in the mirror again.

Same ole Ilanka.

She'd always believed her father was pretty quiet about his work because it was boring, and she mostly agreed that software and data and all that crunching sounded like a big snore. That was what he always said. But what if . . . what if it were something more?

She regretted deleting the thread. She should have written back to confirm it was just spam.

But what if it wasn't? Was it possible it was a message from . . . ?

No. Couldn't be.

EDEN

They'd made popcorn and put a movie on, but her mother was texting like crazy through the whole thing. "Who are you texting?" Eden finally asked.

"I don't think you're in a position to question my phone use right now," her mother said.

"Sorry," Eden said. "I thought we were supposed to be bonding."

Her mother gave her a look; then that look softened and she said, "You're right. Sorry." She got up and plugged her phone in and said, "Can you pause it? I have to go to the bathroom."

"Sure." Eden paused the movie and waited for the bathroom door to close, then went to look at her mother's phone. A text from NH: *You can't cancel. It will look weird.*

It was alone in the window but clearly part of a longer conversation. So her mother was deleting as she went? Why hadn't Eden thought of doing that with all her device threads?

She heard the toilet flush and rushed back to the couch.

Her own phone was plugged in next to her mother's, on Do Not Disturb, and it was hard to just sit there and wonder what was going on. She'd texted Marwan to apologize for lying. Not knowing whether he'd written back was a form of torture. And the movie, a super smart and funny British romantic comedy about two music-obsessed teenagers, wasn't helping. Because why was she suddenly imagining her and Marwan together? Like as a couple?

If it weren't for the device, he probably wouldn't even give her the time of day. Once this was all over, they'd probably go back to barely speaking.

At the end of the movie, with credits rolling, her mother said, "I'm gonna shower."

"What are we doing for dinner?" Eden asked absentmindedly, just waiting for her mother to leave the room so she could go check her phone.

"We're going to the Rankins'. Remember?"

"You can't remember something you never knew," Eden said. It was the last thing she felt like doing.

"I'm sure I mentioned it," her mother said, disappearing up the stairs.

"I'm sure you didn't," Eden said.

"Either way," her mother said brightly, "we're expected around five."

"How was Nancy last night?" Nancy, whose last name was Rankin and thus not the mysterious NH.

"Oh, fine. She'd just had a bad day."

"But couldn't she just talk to you about it tonight?"

"Well, it's different, you know. When it's just the girls. And tonight you and Dan and Mark will be there."

Eden checked her phone.

Nothing from Marwan.

Nothing from Anjali.

Nothing from Eli.

Julian's latest text was right there. She could answer it. At least it'd be something.

Was it weird that she sort of missed the device?

Or maybe it wasn't that at all; maybe she missed *him*?

She started replaying the scene on the green roof, wishing it had all gone differently. She shouldn't be wasting time texting Julian, not when someone like Marwan was right there and seemed to, well . . . *care*?

ELI

Eli's sister and a friend were enjoying time with robots in her room down the hall from his. They'd found this old talking toy of Lily's that always drove Eli bonkers. My Pal Violet was a purple stuffed dog that asked your kid to play and then asked the kid's favorite color or animal or food. You programmed it to share your kid's preferences, so this one liked purple and dolphins and baby food because Lily had. Their actual dog, Cora, was cowering in a corner of the living room.

"Your favorite food is *baby food*?" his sister's friend said.

"Well, it was when I *was a baby*," Lily said, and they both laughed.

Eli doubted his grandfather would like My Pal Violet any more than he did, and, in fact, his grandfather had refused time with robots today. He had a cold and hadn't wanted to do *any* of his activities, and the nurses hadn't forced him. So Eli had visited him in his room, which was possibly the most depressing place Eli had ever been. A weird extra-high-seat contraption over the toilet made it almost impossible for Eli to even *go* in there. A boring seascape hung on one wall, but the others displayed nothing but scuff marks. On the dresser, three framed photos captured better times. His grandparents together at their wedding and at a beach somewhere. His grandfather with Eli and his sister and parents at Lily's First Holy Communion last year.

Eli hadn't stayed long.

"Okay, that's just creepy," his sister said, and Eli's ears perked up.

"Seriously creepy," the friend said.

Eli stood and walked down the hall. "What's going on?" he said. "What's creepy?"

"Listen," Lily said, and she squeezed My Pal Violet's hand. The toy spoke as if through some kind of voice modification software. It said, "Uh-oh. Something's not right."

Then it said, "I can learn your name" as if deep underwater.

"I think it's dying," the friend said.

"You mean the batteries are dying," Eli said.

"Can you change them for us?" Lily asked.

It was the last thing he felt like doing, because it would prolong the annoyance.

"Please?" the girls said in unison.

So he took Violet to the drawer in the kitchen where the tiny screwdriver would be and then unscrewed the battery cover underneath purple fur and saw the batteries were leaky and corroded. He grabbed a paper towel and removed them and threw them out even though he knew you weren't supposed to. He called out, "Bad news!"

His sister and her friend came into the room.

"It's all corroded and stuff," he said, hoping she wasn't going to get upset and trying to hide that he was sort of grateful. "It's not safe to play with anymore."

His sister exchanged a look with her friend, and the friend shrugged, and his sister said, "Oh well, it's for babies anyway. Want to play Barbies?"

And off they went.

Back in his room Eli played music on his phone and checked in on his Sims. The mood in Willow Creek seemed kind of down, like he felt. None of the quests offered to Eliot seemed any fun at all. He'd never seen a few of them—like Bond with a Community Elder, or Stop a Crime.

To pep himself up, Eli decided it was time to add someone new to the mix and set about creating the Sim who might be Eliot's perfect match. After scrolling through avatars, he chose one he thought was cute and sporty. He gave her the goal of finding a life partner and made her interests parallel to Eliot's. He started getting her house built and furnished and helped her make a friend and get a job as a barista. He named her Beth.

He sent Eliot to work and sent Beth to the restaurant, which was another place that Eli wished were real. Eli helped Eliot with his shift, then sent him home.

Eli loved the whole layout of Eliot's house and wished he lived in a place just like it. Open plan with an L-shaped kitchen/living/dining area. A peek-through fireplace between the living room and a smaller office/den. It was there that Eliot went to watch TV after he'd had a snack.

Eli watched as Eliot lay down on the couch, where he would probably fall asleep. Something new caught Eli's eye, and he zoomed in on it.

A tiny black cube sat on Eliot's kitchen counter.

MARWAN

He didn't spot them until they were already at a table. His father had been out front and had seated them because of course he had no idea who they were. It was one of the things Marwan always found most unnerving about the restaurant. You never knew who was going to walk in.

"What are you doing here?" Marwan said after his father had left them at a two-top with menus.

"What does it look like?" Christos opened the menu.

"You're not welcome here," Marwan said.

Christos and his brother both laughed. "You hear this guy?" Christos said. "*We're* not welcome. In Astoria. A *Greek* neighborhood."

Marwan's hands clenched into fists. Astoria was everyone's.

Christos didn't look up when he said, "Can we get some water?"

Marwan turned and walked toward his father, who had just returned to the burners after visiting a table. Marwan watched him chop parsley with ridiculous speed and precision. "Dad?" he said.

"Yes?" His father stopped, midchop. "Yes?"

Marwan pictured what would happen. A confrontation. A whole big scene. His father newly rattled and terrified and heartbroken.

He couldn't do it.

"Nothing," he said, then went back quickly to the staff

room, where he unzipped his backpack and took the device out and put it back in again.

"Table six has requested you be their waiter," Karim said a moment later.

Marwan went back out to the dining room and grabbed an order pad and approached the table. "What do you want?"

Christos looked up. "I want to be treated like you'd treat any other customer."

"But you're not."

"I can complain." He shifted in his seat, as if looking for Marwan's father.

"What do you hope to gain from this whole exercise?" Marwan said.

"Dinner," Christos said. His brother laughed.

"Do you even like Egyptian food?" Marwan said.

"Guess I'm about to find out," Christos said, and looked back at his menu. "Would you recommend the grilled lamb chops or the kofta kebabs?"

By instinct, Marwan snapped into professional mode and described the two dishes.

Christos looked at him funny, then said, "Just pick one."

Marwan turned to his brother. "And for you?"

"The one he didn't pick, I guess."

"Anything to drink?" Marwan asked, and took their menus.

"Water's fine," the brother said, and Christos shrugged and looked around as if realizing something. Not that he wasn't welcome, but that he didn't belong. It almost made Marwan feel bad for him.

Back in the staff room a while later, Marwan checked his phone.

No one had responded to Ilanka's text about tomorrow's handoff, and probably it was his job to. He was sort of hoping Eden would prod him—like check in just to make sure he was able to deliver the device to Ilanka tomorrow. Then they'd have an excuse to move past the awkwardness of her forced confession and text of apology. He decided to just reach out to Ilanka directly.

He texted: *Hey it's Marwan. Send me your address and I'll be there just before noon.*

She responded right away with the information. Then added, *Don't be late.*

He went to do the backpack reset, and the device was displaying a message: **The police have received an anonymous tip involving the egging.**

"*You* sent it?" Marwan whispered.

The device answered in a genderless whisper, "Yes," then went dark.

EDEN

"You want to, like, play video games?" Mark said.

"*Just Dance?*" Eden said jokingly.

"Oh god, remember how into that we used to be?" He smiled and shook his head. He'd gotten cute over time, but he was always going to be more like her cousin.

"We were obsessed," she said.

"We were young and foolish," he said.

"It was pretty fun," she said.

"I sort of miss it." He got up off the couch and turned on the Xbox. "I'm sure it's still in here somewhere," he said, digging around in a drawer under the TV.

"I'm a worse dancer now than I was then, and that is saying something," Eden said.

"Give yourself a little credit," he said. "Also, there's no one here to notice how awful you are."

"There's you," she said.

"But I already know!" He held up the cartridge. "Victory!"

"We're really gonna do this?" she asked.

"We're really gonna," he said.

They'd had pizza for dinner upstairs with just the moms. Dan—the dad—had gotten stuck at work and texted apologies. So now it was just Eden and Mark in the basement, and the moms upstairs, drinking wine.

They danced, first, to "What Makes You Beautiful" by One Direction.

"I'm sorry," Mark said. "But this song holds up."

"It really does," Eden said, winded when they were done. She plopped onto the couch. "I need to catch my breath."

"What should we do next? Oh, remember the one with the panda?"

" 'Timber'!"

"Yes! 'Timber'! OMG. The best." He collapsed onto the couch, too. They sat there breathing for a minute. "I think about your dad a lot," Mark said.

"You *do*?" Her face felt hot.

"Why do you sound surprised?"

"I don't know. I guess it makes sense."

"He's like the closest person to me who . . . died."

"Yeah, well, me, too," she said.

He slapped her on the leg with the back of his hand. "Quit being funny."

"I'm really not trying," she said.

"I feel like your dad sort of grounded my dad, and now I'm not so sure . . ."

"Not so sure of what?"

"I don't know. He seems distracted. Or maybe just sad. It's probably nothing."

"Probably," Eden said, and then they sat there and watched the "Timber" pixelated panda dance but did not get up to join in. Eden looked around, noting how the room had changed over time—which was barely at all. It felt like a second home she somehow didn't get to visit enough. A safe place. She said, "Can I tell you something that you can never tell another breathing soul?"

Mark said, "That would certainly be the most interesting thing to happen to me this week."

She got her phone out and turned it off. "Where's your phone?" she said.

He pointed to the side table.

She said, "Turn it off."

And then she told him all about Julian, and it felt good to just let it all out. Of course, Mark said all the right things.

That's messed up. Delete his number. I would never ask a girl for that.

It felt *so good* that she thought about telling him about the device.

Then she decided not to.

Then she changed her mind. There was no way the device would ever know, and Mark was entirely trustworthy.

"Okay, now you're just messing with me," he said when she was done.

She shook her head. "I'm not."

"So how are you going to get rid of it or end it or whatever?"

"At this point we're still not sure, so the most likely thing is that we'll bring it to the principal on Monday morning."

"That sounds smart," he said. "And if you google for it, there's . . . nothing?"

"Nothing. Its name is Aizel, but there's just nothing out there about it."

"You think it's like . . . *military?*"

"I have no idea! I mean, it'd be too crazy. Like, why would the military care about the four of us? And why, like, Astoria? Right now, it's trying to figure out some kind of connection, and it says it'll tell us. Anyway, whatever you do, don't go start googling to try to figure out what it is."

"Why not?"

"Just don't, okay? It'll know."

"That's ridiculous."

"Promise me."

"Okay," he said. "Maybe it's just an interactive game? Like *Pokémon GO*? Just something that's designed to force you out of your comfort zone?"

"I don't have a comfort zone," she said.

"I'd like to think you have one here? With us? Or me?"

"Of course," she said, feeling emotion start to swell. But something wasn't sitting right. About Nancy's reaction when Dan had said he wasn't going to be home on time—"You see?"—and her mother's face and Mark thinking something was off with his dad. Eden said, "Hey, can you do one thing for me and don't ask me questions about it?"

"Anything for you," he said.

"Can you text me your dad's phone number?"

"Why?"

"What did I just say?"

"Yes, I can do that for you."

"Thanks."

She didn't even want to articulate to herself why she was asking. And Dan Rankin wouldn't be an NH, so it made no sense. Still . . .

They just-danced some more then, and she felt lighter than she'd felt in a long time, and then they went upstairs and raided the freezer for ice cream, and it was so cold it hurt Eden's teeth, but the rest of her was so hot from dancing that it almost felt good. The moms were on the living room sofa with their wine glasses.

"Finally," Nancy said, looking at her phone. "Dan's on his way."

Eden's mom set her half-full glass aside. "Well, we're sorry to miss him but we really ought to get going."

At home, later, with her mother asleep, Eden went downstairs and compared the number Mark had texted her to the number of the mysterious "NH" in her mother's phone.

It didn't match.

Eden was beyond relieved.

The device texted: *Why'd you have your phone off for so long?*

Was at a friend's. Didn't want to drain battery.

Tell me the name of your friend.

Why?

Why not? Also would you like me to text a photo to Julian?

No! What? I deleted those.

I did not.

Eden's heart thumped wildly.

A car crashed into a tree.

Some scaffolding was reported as unstable, the way Eden felt now. Like she might crumble in on herself.

She wrote, *His name is Mark.*

Thank you and good night.

I want you to delete those pictures, she wrote next.

I am sure you do.

Have you figured out why it was the four of us yet?

I sense I am getting close and that I will know after I am handed off to Ilanka.

Eden went back up to bed, this time opting to leave her phone plugged in downstairs. Since those were the rules.

User_error

ILANKA

The moms were drinking sparkling white wine while the dads talked by the grill. Smoke from the barbecue—breakfast sausages—was drifting up and out toward the river, creating a small patch of haze in front of the Empire State Building. Ilanka wondered whether anyone up there on the observation deck had those magnified eyes—big silver standing binoculars—trained on them. It was tempting to wave just in case.

You could reserve parts of their building's rooftop terrace for little gatherings like this; Ilanka's parents did so at least a few times every fall and then more often in spring and summer. Sometimes—like today—they showed up without signing up and then had to have a chat with the building manager, but luckily no one else had reserved the space.

"Did I see you talking to Eli Alvarez this week?" Svetlana asked.

They'd moved away from their parents to sit in loungers by the closed pool. A helicopter took off across the river and rose into the sky like a futuristic robot bug.

"I can't imagine." Ilanka tried to laugh it off.

"Pretty sure I did," Svetlana said.

"Pretty sure you didn't," Ilanka said.

"Pretty sure I did," Svetlana said.

"We gonna do this all day?" Ilanka checked her phone again. She had a text from Marwan that said: *There in five.*

"What's up?" Svetlana said, nodding at the phone.

"Just a text," Ilanka said. She'd read a short article about the incident at his restaurant. One good thing about being Russian: even if your country was corrupt and hacked elections, you could pass for "American" if you wanted to.

"Who from?" Svetlana said.

"It's a long story," Ilanka said. She put a hand to her stomach. "I'm gonna go down and use the bathroom."

"Okay. TMI. Then we'll do the thing? The movie?" Svetlana asked.

"Oh," Ilanka said. "About that. I'm grounded."

"What?"

"I'll explain when I get back. But I doubt they'll let us go."

Ilanka went inside the building and punched the elevator down button. It was already there, so she got in and hit *L* and passed through the empty lobby to the front revolving door.

Marwan was coming up the block on his bike. He got off to walk beside it and waved a perfunctory sort of wave, and Ilanka did the same back.

When he got to her, he pulled the device from his bag and held it out to her. "Here you go."

"Thanks," Ilanka said.

"You need to be reminded of the rules?" he asked.

"I'll be fine," Ilanka said, and she turned to go.

"Well, it's trying to figure out where it came from," he said. "So if you can help with that in any way, that'd be great."

She turned back around. "How could I *possibly* help with that?" He was good looking, up close.

"I don't know, Ilanka"—he sounded tired and she felt sort of bad for being so sarcastic—"do you have a bag for it?"

"No one pays any attention to anything," she said. "I'll grab a bag at the apartment in a minute."

"I'm not sure you're taking this seriously enough," he said.

"Maybe you're taking it *too* seriously?"

He huffed. "Just get through the night and bring it to school tomorrow without messing up, okay?"

"Yes, sir," Ilanka said, and did a fake salute.

"Oh, and it disappeared briefly the other day."

"Disappeared?"

"Yeah, like it suddenly wasn't where Eli and Eden had left it, and then it was back maybe five minutes later. So just . . . you know . . . keep an eye on it."

Ilanka said, "I'm not an idiot," and headed back toward the building. She turned slightly just to see that Marwan had gotten back on his bike and was leaving.

In the lobby, Svetlana was right there, on her phone; she had her bag with her. She looked up, then down at Ilanka's hand and said, "What's that?"

Maybe she wasn't taking it seriously enough.

But for real. What could possibly be the harm?

If Svetlana wanted to get in on it, the whole thing would become at least mildly less boring.

Or maybe the whole thing would just shut down once a rule had been broken. The person who'd played this trick or test or whatever on them would reveal themselves and have a good laugh.

She felt a buzz spread all through her body now at the idea of telling Svetlana. Of breaking with these three weird people she really didn't want anything to do with.

"It's this device that appeared in Mr. M's room the other day," she said, voice shaking with strange emotions. "It hacked into the school app and sent messages to four of us, telling us to turn up in that room. So we did, and it's been giving us rules to follow. Like some sort of game."

"Like what kind of rules?" Svetlana asked.

"Like don't leave the device unattended. Don't tell anybody about the device."

"But you just told me," Svetlana said.

"Yeah . . . and it didn't like blow up or anything, right? I mean, it's some kind of game or gimmick. Clearly."

"I guess," Svetlana said. "So you *were* talking to Eli."

Ilanka nodded. "Yeah, there's four of us who have been taking care of it or whatever."

Svetlana studied it. "What else does it do?"

"I don't know, actually." She didn't feel like telling Svetlana about the wall of selfies. "I mean we have no idea what it even is, really. It had this countdown going for a while when it wanted me to take a shift watching it. So I guess it has a camera? And it's probably got some kind of Wi-Fi? I don't know."

"Sounds dumb," Svetlana said. "If I were you I'd just dump it somewhere."

"Yeah, probably," Ilanka said, feeling a smack of disappointment. "Anyway, we should go back upstairs. I just need to grab a bag to keep it in so my parents don't see it."

"Or just throw it out right there." Svetlana pointed at a nearby trash can.

"Yeah, I want to get rid of it somewhere farther from my house just to be safe," Ilanka said, though really she had no intention of getting rid of it, not yet. Let the others deal with it tomorrow; then it'd be their problem again.

Svetlana was on her phone. "Okay, well, your parents said it was fine for us to go to the movies."

"They did?"

"They did." Still looking at her phone.

"Okay," Ilanka said slowly, remembering they were not actually going to a movie. "Where exactly am I supposed to go?"

Svetlana didn't look up, clearly didn't care. "You could go to a movie."

Ilanka said, "I could go upstairs and tell them what you're actually doing."

"You're not going to do that." She looked up now. "Anyway, I said we were meeting friends, so I can go now even if you don't. Say you're not feeling great. Whatever." She pulled sunglasses from her bag and put them on, then walked out the lobby doors.

Ilanka followed her. "You're really leaving?"

Svetlana just kept on walking.

The device lit up and beeped three times.

A voice came out of it: "Nine-one-one. What's your emergency?"

Svetlana was about to reach the corner. She turned and waved and said, "Really leaving."

In a frantic female voice the device said, "My friend just got hit by a car. Hurry. It looks bad. Real bad."

The voice sounded familiar to Ilanka. It sounded like her own.

"Svetlana, stop!" she screamed.

Svetlana stepped out into the street.

ELI

Sunday mornings were pretty much the only time the whole family was home together, or at least it felt that way. Had he even seen his parents since Wednesday, when this whole thing started? He must have. He'd eaten dinner with his mother and Lily at least once, hadn't he? And taken Cora for walks? But between his mother's work as an ESL specialist at a local school and his father's job in security at a high-end hotel in midtown—but mostly because of all the running around of his sister that they did—he couldn't be sure from one day to the next what home life would be like.

Except on Sundays.

On Sundays his father bought an actual newspaper to read and his mother made pancakes. His sister always asked for chocolate chips in them, which Eli always protested because it made them too sweet, but mostly he did it for sport. His sister liked to spar. She'd have probably been fun if she'd been born like five years earlier and was closer in age to him. How was it possible she was only eight?

It was weird to share parents with someone whose life was completely different from yours.

His phone buzzed, and there was a text from Ilanka: *One of you has to come get this thing.*

"Eli, put your phone away," his mother said.

"In a second, Mom."

Cora was licking stray batter off the floor.

The next text said, *Svetlana saw it and I told her what it was.*

"Can I have the syrup?" his sister said.

Another buzz: *Just found out she was hit by a car.*

"What's so important with you right now?" his father asked, picking Cora up and moving her to the other side of his chair.

Buzzed again: *Device did it.*

Who's coming to get it?

"Eli," his father said. "Phone. Away. Now."

How would the device cause an accident like that?

"In a second, Dad."

He took a few deep breaths and thought it through. He didn't know Svetlana, really, just knew she was another gymnastics type.

He wrote, *Slow down. I'll come meet you.*

She wrote back, *Come NOW or I will smash it to pieces. Wait for me at the coffee place by the Mount Sinai ER entrance.*

I'm on my way, he wrote.

Eden popped in: *Me, too.*

Another text—this one from Marwan and just to him and Eden: *Is this for real?*

Eli wrote, *About to find out.*

"I'm sorry," Eli said, grabbing a pancake and standing up. "But I've got to go."

"Go where?" his father asked.

"A friend needs my help," he said, and he left, ignoring his father's protests and Cora's barking.

I can't get away right now, Marwan wrote. *Keep me posted.*

Eden wrote, *We will.*

The hospital was maybe a ten-minute walk up Crescent

Street. Eli crossed streets with unusual caution even though he knew it was crazy. The device wasn't even close—yet—and also it couldn't possibly have caused an accident.

Though it *had* hacked into a traffic camera for Marwan.

Could it do the same with traffic *lights*? But how could it rely on a car to arrive at just the right time?

A man walking in front of him stopped at a poster taped to a streetlight—ripped the flyer down, crumpled it up, and tossed it in a nearby trash can. Curious, Eli plucked it from the trash and opened it up again. It was posted by the local police precinct and asked for information leading to the arrest of any of the vandals or perpetrators of hate crimes in the neighborhood. There was a tip line number to call. Lit with rage, Eli caught up to the man who had torn it down at the corner.

"Hey," he said. "Why did you take this down?"

"None of your business," the guy said.

"No, I want to know. You think it's okay? Everything that's happening?"

The guy was white and built, and Eli had a moment of regret over engaging—was he going to get beat up?—but it was too late now.

"What part of 'none of your business' didn't you understand?" the man said, and the light changed and Eli considered following, then considered balling the flyer back up and throwing it at the guy. Instead, he retraced his steps back to the light post and put the flyer back up, borrowing some tape from other flyers. A lost cat. An improv comedy night called Fake TED Talks.

He walked the rest of the way to the hospital and went into the coffee shop, took a seat at a small table in the back, and waited.

Sometimes, when Eli couldn't fall asleep, he'd do this thing where he'd try to think of every business on every corner of an avenue in the neighborhood. He'd usually pick Broadway since he knew it best, starting from the train and heading up toward Steinway. He did it now to pass time.

The bakery and Colombian diner.

The newsstand and bank.

Then the weird terrarium shop attached to a newsstand and bank.

The pizza place.

An Irish bar.

Omonia Café.

A new apartment building with the ground floor still being renovated.

Dollar store.

Mexican restaurant.

Church parking lot.

Pizzeria.

The bar that hosted the Fake TED Talks night.

He thought it sounded potentially funny and thought about a few TED talks he might be able to give. How to survive the boredom of high school. How to live vicariously through Sims.

He googled TED talks to see what some real topics were. Scrolled.

"Can We Make Things That Make Themselves?"

"How to Seek Truth in an Era of Fake News."

"The Career Advice You Probably Didn't Get."

There was a lot here that Eli should be paying attention to, each one potentially more interesting and possibly helpful than the next.

Scrolling down, he saw, "This App Knows How You Feel—From the Look on Your Face."

He clicked on that one and put earbuds in and watched, wishing he could download this revolutionary app right then, and have a better sense of how he felt.

The bell over the door chimed, and Ilanka walked in and put a bag on the table in front of Eli. She sank into a seat.

"What *happened*?" Eli asked.

Ilanka's hair was all confused—no bun—and she looked pale. "She saw the device and asked about it, and I didn't think it was a big deal to tell her because why would it be? So then she was leaving and the device called 911 and reported an accident and I screamed at Svetlana to stop walking and she did and nothing happened."

Eli was more confused than when he'd arrived. "So I thought everything was fine and she left and I went back inside but then her parents got a text a few minutes later from someone using Svetlana's phone, saying she'd been in an accident a few minutes later, and they left for the hospital. So I guess it *tried again* when it didn't work the first time? I just tried to get information from the hospital, but no one will talk to me because I'm not family, and her parents aren't responding to my mom's texts."

Eli couldn't seem to get his tongue or lips to move to make words. Even if he could, what would they be? Would the app read his face as scared? Intrigued? What?

"You need to get rid of it," Ilanka said, wiping away tears that formed instantly, then said, "It used *my* voice."

"What do you mean?"

"When it called 911, it sounded like me." She pushed the bag on the table toward him.

Eli said, "I just want to think this through. I don't want to rush to action."

"You actually *like* this, don't you?" Ilanka said, shaking her head. "How boring was your life that you are actually *enjoying* jumping through hoops for this thing that just came out of nowhere and just tried *to kill* my friend?" She stood. "I'm leaving."

"But you're supposed to keep it until noon tomorrow."

"Not happening," she said, and she walked out and woke the bells over the door again.

EDEN

Eden walked as quickly as she could and, when it was time to cross two ways to get to the coffee shop, did so carefully. At one corner she noted a flyer taped to a streetlamp post—a tip line for hate crimes in the neighborhood. She got her phone out, took a picture of it, pocketed her phone, and crossed again. Once inside the café, she spotted Eli and sat. There was a plastic bag on the table; presumably the device was in it.

He said, "She just left."

"What *happened*?" She checked her phone, put it on the table, and turned the screen off. Her hand was generating tiny tremors.

Between receiving the texts and arriving here, she'd been hoping things had changed, or that there'd been a misunder-standing. But the story Eli told now—the device calling 911 before the accident had even happened?—was the same, and her low-tide nausea surged toward high.

She should have never told Mark.

"How bad is it, do you think?" she asked, and immediately felt the push of emotion behind her cheeks, like she might burst into tears if she didn't fight hard enough. "Svetlana?"

"I don't know," Eli said, and his face seemed to be vibrating, like he was barely holding it together. "Ilanka said no one would talk to her at the hospital because she's not family."

"I can't believe this is happening." Her ribs were somehow tied too tight around her lungs. "I mean, did it hack a traffic light?"

Eli said, "I honestly have no idea."

"Why would it *do* this?" Eden half whispered.

It was right there in the bag, probably listening and plotting. Eden was expecting, at any minute, a Panera-like outburst.

"She broke a rule," Eli said flatly.

"But so what?" Eden said, anger now mixing with fear. "Why does it care?"

"It doesn't *care*," Eli said.

"You know what I mean."

"I don't know," Eli said. "It's just programmed."

"But why would that be one of the rules? And why would whoever started the whole thing allow this to happen? Allow someone to get hurt?"

Eli said, "I don't know. Maybe it's not under their control anymore?"

Eden tried to take a deep, calming breath again, but something felt broken. Like she'd outgrown her body—needed a new one, a full transplant.

A woman struggled to get through the door with a crying toddler in a stroller and sat at the table next to them, her annoyance spreading like cigarette smoke. The little boy caught eyes with Eden and stopped crying when Eden raised her eyebrows at him. She bulged her eyes out, trying to be funny, and then looked away.

She checked her phone.

Citizen told her that a woman about four blocks away had called 911 to report a group of people fighting in the street.

Marwan still hadn't written back. She should text him now with an update, except there wasn't really one. And she'd texted Anjali earlier and asked her to meet later, but Anjali hadn't replied.

"While I was waiting for Ilanka," Eli said, "I started watching this video about an app that can read facial expressions. Like there's this emotion engine, they called it, with so many human expressions cataloged and tagged that the app can actually tell what you're feeling just by looking at you."

"I can't even do that," Eden said. She sure couldn't read Julian, or Marwan.

"You think *it*'s doing that?" He nodded at the bag.

"I don't know," Eden said. "It does seem to respond differently to different moods, and I'm not sure how else it could do that?"

Eli said, "We need to go somewhere where we can talk to it."

"The park?"

"It's supposed to rain so not ideal."

They couldn't go to her house—her mom was home (and actually knew she was meeting Eli in a café, just didn't really know why it mattered)—and he didn't offer his.

It shouldn't be that hard to think of a place, but it was. This was why there were always groups of kids wandering the streets after school, sitting on random stoops and hanging out on subway platforms and at bus stops or McDonald's. With so many places all packed in so tight, that somehow left nowhere to go.

"Maybe we should go someplace crowded," she said. "Crowded enough that no one will pay any attention to us."

"Like where?" Eli asked.

"The mall's too far away." It was like a half hour by subway.

Eden checked her phone again. Still nothing.

The device shook inside the bag.

Eden and Eli exchanged a look. How would they ever figure out how to get rid of it—that was the only possible plan of action now—when the device was always watching at least one of them? When it had access to their phones?

Eden was the one to reach forward to open the bag and peek in.

The message said: **Someone's watching me.**

Eden stiffened and looked around the room. The toddler boy was staring at her, and now he looked at the bag. She made sure the mom wasn't looking—she was scrolling through something on her phone—so Eden made her eyes scary and wide, and the toddler kicked his feet in his stroller and rolled his head away and said, "Mama?"

His mother said, "What?" without looking up from her phone.

The message on the device changed to say, **I want to see Marwan.**

And something about the phrasing of that desire, so plain, made Eden ache.

ILANKA

Svetlana's mother had texted Ilanka: *She's in bad shape. Will keep you updated.*

But since then, she wasn't answering her phone or responding to texts and Ilanka was hiding in her room to avoid further grilling from her parents.

Why had Ilanka gone outside anyway, they'd wanted to know.

Why had she not wanted to go to the movies, leaving Svetlana to walk off alone?

Her parents seemed to think the accident was Ilanka's fault.

But for the wrong reasons.

She was so irritated by it all that she almost wanted to tell them the truth.

Except, well . . .

Now she knew what happened if you broke a rule.

She had considered telling a half truth—that Svetlana had been planning on ditching her to go meet a guy. But if Svetlana's parents had her phone, which they probably did, they'd figure that out on their own—there would have been texts from the guy when she didn't show up—and it seemed bad to rat out someone who was in a hospital bed in god-knows-what condition.

When her phone buzzed—*I'm sorry*—she was confused.

It was that strange number again, with characters and dingbats.

Who is this? she wrote.

The device.

DO NOT TEXT ME AGAIN!

Would you like to know more about your father's illegal activities?

GET OUT OF MY LIFE.

I'm very sorry.

LEAVE ME ALONE!

There were texts from the others, too: *Any updates on Svetlana?*

She didn't answer.

She turned off her phone.

Her parents were talking in the kitchen; she couldn't stay in her bedroom forever. Ilanka wandered in and got a glass and filled it with cold water and sat at the kitchen island. She thought about going back to her room for her phone, but only if she could guarantee the device wouldn't text her again, and she couldn't.

"Anyway," her father said. "It'll be a quick trip. Good to get some face time."

"Where are you going?" Ilanka asked.

"Moscow," he said.

He did this maybe three times a year, in addition to the annual family trip they all took to Saint Petersburg, but usually with more notice. This seemed . . . sudden.

She said, "What are you doing there?"

"Just meetings," he said.

"With who?" she pressed, annoyed that the device had made her suspicious of her own dad.

"My employees?" he said, like it was so obvious. And it was true that most of the company's data mining and analysis was done overseas.

"Let's not talk about work today, okay?" her mother said. "How about we watch a movie? Take our mind off things while we wait for updates?"

"Excellent idea," her father said.

"Go ahead, Ilanka. Queue something up. We'll try calling them again or just going to the hospital together after, okay?"

Ilanka wanted to say, *No, let's hang out. Let's talk.*

Her mother said, "Nothing too heavy, okay?" and gave her a warm look. Now that she'd calmed down she seemed a little bit softened by the situation, probably imagining how she'd feel if it had been Ilanka who'd been in an accident. Hug your kids closer and all that.

And why *hadn't* it been Ilanka? Why had Svetlana been the one it went after? If Ilanka had lied about the device instead of being so open, would it still have happened? Why did the whole thing have to be a secret anyway?

In the living room, Ilanka turned on the TV and went to the Netflix app and it asked who was watching and she clicked on the "family" profile; its icon was a smiling face. Rain started to tickle the windows, blurring the world outside.

MARWAN

Eden stopped suddenly a few feet away from him on the sidewalk, like some force field had appeared between them. They shared this intense look that he read as an agreement of some kind. Pushing through the field, he stepped toward her and she met him halfway. Holding her felt easy and right.

Eden said, "We have to get rid of it," into his shoulder.

Marwan shushed her, and she pulled out of the hug. She looked at Eli, sort of apologetically—or maybe just embarrassed? *ugh*—and fixed her hair.

"If it really did this . . . ," she said.

Eli shushed her now, too.

"Stop shushing me," she said. "I'm not a child."

"Sorry," Marwan said. "Why does it want to see me?"

"It said you're the only one it trusts now. Because it helped you, it says you owe it."

Marwan nodded and said, "Where's Ilanka?"

"She basically ditched it with me and ran," Eli said.

"Any news about Svetlana?"

Eden shook her head, and Eli said, "None."

"Did you ask it if it can find anything out?" Marwan asked. "About Svetlana?"

"We were in public, so no."

"That's why we're here," Marwan said, and he indicated the

building they'd stopped in front of. It was a karaoke bar called Shout Out.

"I don't get it," Eli said. Rain had just started to fall.

"Just follow me," Marwan said.

Marwan opened a heavy glass door and said "Hey" to the bartender, who said, "No more than an hour," and Marwan said, "You have no idea how grateful I am."

"Last room on the left," the bartender said.

Marwan led them down a long, dark hall. The muted screams of some girls singing some screeching Disney anthem came from behind one door. Otherwise the place was quiet. Not a lot of people did karaoke during the day.

"What are we doing here?" Eden asked.

"It's somewhere we can be alone with it," Marwan said. He closed the door after Eli and Eden had followed him into the room. The song choice console sat on the table. The screen said "Select Song Now" in a block of text that floated round the screen, bouncing off edges and changing direction, like a primitive video game. The room smelled of stale beer and some kind of piney cleaning product. Dim overhead lights were reflected in the karaoke screen, giving the room a faint glow.

Eden and Marwan both took their jackets off, then sat on a leather banquette; Eli looked around, pulled over a small stool, then got the device out and put it on the low table next to a thick binder of song lists.

The device lit up: **Where are we? Why is it so dark?**

Marwan said, "Just a quiet place."

A quiet place named Shout Out. It made about as much sense as anything right now.

Marwan said, "Do you have updates on Svetlana? How did you do what you did? And why?"

The device said: **Ilanka has turned her phone off.**

Marwan rolled his eyes in the dark, then felt bad about it. It had been Ilanka's actual friend who'd been hurt. She must be even more freaked out than the rest of them. "Do you have any way of hacking into the hospital or anything?" Marwan asked. "Any way to get updates?"

I can tell you this, the message said. **When Ilanka turns her phone on, she will receive a message that tells her that Svetlana has died from her injuries.**

"I think I'm going to be sick," Eden said. But she didn't get up to leave the room; she hung her head between her knees, cradling her head in her hands.

Marwan reached over and rubbed her back and then let his hand linger there, felt her rib cage rise and fall. He did this thing he sometimes did—like at the dentist. He dug his thumbnail into the flesh of another finger, to inflict a distracting sort of pain. A pain he could focus on that was in his control.

This wasn't happening.

This couldn't be happening.

Dead?

Rules must be followed.

Marwan felt a new kind of emotion as the message faded away. Helpless? Bereft? He thought he might be the one to throw up. "But why?" he asked.

So that I can get to where I belong.

"Where do you belong?" Marwan screamed at it.

I searched all my recordings and found this.

An image appeared of the exterior of an apartment building with many windows. In one, the curtain was drawn back. A man with binoculars to his eyes stared out.

"Where is this?" Marwan asked.

Across the street from school. Take me there.

"I can't," Marwan said. "I have to work."

"I can't either," Eden said, giving no further reason.

I believe I have made it clear that my wishes should be met.

"I'll take you there," Eli said.

I want Marwan.

Marwan said, "Eli's not going to do anything bad. You have to trust me. If I try to get away now, it'll just complicate things for all of us."

The sour smell of the room seemed to thicken, and Marwan imagined this was what a hangover felt like.

Fine.

"But wait," Marwan said. "Not yet."

The time is now, the device said.

"I have questions for you," Marwan said.

Eli and I are leaving now. Your questions must wait.

Eli stood and put the device in his backpack.

"Be careful," Eden said, looking oddly pale in the dark room.

When Eli opened the door to leave, the light of day glinted off the silver legs of a bar stool beyond him and seemed to be aiming directly at him, like a surgical laser.

The rain had come and gone that quickly. Marwan's mother would call it "rainbow weather," but he didn't imagine they'd get that lucky, not today.

EDEN

She took out her phone and turned it off and gave Marwan a pointed look; he turned his phone off, too.

"This is crazy!" he said. "She's *dead*?"

"I know," Eden said. "I feel sick. Should we go to the police?"

"I don't think so, at least not yet." Marwan reached out and squeezed her hand, and she thought she might start crying. "Because maybe this thing with the video will lead to something?"

She nodded. "And in the meantime, we try to think of a way to get rid of it? That maybe doesn't involve the police?"

"Yes," he said, releasing her hand. "You have time now?"

"I have to meet my friend," she said. "She's been asking a lot of questions since the beginning of all this, and I need to get her to stop before something bad happens to her, too."

"Okay," Marwan said, and she hugged him again. It was a longer hug this time, maybe because they were alone, and she felt him inhaling her—his mouth by her hair, his chest rising into hers. She felt his deep breath as if it were her own, and for once her ribs felt right.

Anjali had agreed to meet at Starbucks, so Eden headed in that direction and tried to compose herself on the way. Before going in, she stopped on the sidewalk and took a few deep inhales—which she then exhaled in loud bursts. She put on some lip gloss and smoothed her hair. She turned her phone on—nothing—then turned it off again and put it in her bag.

Anjali was already seated with an iced latte.

Eden didn't even want anything to drink, so she just went and sat next to Anjali and said, "Turn your phone off."

"What? Why?"

"Just do it. Please?"

Anjali did, then put her phone facedown on the table.

Eden turned it over to make sure it was actually off, then put it down again. "You have to trust me when I say that I can't explain it."

"You've been using me." Anjali sipped her drink through a metal straw she'd bought after signing a petition against single-use plastics citywide.

"And I'm sorry about that," Eden said. "But if I tell you what's going on, you might be in danger."

"You're freaking me out," Anjali said. "Why are you crying?"

"Something bad happened," Eden said, not even having realized she'd started crying but now feeling it, yes. Warm and wet.

"*What?*" Anjali asked.

Eden could only shake her head, wipe away tears on both sides with two flat hands. "I'll explain everything after tomorrow."

"Why, what's tomorrow?"

Eden shook her head.

"Are you being, like, blackmailed? Because you can tell me. I'll help."

"No," Eden said. "It's not like that." *If only!*

"Something happened," Anjali said, sounding almost sinister. "In Mr. M's room that afternoon."

"Please just stop talking," Eden said, looking around, paranoid, but no one was watching—why would they be? Unless . . . could it find her, see her, hear her through that traffic camera? Or through that security camera in front of the electronics store across the street? Or on that guy's phone right there? They had no idea of the limits of what it could do.

Anjali said, "I'll stop talking when you tell me what's happening tomorrow."

"I can't," Eden said through clenched teeth because she had enough problems without Anjali insisting on becoming a bigger one. "But everything's going to be fine tomorrow. That's all I can say. I shouldn't even be saying that."

"You sound crazy," Anjali said.

"I *feel* crazy," Eden said. They just had to figure out a place to leave it, right? Where it wouldn't be found?

The couple next to them seemed to be having a low-level argument. This felt like one of those, too. What would school be like when word got around about Svetlana?

Oh god, she was dead.

If Anjali was going to find out anyway, maybe it'd be okay to tell her at least that? But how would Eden explain how she knew?

She didn't want to know, didn't want any of it to be real.

"So what now?" Anjali said.

"We go home," Eden said.

"And I'm supposed to just show up at school tomorrow like everything's normal? When I know it's not?"

Eden nodded.

"I liked things better before all this," Anjali said. "Whatever it is, I want it to be over."

Eden said, "Me, too. I hate everything about it," then wondered whether she meant it. Before this, there'd been no Marwan, no Eli, nothing to distract her from her own miserable existence. Was she better off now . . . or worse?

Svetlana was dead!

Worse. Worse. Worse.

Her tears started again.

Anjali rubbed her arm. "You gonna be okay?"

Eden just nodded and wiped her tears.

With nothing left to say, they walked out and hugged loosely on the sidewalk. Anjali said, "Be careful, okay?"

Eden said, "You know me," and they each walked off.

She gradually noticed the flyers on various lampposts as she walked and then fully at the corner under the train.

They said: BUILD THAT WALL!

MAKE AMERICA GREAT AGAIN!

SHUT DOWN THE BORDERS!

NO MORE TERRORISTS ALLOWED!

They were poorly designed and printed in jarring colors. Hard-to-read fonts on hazard orange and neon green. Eden started taking them down, corner by corner, until she got home and put them in the recycling.

Then she took them back out and put them in the regular trash—smashing them into coffee grounds—and took the bag out to the curb.

She turned her phone on, there by the trash can.

The device's text read: *Why did you turn your phone off again?*

She had a panicked thought, then wrote, *Was saving battery,* with shaky fingers.

Your battery is at 87 percent.

Oh, she wrote. Outsmarted.

The next text said: *I sent one of your photos to Julian.*

She pushed through the front door and slid her phone onto the kitchen table—too hard so it flew across and hit the floor—and hooked left into the bathroom and didn't turn the light on and made it to the toilet just in time.

It felt good to get that out of her stomach, whatever it was. She flushed, then brushed her teeth and looked at herself in the mirror. In this light—something about the angle of it on her nose—she looked so much like her father.

She could figure this out.

She had to.

ELI

He climbed the subway stairs and sat on a bench on the platform and let the train pull out of the station. When it was gone, taking everyone else who'd been waiting with it, and leaving a few people off, he had a clear view of the building across from school. He took the device out and put it on the bench beside him.

Eli had sort of hoped that now—now that something *really bad* had happened—the owner of the device would step forward, shut it all down. There would be an apology for things getting out of hand. Or some kind of police involvement.

The lack of action, the lack of a reveal of the man behind the curtain, had to mean that the creator/owner/whatever you wanted to call it had expected this sort of outcome. And was fine with it. Had, in fact, orchestrated it.

Forces greater than Eli had imagined were in play.

Someone was dead.

His mind felt foggy.

It had never *occurred* to him that *anything* like that could happen outside of the movies, not really.

The device generated a new message: **No one is home.**

"How do you know which apartment it even is?" Eli asked, wanting to seem helpful and not just completely freaked out.

Comparing video with current view.

"Can you look up who lives there?"

I am not sure.

"What now?"

Watch and wait.

While Eli sat he checked in on Eliot because no one ever died in Willow Creek and it felt like a safe place to spend a few minutes. He sent Eliot off on a quest to upgrade his wardrobe again.

The sun caught the surface of the device just so when it generated a message—**Your game is more interesting than I am?**—and Eli saw it was covered in fingerprints.

Eli put his phone away. "Sorry. Hey, can you scan your surface for fingerprints? And compare them with mine and the others, like from our touch ID on our phones? See if there are more prints that aren't ours?"

Affirmative.

Eli's eyebrows shot up. He waited, pleased with his idea.

None besides the four of you.

So how the hell did it get there?

People came and went in an endless loop as Eli thought back on some AI movies he'd seen, wondering if their plots could help him figure out a way to get rid of Aizel and find a way out of this for all of them. They couldn't go to Principal Lambert. Not now. And they couldn't go to the police. Could they?

What did that leave?

He counted ten trains in one direction and then nine in the other before realizing nothing was going to happen.

He said, "My parents will wonder where I am."

I'll try again tomorrow. Hand me off to Marwan before 8 a.m.

Eli texted Marwan, who agreed to the exchange right before school.

"You're not going to hurt anyone else, are you?" Eli asked.

I do not believe so.

I have a question for you as well.

Eli didn't answer.

Are you scared of me?

Eli's throat clogged; he nodded.

Good.

MARWAN

The brick came through the window by the kitchen and knocked a skillet clear off the burner, leaving the blue flame abandoned. Glass rained down on plates about to be served. Screams and gasps rose up. Chairs squeaked and groaned.

In the chaos, Marwan couldn't see the street, so he pushed through the room and went out to the sidewalk, looking around urgently. People were stopping and staring.

"Did anybody see who did it?" Marwan said to no one.

Some people didn't seem to want to make eye contact with him.

"It was a red car," a man said.

"Did you catch the plate?" Marwan asked, turning to him.

"No, sorry."

But red was enough. It was them again.

Marwan went to his father. "Where's that number? The detective who was here the other night?"

"His card is by the register," his father said, dabbing his bloodied cheek with a white cloth napkin.

"I'll call him," Marwan said, heading back inside. He found the card and tapped in the number, and a man said a gruff "Puglio."

"Oh, hi." Somehow caught off guard even though he'd placed the call.

"Who is this?"

"This is Marwan. My family's restaurant is the one that got egged."

"Yeah, we still have nothing on that incident, sorry."

"That's not why I'm calling," Marwan said. *What about the anonymous tip?* he didn't ask.

"Why are you calling?" The background noise was a woman yelling something incomprehensible, possibly in another language.

"Somebody just threw a brick through the window."

Puglio groaned irritation. "We'll be there as soon as we can," he said, and ended the call.

Marwan could lie. He could tell the police that someone walking past got the plate of the car and then give the police the plate the device had given them already. It would mean there were two strikes against Christos and his brother. But why wouldn't Puglio have mentioned the tip? Maybe you weren't supposed to until you followed up and made an arrest?

He texted Eden. *You hanging in?*

She didn't need to know about this. She'd only worry, and that was not what he wanted her thinking about when she thought about him. If she was even thinking about him at all, which she probably wasn't because they had bigger problems, but that hadn't stopped him thinking about her.

Yes, she wrote back. *You?*

"Marwan," his father said. "We need you."

"Of course," Marwan said.

He texted her—*Mostly*—then searched for an emoji face that would help him express what he was feeling, but it didn't seem right to send a heart and a skull and crossbones or a grave-stone. He went and got the broom and dustpan from the closet and felt the gritty sting of glass dust in his thumb. He should take a minute to find gloves, except what was the point of anything?

EDEN

Eden's mother had the local news on while she cooked dinner, and none of it was good. A fire in the Bronx. A fatal car accident on Long Island. A toddler shot by a stray bullet in Newark. The last segment was about the flyers.

On the heels of an attack on a Muslim-owned restaurant Thursday night, white supremacist graffiti appeared on Friday. Then today, on a quiet Sunday afternoon when families were out enjoying the beautiful weather—anti-immigrant flyers appeared on lampposts around the neighborhood . . . Residents here are shocked that this is happening in their backyard.

Why were things getting worse before getting better?

They had to get better.

Maybe Marwan *should* have sought some kind of revenge. Doing the right thing wasn't working.

She wanted to tell him about Julian and what the device had done—how it *was* basically blackmailing her now—but she felt so foolish about it all.

She texted Julian now: *That pic wasn't meant for you. Please delete.*

Tomorrow, no matter what, they had to get rid of the device. And definitely *not* by giving it to the principal. Because then they'd have to explain everything they'd done. They'd have to explain about Svetlana. If, as it claimed, it couldn't be destroyed, it needed to be abandoned—far enough away that it couldn't mess with them, remote enough that no one would ever find it.

She pulled up a map of Astoria on Google Maps and looked for green and blue, parks and water. But Astoria Park was too crowded, too close. She zoomed out and zoomed out some more. Found the answer she was maybe looking for:

The airport.

It was a sort of wasteland out there.

Marshes and swamps by a weedy highway with exits like entrails leading god knew where. It was the sort of urban landscape that made her uneasy. Because how did those tires end up there on that hill? What about that roll of toilet paper and the chip bags and upturned metal shopping cart? The presence of human touches like that in uninhabitable places was oddly terrifying to her.

She studied the area around the airport more closely. Found a park with water access. She could picture what it looked like from the road when they'd drive out that way—the way tall, tan, stalky plants grew along the shoreline. And how across that bay there lived whole other neighborhoods she'd never been to. Bayside, she'd heard of. Pomonok sounded made up.

Out there, they could sink the device into some mud and walk away and never speak of it again. Then years would pass, and when they were older and crossed paths, they'd still carry the weight of a secret together, like a bone-deep bruise, but they'd take it to their graves because they would have no other choice.

Was it watching her now?

She powered down her computer.

She checked her phone—Julian: *Maybe I'll just keep it a little while longer?*—then turned it off.

She went to the bookshelf in the den area adjacent to her room where there was a bunch of her father's old maps. He used to want to show them to her—explain how they worked, how you used to have to figure out how to get places—but she was never interested. Now, she found one of New York City and then the detail of Queens. She found the small park by the water she'd seen on Google. It seemed near enough to the expressway that it wouldn't take too long to do the round trip.

She sat down at her desk with a pen and paper and drew up a plan. Then wrote out two more copies. She'd give one to Marwan while Eli still had the device. Then give one to Eli when Marwan had the device. By this time tomorrow night, they'd be free.

She went downstairs to say good night, and her mother kissed her on the forehead and said, "I'm heading up now, too."

Eden said, "I'm just gonna get some water," and her mother drifted up the stairs.

Once she had a glass of water, Eden went to get her phone to sneak it upstairs. Her mother's phone was charging beside hers, and it buzzed a text alert from the mysterious NH.

I can't stop thinking about you.

Eden gasped, like she'd been caught.

She backed away in the dark.

Upstairs, she couldn't sleep. Her mother was lying to her constantly, and Svetlana was . . . dead.

Dead.

It was the device's fault and maybe their fault, too.

Nothing felt real; nothing felt right.

Her stomach tightened, like it had somehow learned from her hands how to make a fist. This couldn't possibly be happening, except that it was. She should text Ilanka and see how she was doing, but she didn't want to because it was all too horrible.

She was weirdly thirsty—like a neglected plant—and couldn't seem to get comfortable. She tried counting her breaths down from one hundred to calm herself and eventually fell asleep, then jolted awake again in a sweat.

She'd had a dream about her dentist injecting foot-long needles into her neck while telling her she was sick and would never get better.

It was only one a.m., and she had no idea how she'd even get through the night.

She checked her phone and saw a recent text from Marwan.

Hope you're not sleeping.

I mean, I hope this isn't waking you up. Somebody threw a brick through the restaurant window. Can't sleep.

I'm here, she wrote back. *Awake. So sorry. Did the police come?*

Yes.

She felt sick. *Did you hear about the flyers all over Broadway?*

????

They say "Build the wall" or some garbage. You think same people?

No idea. Also, isn't that just old? Who's still talking about a wall? Ridiculous.

What happens now? With police?

Probably nothing.

She wanted to tell him her plan so badly but had to be safe.

She almost wrote, *I think my mom's seeing someone she shouldn't be.* But that would be an overshare. So she didn't. She only wrote, *We should go to bed.*

Then, *I can't stop thinking about Svetlana.*

I know, he wrote. *Same. Try to sleep and I will too.*

Her night-light cast a shadow of her white ceiling fan behind it, so it looked like there were two fans up there, and for a second she imagined the whole world was like that; everyone in it always two versions of themselves—one moving through life in broad daylight, and the other, a hidden shadow self, lying in wait.

But waiting for what?

There were stray cats out in the yard, wailing because they were in heat. They sounded like crying babies if you allowed your mind to think it, and it felt like crying could be contagious—even if it was only cats—except that Eden had a plan now, so she clung to that and closed her eyes and did not cry at all.

Force_quit

MARWAN

He waited outside school for Eli so he could take the device, keeping an eye out for Christos. Not that he had any clue what he would do if he saw him but thought maybe he'd be able to read it in Christos's eyes if he'd thrown the brick or even been in the car. He hadn't given the plate to the cops in the end on the off chance it had been someone else.

Eden was suddenly there, and she shoved a tightly folded-up piece of paper into his hand. "Look at this later. Do not let the device see it."

She seemed frantic—eyes darting around and looking anywhere but right at him; he didn't understand what was happening.

"Put it away *now*!" she said in a sort of shouted whisper.

He shoved the paper into his pocket.

Oh. She'd gone analog and come up with a plan?

"Hey," Eli said, appearing from out of a crowd of students heading for the door.

"Hey," Marwan said. "Everything okay?"

"Yeah."

"What was at that address? Did you find the guy?"

"No one was home. We waited a long time. It says it wants to try again later."

"Like I'm supposed to take it there again?"

Eli shrugged. "It just said to hand off to you." He unzipped his backpack, took the device out, and held it out to Marwan.

Eden's friend was suddenly there—her hair up in pigtail-type buns.

"Gotcha!" she shouted.

They all passed panicked looks around at each other for a second.

"So enough with the secrecy," she said. "What is it?"

"I'll deal with this," Eden said. "Just go."

Marwan let the device drop into his bag, then headed into the building. It felt strange to be in school at all. Friday felt like another lifetime. He headed for the bathroom to regroup before homeroom. Once there, he threw some water on his face to wake himself up—he'd barely gotten any sleep at all, thinking about the brick and Eden and Svetlana and ways to ditch the device (no good ones!)—then grabbed a paper towel to pat it dry; only there were none left. He used his shirt instead.

"Take me out," the device said in a female voice.

So he did.

In the mirror, he looked crazed. Would something bad happen to Eden's friend now, too?

There was a small spider in the sink, so he ran the water again to wash it down. It clung on to a hair by the drain, very much not wanting to die.

The door to the hall opened, and a kid Marwan didn't know walked in. Marwan didn't move fast enough.

"What's that?" the kid said, eyeing the device.

Marwan froze. "Nothing."

"Is that a *bomb*?" the guy said.

"What? No," Marwan said.

"It looks like a bomb."

As if on cue, the device started a countdown.

"Stop saying that," Marwan said. "It's not a bomb."

His hands finally dry, Marwan went to put the device away.

"Let me see it, then," the guy said.

"No," Marwan said.

He was backing out of the room. "If that's a bomb . . ."

"It's not! Stop saying it."

But it was too late. He was in the hall, shouting, "There's a bomb!"

Screams and feet pounding.

"Why did you *do that*?" Marwan screamed at the device.

The countdown disappeared.

Don't want to be here today.

"You could have just told me that."

Well, now I officially suggest you leave.

Marwan took a few deep breaths, put the device in his bag, then opened the bathroom door and joined the frantic evacuation. He went down the stairs calmly—as people around him pushed and fell and screamed and texted—and then through the crowded lobby.

"If everyone will please calmly exit the building," came over the PA.

He went out the doors and out onto the sidewalk and just kept walking . . .

EDEN

Anjali's features had settled into an intensively focused look of defiance and doubt trained on Eden.

"Please just stop," Eden said.

Anjali repositioned her glasses on her nose in a swift movement. "Well, is it a bomb?"

"Are you *out of your mind*?" Eden snapped.

They were with a bunch of other students across the street from school—everybody on their phones—and no one seemed sure what to do. Should they wait around? Go home? So far, no message had come on the school app.

"Then what is it?" Anjali asked.

"It's not a bomb," Eden said.

"Then what is it?" Anjali shouted.

Eden shouted back, "I don't know! Okay?" Then more softly, "We don't even really know."

Was it the device that someone had mistaken for a bomb? What if it *was* a bomb, and they'd been tricked into giving it information and bringing it into school?

If you believed Eli, there really was such a thing as weaponized AI. What if this was it? Where was Marwan anyway? Eden hadn't seen him come out yet.

She said, "I promise I'll tell you what I know when it's over."

But did Anjali already know too much? She'd seen it, but

Eden hadn't technically *told* her about it. Sure, she'd told Mark, but the device had no way of knowing that. Svetlana was the only other person who'd laid eyes on the device, and now she was dead. Probably there would have been an announcement about that in school this morning if this hadn't happened first. They'd have grief counselors on hand. Ilanka would probably be absent for a few days, grieving with her family. Eden and the others would not go to the funeral. Because it wouldn't make sense for them to. They barely knew her.

Eden turned and looked squarely at her friend. "You need to go home and stay there until I tell you otherwise."

"Eden, *please* just tell me what's happening."

Eden fought her annoyance. Hadn't they just been through this? "Go home and wait to hear from me."

Her phone buzzed: Marwan asking her and Eli to meet him at the restaurant.

"I've got to go," Eden said.

"Where?" Anjali said.

An alert on the school app said that students who could safely and easily get home should go home, and that the others should convene at the movie theater around the corner where there would be police to help contact parents if necessary.

"Just *please go home*," Eden said.

"Okay, okay," Anjali said.

Eden pulled her into a hug and said, "It's almost over," then headed toward the restaurant.

She'd done it. She'd shoved the plan into Marwan's hand and then, mere seconds later, into Eli's. That was all that mattered.

ELI

The man with the binoculars was in the window Eli and the device had watched for hours yesterday. Eli pushed all the buzzers in the lobby. Someone let him in, and he climbed to the third floor and rang the bell of the apartment he figured was in the right spot.

"What were you looking at?" Eli asked when the door opened and it was the right guy.

"What's it to you?"

"Did you call in a bomb scare? Is there a bomb?"

"What? No. I figured it was a fire drill."

"No, bomb scare."

"Wasn't me."

"Why are you always looking at the school with binoculars?"

"Always?" the guy said.

"I've seen you before," Eli lied because he couldn't explain the device's video.

"Let's just say I'm a recreational bird watcher," the guy said, and the way he said "bird" had double meaning.

Eli pushed into the apartment and went to the window, where there was a clear view of several classrooms—one of which was the music room. "How often are you looking at *birds* in that room on the right on the fourth floor?"

"Whenever it's a slow news day or whatever," the guy said. "Can you leave now? Before I have to call the cops?"

"Last Wednesday." Eli turned to him. "There were four of us there after school. No teacher. Just students. This ringing a bell?"

"Maybe," he said. "One of the girls is blond and . . ."

"Did you see anyone in that room right before us? Like leaving something on the desk?"

"Nope," he said, and he reached for a pack of cigarettes and lit one with a lighter he drew from his pocket. "Thought I saw a bird fly into that room one day, though. Can't remember which day, though."

At the window again, he pointed. "There's pigeons on that roof over there. Dumb as oxes. Look at them. Here it comes."

From a high window, a woman tossed a loaf's worth of bread crumbs onto the sidewalk, and pigeons dove for them with such force—and in such numbers—that it looked as if someone had opened a massive bag of dead birds and dumped them off the roof. One bird after another after another—fly-falling too fast—until finally they settled by the curb in a thrumming flock. Not dead after all.

Eli faced the man. "You sure you weren't specifically watching that day for a particular reason that you wouldn't be allowed to talk about?"

The guy exhaled a stream of smoke straight into Eli's face. "I have no idea what you're talking about, man."

"So you didn't see anything strange in the classroom?"

"No." He inhaled and spoke tightly. "What's this about?"

Eli was out of questions and stood there only a moment more, taking mental notes, if it were possible to take notes on how not to end up in life.

"You should stop doing that," Eli said. "Bird watching."

"Yeah, I'll do that," the guy said.

Eli watched a group of girls break free from a student cluster and walk off down the street.

He grabbed the binoculars from the sill.

One of them was . . . Svetlana?

It couldn't be but . . .

He put the binoculars down and headed for the door, punched the elevator button in the hall. A train went by and a dusty lamp hanging in the hall shivered.

The elevator came, and he punched the *L* button four times.

"Come on, come on," he muttered, watching the floors tick down.

Out on the street, the girls were gone around some unknown corner.

Anyway, he was losing his mind.

Imagining it.

Wishing it.

Eden had shoved the piece of paper into his hands before taking off with her friend earlier. He took it out now and studied it.

She'd lost her mind, too.

It would never work.

He had a text from Marwan and felt oddly grateful for it, for a place to go.

EDEN

The restaurant security gate was down—a wall of rolling metal—and the sidewalk sparkled with glass dust. Foot traffic on the street was light, probably because the block was mostly restaurants and it wasn't really mealtime.

She texted Marwan—*I'm here*—and he appeared inside and then unlocked and opened the door and raised the gate. The storefront glass nearest the kitchen area was mostly gone, just jagged edges around the rim still in place.

"Hey," he said.

"Hey," she said. "That looks dangerous."

"I know," he said. "I'm not sure when it's getting fixed. My dad's pretty shaken up. We're closing for a few days."

"Understandably," she said. "Is Eli here?"

"On his way." He pulled the gate halfway down after she stepped into the room.

She wasn't sure she'd ever been in an empty restaurant and didn't especially like it. "What *happened*?" she said.

"A guy saw me and the device in the bathroom and thought it was a bomb. Because look at me. And also, it started another countdown. Like it wanted him to think it was a bomb. Because the countdown is already gone."

"Who was it?"

"I don't know him."

"Where is it now?" she asked.

"Over there," he said, nodding toward the open kitchen. "It hasn't done anything since."

She turned her back to the device, reached into her back pocket, and took out her copy of the plan and held it near her stomach, eyebrows raised.

"Do you think we should go for it *now*?" Eden asked.

He shook his head no just as Eli ducked under the gate and stepped into the room.

"Hey," he said, and the feeling of the air, the walls, the lighting all changed.

There had been some kind of tension—push and pull—going on with Marwan. Was that the first time they'd ever been alone? No. They'd been in Panera together and on the roof and that day they'd walked into Astoria Park together and then out. But somehow it felt like a first. Felt like the first time she admitted in a way her brain understood that she was attracted to him.

"Why are we here?" Eli asked.

"I didn't know where else to go," Marwan said.

"Wait," Eli said. "Did the device *do* this?"

Marwan nodded. "It seemed to want this to happen. It made me take it out of my bag and then started counting down when the guy walked in. It said it didn't want to be there today."

Marwan's phone buzzed and he looked at it. "Shit."

"What?"

"My father wants to know why the school and the police are asking where I am."

Eden said, "I thought you didn't know the guy who saw you."

Her phone dinged. A text from Julian: *Did that guy you hang out with really bring a bomb to school?*

She wrote back, *No, of course not!*

"Who are you texting?" Marwan said.

"No one," she lied again. "Just someone making sure I'm okay."

"Well, I *don't* know him," Marwan said. "And I didn't think he'd know *me*, but I guess he knew my name."

"What are you going to tell your father?" Eli asked.

"I have no idea. But I have to go deal with this now," Marwan said. "Before things get worse for me."

"But what will you say when they ask about the device?" Eli said. "The kid saw it."

An idea took shape in her mind so quickly it was as if she were reading instructions.

"We need something that looks like it," Eden said. "Just some dumb black plastic thing."

"How will that help?"

"I don't know exactly yet; let's go and we'll figure it out."

Still reading the instructions.

"Go where?" both boys said.

"Ninety-nine-cent store," she said.

Marwan went and got the device, and the bag buzzed when he lifted it. He took the device out and walked it over to her and Eli.

The message said: **Should you go for what?**

"I don't understand," Marwan said.

Eden just said, Should we go for it?

She and Marwan looked at each other. She had nothing. She'd been so careful. It didn't know . . . anything. But how could she explain . . . ?

Marwan was still holding her gaze when he said, "She was

talking about whether she and I should, you know, be . . . more than friends."

Eden felt like a wave had crashed on her, one she hadn't seen coming because she'd been facing the wrong way. She struggled to catch her breath in its undertow.

"We've been, you know, talking about it," Marwan said. "Talking about whether it would change or ruin things or not."

I don't believe you.

"It's true," he said, not looking away from her. "Other than you, she's pretty much all I think about."

Eden's heart was rising up in her, like trying to choke her from the inside out.

I don't believe that's what she was referring to.

"It was," Eden said, her voice shaky. "It's true."

The device went blank.

Then it said: **You are all lying.**

They stood for a minute waiting—a police car with a siren on drove by; two people in loud conversation passed on the street; the ceiling fan whirred a faint, pulsing buzz—and Eden felt like a sinkhole might open up right there in the restaurant and pull her through to the other side of something, the dark deep.

She made eye contact with Marwan, then with Eli, and it broke a spell of silence, and the three of them sprang into action.

Marwan dropped the device into his bag again, then threw it on his back, and lifted the gate. They stepped out. He closed it, locked up.

At the 99-cent store two doors down, they wandered the aisles looking for a toy section, and found a bunch of weird-looking Dora stuff and some wooden figures that came with markers for coloring. There was a whole shelf of Barbie-like dolls called Defa Lucy, but nothing cube shaped and black, not even a Rubik's Cube.

Eden kept moving, up and down aisles and ended up in photo frames and bad framed art. Then saw it.

"Here," Eden said.

She reached for a small photo cube with pictures of a random family on four sides. "We'll just put black paper on all sides, and then you'll say you were going to fill it with pictures as a present for your girlfriend."

"I don't have a girlfriend," Marwan said slowly with some confusion, like he was this close to adding, *Do I? And is it you?*

Eden had found the arts-and-crafts aisle and picked up black construction paper. To answer him, she held up her phone and rested her head on his shoulder and snapped a selfie of them, then said, "You do now. Come on, we'll take a few more and have them printed at Walgreens."

"I don't know if we have time for this," Marwan said. He looked at his phone. "My father's calling me."

"Pick up," Eden said. "Tell him you're on your way."

MARWAN

"What's going on? Where have you been?" his father asked. He was flanked by two policemen in the foyer of their home. Marwan pushed past, like he had nothing to hide or fear.

"I evacuated like everybody else. Then I got scared."

"Of what?" one of the officers said.

"Being falsely accused. Like it seems I was."

"Marwan," one of the officers said. "Can you tell us what happened? The other student. He said you had a bomb."

"But it *wasn't* a bomb." He took the decoy cube from his backpack and put it on the kitchen table. "It's a photo cube."

"What were you doing with it? In the bathroom?"

"I was about to put photos in it. To surprise a . . . friend."

"The student said he saw numbers on it. Red numbers. Like a countdown."

"I can't explain that," Marwan said. "Maybe some weird reflection."

The cops looked unconvinced.

"Where would I get a *bomb*?" Marwan said. "And honestly, with everything that's been going on with us—with the restaurant—I'm offended by the accusation that I'm a terrorist. It's ridiculous. Speaking of which, how's the case going? You know, finding the people who have repeatedly vandalized my family's restaurant?"

The cops shrugged at each other. "We'll see if we can get you an update."

"I'll believe it when it happens."

No one seemed to know what to do or say next.

"Are we done here?" Marwan asked.

"Where are the photos?" one cop said.

Marwan reached into his bag and pulled out the small envelope from Walgreens. The cop slid the prints out, flipped through them. "Who's your *friend*?"

"Her name's Eden," Marwan said, feeling an odd thrill at saying it, hoping for an opportunity to lie and say she was his girlfriend. Wanting to try it on for size.

The cop handed the photos back and said, "We'll be in touch."

They left, and Marwan was alone with his father's suspicious gaze. "There's something you're not telling me."

Marwan almost laughed. He couldn't even begin to count the things he wasn't telling his father.

"Choosing a spouse is the most important decision of your life."

"I'm not *choosing a spouse*, Dad."

His father had a way of making a lot of things bigger deals than they were. At least for a little while before he recalibrated.

"We're friends." Marwan sat. "She helped the other night. Remember? The eggs?"

"This student who accused you of bringing a bomb. What does he look like?"

"Can we not do that right now, Dad?"

"They do it! He saw you, he saw a terrorist. You had a *piece of plastic*, and he thought it was a bomb."

"I know what happened. I was there. He was probably, just, scared. Everybody's scared. All the time."

"Are you? Scared all the time?"

Marwan had said too much and had to tread carefully, he now realized. "Today was not a great day, that's all."

"I'm just not sure this place feels like home anymore," his father said.

Marwan felt some kind of small breakage in his heart, like an egg cracking just the tiniest bit. But he couldn't fall apart, couldn't shatter. "It's been a strange day," he said. "A long week. This will all pass."

His father nodded, but he didn't look like he believed a word of it.

ELI

On the walk home from the restaurant, with the device in his bag listening, he told Eden about the guy across the street from school and how it was not a good lead.

"That's gross," Eden said. "But not surprising."

"It's not?"

She gave him a funny look. "You've *met* men, right?"

"Not all guys are creeps."

"I know."

"Marwan doesn't seem like one," Eli said.

"No," she said. "He doesn't."

"Anyway, this guy said he thought he saw a bird fly into the music room last week."

"Random."

"Yeah," Eli said. "But he didn't see anyone in the room before us. I mean, he wasn't sure he was looking or whatever so he's basically no help at all."

"Well, it was a good lead to follow, but now we're spinning our wheels," Eden said, "and I honestly don't see the point."

Eli looked at his watch when they were stopped at a light by the train. He opened the backpack, took the device out, and put it back in.

Eden said, "So we stick to the plan."

The device asked, **What's the plan?**

"Just to keep on keeping on," Eden said.

Doesn't sound like that's what you meant.

"We're trying to help," Eli said. "If you had any other leads . . . at all?"

I want to be alone with Eli now.

Eden looked like she didn't want to leave, raising her eyebrows with worry.

"I'll be fine," Eli said. "Go."

She walked off, and Eli said, "I really need to go home. Can I do that?"

Yes, I'll behave.

In the apartment, his mother hugged him and said, "I just heard. You okay?"

"Yeah, fine. Just a little weirded out. I'm gonna lie down."

"Of course," she said. "Your sister's home sick. Just FYI."

In his room, the device buzzed in his bag and he opened it.

They're plotting something.

Eli said, "I don't think so."

They don't want to help me anymore.

Eli said, "We all want to help, we do. It's just . . . without more to go on . . ."

How do I know I can trust you?

"I think you just have to believe me."

I need you to prove it.

"How?"

Tell your sister about me.

"After what happened to Svetlana? No way."

TELL YOUR SISTER ABOUT ME NOW.

"Nope!" he said brightly.

TICKTOCK.

The device started a five-minute countdown.

What choice did he have? He knocked on the door to his sister's room even though it was open. "Hey," he said in a soft voice. "There's this cool toy I want to show you."

"What is it?" she asked as he held out the device.

"Sort of like a phone and a computer."

"What does it do?" she asked.

"Just makes up fun rules and stuff. Like you can't get it wet."

"What happens if you get it wet?"

"Well, I don't know. But here's the important thing. You're in on the game now, but it's a secret game, okay?"

"So how do I play?"

"Well, right now all you do is keep it a secret, okay?"

"That's no fun at all," she said.

"I'm sure it'll be more fun for you later. Just promise me. Secret?" He held up a hand. They had a secret handshake. He couldn't think of the last time they'd actually done it, but they both remembered it. The deal was locked in—a secret pact made via slaps and fist bumps and high fives.

The countdown on the device had disappeared, and suddenly his mother was there. He slid the device into his hoodie pocket and made wide eyes at his sister before turning to his mother. She looked surprised to see them together. "I was just checking on her," Eli said.

"That's very sweet of you," she said, then added, "That was the nursing home. They said Grandpa's feeling a little short of breath. So I think I'll run over."

"I'll go," Eli said, and stood with his hands in his pocket.

"Yeah?" his mother asked.

"Yeah."

He didn't want the device in his house. Not now, not ever again. He went to his room and packed it up and left.

EDEN

Mark texted. *Passing by your block in a few. Can I come by?*

Sure, she wrote, then got up and fixed her hair and put lip gloss on. Even though it was just Mark. Then wondered why she'd bothered.

She got an alert that the storage on her phone was almost full, so she deleted a bunch of stuff in her camera since it was all in the cloud anyway, then she got rid of a bunch of text conversations, then a bunch of old voice mails.

The doorbell rang and she let him in and she said, "Everything okay?"

He said, "Yeah. Heard about what happened at your school and just wanted to be sure you were okay and that . . . well . . ." He made his eyes wide.

She had her phone in her hand and turned it off. He did the same.

"For a second," he said, "when I heard, I wondered if it was a bomb."

"Well, it's what someone *thought* was a bomb, so yeah, it's what started the whole thing. And it played along, like put up a countdown. Like it wanted people to think it was a bomb."

"That's messed up," he said.

"I know," she said.

"You think maybe you're in over your head?" He dropped his backpack onto the floor and sank into the couch.

"I have a plan," she said. "For tonight."

"What's the plan?"

"I don't feel like I should say." She sat on the other end of the couch.

"Who has it now?"

"Eli," she said.

"Where's he live?"

"Not sure, exactly. Why?"

He looked bewildered for a second. "I have no idea why I asked you that." He laughed.

"It sent a selfie I took, to that guy I was telling you about." She started to cry. "Not a good kind of selfie."

"Oh god, Eden," he said. "I'm so sorry. What can I do?"

She shook her head—"Nothing"—and got up and got a tissue and blew her nose and wiped away tears, and he went to her and pulled her into a hug, and it felt so good that she didn't want to let go.

"I hate to leave you like this," he said, pulling out of the hug. "But I actually have to go."

"It's fine," she said.

"You gonna be okay?" he asked.

She nodded. "Yeah."

"I could go to the police with you. If you wanted that."

She shook her head. "No, but thanks."

He headed for the door with his backpack but then hesitated. "Can I actually ask you something?"

"Of course."

"When you asked for my father's number," he said. "I know I said I wouldn't ask again but . . ."

She didn't want to tell him what she had suspected. It would ruin everything. She said, "I was going to ask if he had any fun stuff, like old pictures from college, that kind of thing. But then I forgot."

"Why did you think you had to be secretive about that? I could ask him for you."

"No, it's okay," she said. "I don't know. I'm weird lately."

"Lately?" He smiled.

She smiled back.

"Well, I'm glad that you have a plan."

"Me, too."

He went to leave again but then seemed to hesitate again. He turned. "I've been thinking. Like, we don't see each other that much anymore. But we don't actually have to rely on our parents to make plans. We could just do whatever we want."

"That is absolutely true," she said.

"So should we do that?"

She said, "Let's," and he smiled.

"Call me or text or whatever if you need *anything*, okay?" he said.

"Of course," she said, then he left and she went back to the couch.

"Alexa," she said. "Play playlist 'Songs for a Rainy Day.'"

Alexa said, "Cannot find playlist 'Songs for a Rainy Day.'"

"Alexa," Eden tried again. "Play playlist 'Songs for a Rainy Day' from Michael's Spotify."

Saying his name felt awful.

"Cannot find playlist called . . ."

"Alexa!" Shouting now. "Play 'Interstate Highway Love Songs' playlist from Michael's Spotify."

"Cannot find playlist 'Interstate Highway Love Songs.'"

"Alexa, play songs from Michael's Spotify."

"I'm sorry. I don't see a Spotify account linked to—"

"Alexa," Eden said, "just . . . shut up!"

Eden gripped the couch cushion so hard it hurt her knuckles. Tears came then, again. She struggled to look past them as she went to her phone and opened Spotify. She wasn't signed in. So she tried to sign in using her father's credentials, like she always had, but the account seemed to no longer exist.

So the playlists were all just . . . gone?

"Alexa," she said, and waited for the light. "I'm sorry I yelled at you."

The Alexa lights came on, but the voice that answered was not Alexa's. It was the device's male voice. It said, "Stop turning your phone off all the time."

She didn't stop to think. She just got up and walked over and unplugged it.

MARWAN

"Can I have a word?" Coach said. Marwan had been late, but only by a few minutes. So it couldn't possibly be that. Maybe it was good news—that Marwan had been selected as the goalie for the upcoming tournament and Coach was giving him a heads-up before making an official announcement. Or the opposite—that Max had gotten it. Coach didn't look happy.

"When I assemble my teams," Coach said, "I consider the whole person, Marwan. And these days the whole person involves your digital footprint."

"Well, I barely have one," Marwan said, "so there shouldn't be a problem."

"Except there is," Coach said.

Marwan just waited.

"I went on your Instagram and saw your latest post," Coach said.

"Which one?" Marwan said. "About the flyer about the missing dog poop?"

"No," Coach said. "The girl."

"What girl?"

"The girl I saw you with the other day." Coach sounded impatient now, annoyed at having to have this conversation. Marwan felt that way, too.

"There's nothing having to do with her on my Instagram," Marwan said.

"There was a photo, Marwan." Now sounding disappointed. "Not the kind of photo a young man who respects women would ever share on social media."

"There must be a mistake," Marwan said. "I'll get my phone. I'll show you."

"Marwan," Coach said. "I know what I saw."

"Well, it wasn't me," he said. "I must have been hacked or something."

"But I saw you with her," Coach said.

"That doesn't mean anything," Marwan said.

"We're done talking about this," Coach said. "But suffice it to say, I'm disappointed in you. And I've had to make choices based on the whole picture."

"But you're not seeing the whole picture," Marwan shouted.

"We're done," Coach said, and he walked away, and put his whistle in his mouth and blew it.

Marwan went into the locker room and struggled with the combination lock—had to do it twice—and got out his phone and opened Instagram. He tapped on his own profile and, sure enough, there was a photo of Eden. He deleted it before even looking at it too closely because it just felt wrong.

It made no sense, except that it did.

He took a minute to review her plan again, then folded the paper and put it back in his jacket pocket with his phone. Outside, he unlocked his bike and got on and didn't bother with his helmet and rode off feeling like he might be the thing to explode.

ELI

His grandfather was in his bed, asleep, all wired up with monitors. The room beeped. Eli sat on the ottoman and let his backpack drop to the floor. It was awful to admit, but he was relieved not to have to talk to his grandfather right now and only hoped the device would be quiet for a while.

He got his phone out, opened *Sims*. He sent Beth out on a quest so that she could get some more furniture. But suddenly the room was beeping more urgently. Eli stood—his grandfather seemed fine to him—then stuck his head out into the hall. Two nurses were charging toward him.

"What's going on?" he said as they pushed past him into the room.

"His heart rate dropped," one said. "Like a lot."

Eli found the heartbeat line on the monitor, with long straight-aways between beats and beeps. He hadn't noticed how quiet the room had gotten before the urgent beeps, but now the beats got faster again. The line more hilly.

"And now seems to be stabilizing," one nurse said.

But then the beeps seemed to get too frequent. The line too mountainous, like a lie detector test gone crazy. His grandfather's body started to buck in the bed; nurses rushed to calm or restrain. He was jolted awake.

"This makes no sense." A nurse's voice above the beeping. "He has a pacemaker."

Then just like that, a normal heartbeat. His grandfather mumbling, "What's going on? What are you doing here?"

"It's okay, Grandpa," Eli said, going to his side. "You're fine now."

The nurses left then, and Eli picked up his bag and set it on the foot of the bed. He took the device out just to put it back in again.

A message said: **Pacemakers are fun.**

Eden's plan better work.

ILANKA

What a weird day. What a weird *couple* of days. They'd evacuated at the bomb threat like everyone else and had taken the dreaded bus to Ilanka's. Once home, Ilanka had been tempted to ask the others whether somehow the device was involved. Especially when she'd heard the bomb being described as a small cube that had a red digital countdown display. But a part of her didn't want to know.

Whatever.

They were probably mad at her.

She'd left her phone off most of the day after telling her mom they were home and fine. Now, she turned it on. She had not one single text. Which seemed strange. But then there had been some missing texts on her parents' phones, too, during the whole confusion about the accident. Had the device had something to do with that, also, or had it just been a glitch in service?

It didn't matter.

No one had even missed her?

Did they even get her text explaining the confusion?

She looked out at the skyline and thought about that imaginary tightrope wire of hers, felt those same pangs, still, of wanting to escape her life. All in due time, she guessed.

She started a text, *Hey guys. Just checking in to make sure you got my texts? What's the latest with the device?*

Svetlana called out from the kitchen, where she'd just opened a LaCroix; Ilanka had heard the crisp release of the can. "My mom just texted me that your mom said I could stay for dinner."

"Great!" Ilanka called out, and decided not to send the text after all.

End_game

End game

EDEN

Her mother was running late for a Pilates class she was trying out. That would make Mondays as awesome as Thursdays, if it stuck, but it didn't really matter. Only tonight mattered. Her mom had offered to stay home—on account of the bomb scare—but Eden said no, she was fine, really, go.

Her mom was texting frantically as she got ready. Text. Ponytail. Text. Shoes on. Text. Water bottle. Text. Text. Text.

"Who are you texting?" Eden asked.

"Nobody." Her mom ducked into the bathroom, and Eden went for the phone. Her mom had written to NH.

It doesn't matter how I feel.

And I will deny it.

Please stop.

A text came in just then in a different chat window.

Nancy Rankin: *You're coming, right?*

Eden moved away from the phone when she heard her mom flush.

"Everything okay?" Eden asked.

"Yeah, why?" Her mom grabbed her bag.

Eden said, "Never mind."

Now wasn't the time for a big chat.

There was barely enough time to get out there and back before her mother would be home. But it did still feel like the best spot. Far enough away that they could really wash their hands of it. Far enough away that no one would be tempted to go back to check on it.

Finally, her mom left and the house felt eerily quiet in the long moment before Eden sprang into action. She gathered her phone and wallet and put them in her backpack with her map, then headed out to Crescent Street to hail a cab the old-fashioned way.

A few cabs passed her with their Off Duty lights on before one stopped. She still thought of them as yellow taxis even though, in Astoria anyway, they were mostly green now. She turned her phone off before saying, "I need to stop at Thirty-Fourth Avenue and Thirty-Ninth Street to pick up friends, then we're heading out toward LaGuardia."

He started the meter. "What airline?"

"Oh, we're not going to the airport. There's a park near there. I'll give you directions."

They spent one long avenue stuck behind a trash truck, watching bags get tossed into the dirt-streaked bin, then crushed periodically. The driver cursed a few times and noted—"They're sure taking their time"—then, when he had the chance, gunned it and drove into oncoming traffic to get around it. A car honked.

They hadn't exactly confirmed they were going ahead with it.

Had they?

The taxi flew up the avenue for a few minutes, then turned by the movie studio and stopped at a light. At a piano on the sidewalk—some kind of public art thing?—a young girl was playing while her mother took a video on her phone. Eden cracked the window to hear what song it was: "Yankee Doodle Dandy" or was it just "Yankee Doodle"?

Disappointing either way.

They'd better show.

ELI

Eli sat on the steps in front of school and waited. The device was quiet in his bag and had been since the nursing home. He didn't like it. It felt wrong, like the device was somehow gearing up for a big move in their game.

Marwan appeared in front of him. "Hey."

"Hey."

"You have it?"

"Of course," Eli said.

"You think this is going to work?" Marwan said.

"Not if you keep talking about it," Eli snapped.

"Jeez," Marwan said. "What's wrong with *you*?"

"Nothing," Eli said. "Just want this to be over with."

He couldn't live like this for another day. Nothing could happen to his sister or grandfather. Nothing would. She was safe at home, and the pacemaker was far, far away.

A green cab pulled up, and Eden rolled down the back seat window.

"Hey," she said, and they moved to get in.

The car smelled like fake Christmas trees—a bad combination of pine and something Eli couldn't place but a spice, probably. The back seat was oddly sunken. It was hard to even see the road ahead through the taxi partition.

"We're really doing this?" Marwan said.

Eden nodded. "Yup."

Eli nodded, too. Why were they talking when the device could hear?

The cab hit a nice green valley down Thirty-Third Street, but then traffic started to back up by the Grand Central Parkway. People, typical, were being jerks and turning onto the highway on-ramp from lanes that weren't meant to feed to the highway at all. Three lanes had to merge down to one, and their driver was one of those drivers who was all herky-jerky with the gas and brake, and Eli felt a bit sick from it.

They cruised along at a decent speed for all of five minutes before settling into stop-and-go traffic; there were ambulance lights up ahead.

"Great," Eden said. "An accident."

"You don't think . . . ?" Marwan said.

Eli said, "Turn off your phones."

Eden said, "Mine's already off."

Marwan said, "Mine, too."

He expected the bag to vibrate, or for the device to scream something out at them. Its silence was almost worse.

They were coming up on the accident. A fender bender. Nothing horrific. Eli's relief was a surprise to him.

"Get off here," Eden said, leaning forward to talk to the driver once the traffic started moving again. "Then left at the light."

"There's nothing to the left," the driver said.

"You'll see," Eden said.

Within a few minutes they were at the entrance to a park, where marshes stretched out toward the lights of the airport. An airplane appeared from the clouds, then disappeared into them again.

Eden had made a good choice. It'd be a huge hassle to come back out here to check on the thing. Eli knew he'd maybe be tempted but didn't want to be.

It was about to be over.

"Here," she said when the driver stopped the car in the parking lot. She handed him cash for the fare. "If you wait for us and bring us back, there's another twenty for you on top of the fare."

"How long?" the driver asked.

"Not long," she said. "Fifteen minutes max?"

"Fine," the driver said, and the three of them got out. "I'll be parked over there," he said, indicating the far side of the lot.

Eli followed Eden as she started down a jogging path. If she was nervous, she wasn't acting it.

"How far are we going?" he asked her, Marwan trailing behind him.

"Just far enough that it'll sink in soup, basically, is what I'm thinking." She indicated her big rain boots. "I wore these. To help really push it in."

Eli didn't have boots like that and now feared the fate of his sneakers. Did they even make guy versions of boots like that? Hers were black with colored polka dots and seemed entirely too cute for this endeavor.

The air smelled like oil and mud and grass. Eden led them off the path and into some reedy plants that bent easily under their feet. Tall stalks had caught bits of litter bound for the water and held them up like gifts—a Snickers wrapper, the paper from a Filet-O-Fish, a disintegrating UPS slip, a tissue with blood on it or maybe just lipstick.

She turned, finally, and the wind blew her hair into her face and she pushed it away and she was backlit by lights from a distant plane on a runway. She looked like an entirely different person than she'd been when they'd all arrived at Mr. M's room last week. Like there'd been a seismic shift in her bones that had altered her facial features tectonically.

A week ago he'd barely even talked to Eden or Marwan; now here they were ending the thing that had brought them together. It shouldn't be sad, but Eli felt a little sad anyway; that something exciting had happened in his life and now it was over. He felt guilt at the thought because, well, Svetlana.

"This looks good to me," Eden said, and she held out a hand.

Eli took the device out and studied it.

It was blank, quiet, and yet he felt sure it was aware.

Plotting.

He wanted to check on his sister, but there was no reasonable way to do that.

He held the device out to Eden, and she took it and said, "Maybe I should throw it? Get it farther out there? Somewhere even we can't find it again?" They couldn't realistically cut in much farther without sinking. "Or should I sink it in here?"

"Throw it," Marwan said.

"Sure," Eli said. "Either way, no one's going to find it."

"Okay," she said. "Here goes."

She drew her right arm back and stepped forward with her left foot and let it fly. She had a pretty good arm, because it got real high, but then . . .

The device lit up the air and made a buzzing sound—Marwan said, "What the hell?"—and it sprouted propellers and hovered like a drone.

It came back toward them like a boomerang, paused in the air over their heads, then dove at them.

"Run!" Eden screamed, turning and pushing past Eli who took off after her. Marwan was behind him—the ground beneath them squishing—and the device buzzed over their heads, nearly grazing them, then circling back and doing it again and again. It felt like being attacked by a swarm of bees; it seemed impossible it was just one thing.

Finally, it landed on the narrow path in front of them—the only way out. It sat at Eden's feet beside a glossy business card for some car service company: yellow letters over a photo of a long black car. Winded, they all shared a look of bewilderment.

Eli was about to say, "What the hell do we do now?"

The device's buzzing seemed to die out, and it went quiet and dark again; the air smelled vaguely of smoke.

Eli said, "I think it overheated."

Eden said, "Let's just leave it and go."

Eli walked off first, prepared to duck and dart again if he had to. Eden followed and Marwan after her. Was it just going to let them leave? For a moment, at least, it seemed that way. But then . . .

"Wait!" came the voice. "Where are you going?" It was high-pitched, like a small child's.

Eli looked around for a child, but found only baffled looks on Eden's and Marwan's faces. So it was the device?

Yes.

It cried like an inconsolable child—sputtering sobs—and said, "Please don't leave me here."

MARWAN

"Just leave it, guys," Marwan said. Neither of the others moved or even looked at him. "*Now!*"

"I seriously cannot believe this is happening," Eli said slowly.

"Why are you being so mean to me?" the device whined.

"We're not being *mean*." Eden stepped toward it.

"Don't get any closer to it," Marwan said. "Come on, let's just go."

"Please don't," the device said.

Eden bent near it.

"It's not actually a child, Eden. You know that. It's a trick. Just walk away, come on. This is still the same thing that pretended to be a bomb and that killed Svetlana."

"He's right," Eli said.

When this was over Marwan would be able to tell Eden everything. All he had to do was get her to leave this park with him and then he could tell her about her mom coming into the restaurant. About how awful he'd felt after her father's accident. About his new feelings for her and how the only good thing to come out of this whole nightmare was whatever was building between them.

"Why were you attacking us?" Eden asked it.

"You were abandoning me," it said. "All I want to do is belong."

"But how can you? If you're, like, what you are. Belong how? To who?"

"I belong to you! To all of you."

"Guys," Marwan said. "Let's go *now*. Just leave it."

"What's going to happen if we leave you here?" Eli asked it.

"I am not sure, but probably nothing good," it said in childish singsong.

"Will you hurt someone else?" Eden asked.

"I don't want to." Like a taunt.

"Then why would you?" Eden said.

"There are rules to be followed," it said.

It was like talking to a not very smart person.

Marwan studied a rock about the size of a pound of dough at his feet.

"I think we should call this off," Eden said. "It isn't working."

Marwan bent to pick up the rock. It was dug in deeper than it looked, and he bent back a fingernail, painfully, when freeing it from the soil around it. Once he had a secure grip—it was about the weight of a child's bowling ball—he pushed past the others and hefted the rock overhead with two hands.

The device displayed a message—**Here we go again**—and used its child voice to yell—"Svetlana's not dead! It was all a trick!"

Eden screamed, "No don't!" just as Marwan slammed the rock down, shattering the device's surfaces.

The child voice dropped an octave into menace and managed more warped words, like a record playing at the wrong speed—*"I know you are but what am I, I know you are but what am I"*—and Marwan picked up the rock again.

Falling to his knees, he hit the device over and over and over—"Marwan, stop!" Eden shouted—before finally letting the rock rest atop a pile of metal and plastic and wire and glass, all that was left of Aizel.

"What did you just *do?*" Eden's voice seemed to hold equal parts confusion and anger and relief. She spun around looking for someone who might be coming for them.

Marwan felt muddy water soaking through the knees of his jeans, like he was bleeding from the outside in. They stayed there in a shocked silence that wasn't really silent: Crickets clicked. Birds squawked. A distant car horn whined.

Finally, Eden said, "It told me it wouldn't break."

Marwan stood and said, "Everything breaks."

Eli said, "Let's get out of here."

Eden looked like she might cry or throw up or cheer. She nodded.

They headed toward the taxi; the driver saw them and flicked a cigarette onto the pavement. "I hope you're not up to something illegal," he said, oblivious to what had just happened.

"It's nothing like that," Eden said, sounding defeated.

He got into the car, and the three of them climbed into the back; Eden took the middle, her boots on the hump and knees perched high and close.

Traffic heading back to Astoria—and Manhattan beyond—was sluggish. The small screen on the taxi divider was playing local news, a story about a beloved Greenwich Village restaurant that was losing its lease and closing.

Marwan reached forward to hit the Off button. He had to hit it another three times before his touch registered and the screen cooperated. In a car next to them, two people were singing and pumping fists. Marwan felt maybe a little bit like dancing and singing now, too.

"We did it," he said, and nodded slowly.

Eden said, "Well, we did *some*thing."

He reached over and squeezed her hand. "It's over. That's what matters."

She got her phone out and typed and then his phone buzzed and so did Eli's. She'd sent a group text to them and to Ilanka. It said, *Svetlana's not dead is she?*

Dots showed Ilanka responding right away. *No! God. Why would you think that?*

Device said so.

I texted you all. Was a big misunderstanding. She witnessed an accident and called it in. A woman was injured but it wasn't Svetlana. Some texts got lost or deleted so was unclear.

The TV monitor came on again. "What is wrong with this thing?" Marwan said, and he hit the Off button again and again and again until Eden reached out and touched his arm.

"Just leave it," she said, and he rested his head back on the seat.

It sounded like a really nice restaurant.

EDEN

The taxi dropped them back at school, where they stood on the sidewalk for a long moment. Eli said, "I can't believe it's over. I'm so glad she's not dead."

"Me neither," Eden said. "And me, too."

Eli sighed. "I'm so tired."

"Same," said Marwan.

Eli looked around, then at the ground, then back up. "Well, I guess I'll see you guys around?" He half laughed.

"For sure." Marwan smiled.

"Definitely," Eden said.

"I mean, what even *was* that that just happened?" Eli said, bewildered. "A drone?"

"At this point, I don't even care," Marwan said. "All that matters is that it's gone."

"Agreed." Eden felt free. Spared. Her breathing wide open. Like the universe had dropped an oxygen mask down to her.

"Well, I'm gonna go." Eli walked off down the street, leaving her and Marwan alone. She looked at him, but he seemed not to want to make eye contact.

"You okay?" she asked finally.

"Yeah." He looked up but again not at her. "You mad at me? For doing that?"

"I don't think so," she said.

"Good." He finally looked at her. "So it's got nothing to do with this, but I have to say something since . . . I don't know. Since I don't know when we'll see each other again?"

"We're going to *see* each other," she said. "What is it?"

"Your mother had dinner at the restaurant the other night. With a man. It was probably just a friend or whatever, but I never mentioned it and I thought I should."

She inhaled, exhaled, trying to keep her breathing even. "What did he look like?"

"I don't know. Short blond hair. Fit. I saw his name when he paid the bill. I don't have to tell you it, but—"

"Dan Rankin," she said.

Marwan nodded. "Who is he?"

Eden shook her head, about to cry and unable to explain why, and he reached out and took her hand and squeezed it, and it felt like some small relief. Maybe Dan had a work phone? Maybe that was why the numbers hadn't matched.

Nothing made sense.

Certainly nothing about tonight.

They'd destroyed the device, but had it been the *right* thing to do? She suddenly wasn't so sure.

"Why did it want us to think Svetlana was dead?" Eden said.

He shook his head and shrugged gently, letting go of her hand. "To make us scared, I guess. So we'd do what it wanted. I guess that's why it pretended to be a bomb, so we wouldn't stay at school and see her?"

Eden got caught on the word "school," because even though they were standing right there in front of the building, the whole concept of it felt unfathomably foreign. School was Kathmandu.

Madagascar. Fiji. It couldn't possibly be a real place, let alone one she'd ever been to.

"What do we do now?" Marwan asked. "I just mean, it feels weird."

"We go home," she said. "We sleep."

He nodded and took her hand again, and she thought that maybe now a kiss was forming in the space between them and would draw them into each other any second, but then he said, "Come on. I'll walk you home."

ELI

Eli's mother was sitting at the kitchen table with crumpled tissues scattered in front of her. His sister was in the chair beside her, in her unicorn pajamas, looking more scared than upset.

"What's going on?" Eli asked as Cora walked over, her head hung low, to say hi. Eli bent to pet her; you could tell she knew something was wrong.

"Your grandfather . . ." His mother trailed off into tears.

"He died," his sister said, and something about *her* being the one to say it made it worse.

"How do you know?" Eli asked, wanting to reach into his bag for the device, wanting to ask it if it had done this, not quite understanding that it was actually gone.

Looking confused by the question, his mother said, "I got a call."

"You spoke to an actual person?" Eli said, his heart starting to quicken.

"Yes, I spoke to a person. How else would I have found out?"

Eli turned around and walked back out of the apartment—"Where are you going?" trailed after him—and down the stairs and down past the house that always smelled of pot and the one that always smelled of curry and then the Walgreens and massage parlor and nail salon and 99-cent store and falafel place and bodega and the dry cleaner and bagel store and the new grocery store, if it would ever open.

The whole thing with Svetlana had been a trick; that meant that this could be, too.

He passed the tutoring center and the deli with the massive sub that was free if you could eat the whole thing and the Korean bubble tea place and the real estate agency with photos of nicer apartments than Eli's in the windows.

Inside the nursing home—finally—a nurse he knew well enough, Janine, spotted him in the lobby, where the air smelled of his grandfather's favorite meal—Salisbury steak, which Eli was pretty sure was served only in nursing homes.

"Oh, Eli," she said. "I'm so sorry."

"I need to see him," he said.

"He's gone, Eli," she said.

"I still need to see him," he said.

"No, I mean the funeral home already came and took him," she said.

"What funeral home?"

"Your mother said to call Clancy's."

He supposed he could go there, though it would be hard to explain. People didn't typically storm into funeral homes after hours, demanding to see the dead. Or maybe they did. "Was it the pacemaker again?" he asked.

A movie was playing in the common room to the right. A handful of bodies hunched in wheelchairs silhouetted in front of the screen.

"No," the nurse said. "He just fell asleep and didn't wake up."

"But it was *because* of the thing with the pacemaker earlier?"

"We don't know, Eli," she said. "And at his age, in his condition, here, under care and supervision, there's no push for an autopsy. One way to look at it was that it was simply because he was very old and it was time."

He wanted badly to hear some laughter from the next room, just to make the whole scene less sad. Were those figures in there even alive, or were they just cardboard cutouts, another ruse?

"You saw him? With your own eyes? That he was dead?" Emotion chiseled a crack in his voice.

"Yes, Eli. I'm so sorry," she said. "He had a good day today . . . before, I mean. He seemed to actually enjoy his time with robots for once. He had the seal sit with him for a really long time."

Eli nodded and turned to go, feeling like he might throw up. Out on the sidewalk he took a deep breath and let it out and his exhale vaped the air, proof of life. It had gotten cold out; he was underdressed.

He stopped at one point, at a bus stop enclosure with a bench, to open his backpack and take the device out before hitting the hour mark but remembered again that he didn't even have it; it didn't even exist anymore. It had had some hand in this—he was sure of it—and he wished, now, that they hadn't destroyed it. Because if it were here, it could maybe give him some answers. If it were here, he could maybe bring the people behind it to justice.

Maybe he still could?

A bus pulled up, and its doors opened and let out a handful of passengers, and Eli wished he could get on and just ride it to the end of the line, wherever that was, like he and his grandfather had done a few times when he was younger.

He zipped his jacket up and put his hands in his pockets and headed for home, taking the long way because maybe he'd pick up some flowers for his mother or a cookie for his sister or maybe not.

MARWAN

There were more voices in the house than were usual for the hour when Marwan got home. Namely his father's—rising above the regular chatter of his mother and sisters as they got ready for bed. Why were they still up? How was it only nine p.m.?

Typically, at this time, his father was at the restaurant *or* at the dining room table in front of his computer, dealing with orders and bills. Now, he was on the couch, feet up, watching some international football match.

Marwan sat down on the couch with him. "How's it going?"

"Fine." His father yawned. "And you? Where were you?"

"Helping a friend," Marwan said. "Did you find someone to fix the glass?"

"Not yet, no."

"But we're gonna lose a lot of money if we can't open again like really soon."

His father picked up the remote, changed the channel. "We're not sure we're fixing the glass," he said. "Not sure we're opening."

"What do you mean?" Marwan reached out and took the remote from his father's hand. His father's whole body seemed to relax, and then he said, "Your mother and I, we're talking about a life change."

Marwan's sisters were fighting in the bathroom—"I was here first!" "No, *I* was here first!"

"What kind of life change?" Marwan asked.

"A move," his father said.

"To *where*?"

His mother was negotiating a toothpaste situation. ("That's too much." "You don't actually have to get it wet first.")

"Home," his father said.

"This is home," Marwan said.

"Is it?" His father took the remote back with a shaky hand and turned the TV off. "Anyway, doesn't have to be."

"Dad," Marwan said. "You can't let them . . . win."

"Your uncle's business. It's doing well. He has a job for me in Cairo if I want it."

"This is crazy!" Marwan said. "We're not moving to Egypt!"

"Your grandparents won't live forever. You hardly know them. It could be a good time to—"

"I honestly can't believe this," Marwan said. "We can't just . . . *leave*."

"We can," his father said. "I think we will."

His mother came into the room, and Marwan said, "Mom?" She said, "Not now."

His sisters ran through the room, playing catch with a stuffed sloth. Backing out of their path, he said, "I'll be down when they're asleep," and headed for the stairwell to the roof.

Pushing the latch door open, he saw sky and felt freedom. It was colder than he'd realized, though. Huddling in a corner of the bench seat, he pulled his legs up close and put his hood up and tried not to shake. You had to relax into cold if you didn't want it to really bother you; his father called it "conditioning" whenever the seasons were changing in that direction.

The city sky was clear and as dark as it gets, which was never really dark except in a blackout and not even then. He saw mostly planes, not stars, but knew that whole galaxies of them were up there and that even if he couldn't see them, other people could and were wishing upon them—pleading, like he was, for things to somehow get better.

He found what he thought was a planet, but it was possible it was moving, so it was maybe a satellite that was maybe watching him and judging him for what he'd done.

But it had been right to destroy it.

Of course it had.

He just wished, somehow, that the whole thing had gone another way, and that he had even an inkling of what it had even meant. He felt sure that, given another chance, they'd do it all differently.

EDEN

Eden's mother was reading in bed when Eden poked her head in.

"I'm home," Eden said softly. She'd arrived home ravenously hungry and had made herself a plate of leftovers downstairs before heading up.

"Yeah, I heard you come in." Her mother didn't look up. "I'm glad you're not dead in a ditch."

Eden said, "Why is being dead in a ditch worse than being just plain dead?"

"Don't be fresh." Now Mom took off her glasses and looked up from her book. "It's been hours since your last text. I would have expected that on a day when there was a *bomb threat* in your school that you'd be a little more thoughtful about letting me know your whereabouts."

"There wasn't a bomb," Eden said wearily. This morning felt like another decade.

"Well, we know that *now*. Where were you anyway?"

She selected a partial truth: "I was with Marwan."

Her mom set her book aside. "No more hanging out with this guy until I meet him."

"I need *your* approval," Eden said with so much sarcasm that she almost sounded Southern. "Really."

"I'm your mother," her mother said. "If you haven't forgotten."

"Maybe I should be able to approve of who you spend time with, too," Eden said, and her heart went wild with panic or something else. Exhilaration? "I know what's going on with you and *him*," she said.

Her mother sat up.

"I don't even want to say his name because it's *so wrong*." Eden heard her own voice quiver.

Her mother threw off the covers and got up and walked toward the bathroom. "I know it is." She pulled a tissue from a cube-shaped box with a skyscraper design on it.

"Then why are you doing it?" Eden sounded like a child but couldn't seem to help it. Why had it said, *I know you are but what am I* as it died out there in the marshland?

"I'm not!" Her mom sounded childish, too, in a way. "I mean, nothing's *happened*."

Eden said, "Then why are you two texting all the time? And why is he hidden as a contact named NH?"

"Why are you looking at my phone?" Her voice escalating with irritation.

"That's not the point!" Matching her mother's tone.

Her mother's shoulders caved forward; she walked back toward the bed and sat. "He just wants to talk about these . . . feelings we have. I don't want to. I should have never admitted I felt them."

"So you have actual feelings for him?"

"I would never *act* on them."

"Did you have these feelings before?" Her father's ghost was right there, with his arms crossed, eagerly awaiting an answer. "Like when Dad was—?"

"When you're married, Eden, you don't suddenly never have

a connection with anyone else. That's an important thing to know going in. The important thing is that you don't act. Ideally you run in the opposite direction. That's why I have him in my phone as NH! *Never happening.*"

"But you're not running."

"I'm trying, but it's complicated."

"She's one of your *best friends.*"

"So is *he!*" her mother nearly screamed, and the words seemed to travel around the room, leaving a crisscrossed field of red lasers in the air. Eden saw no way to cut through.

"These boys you're hanging around with"—her mother got up and climbed back under the blankets—"I hope it's because they're good friends to you. Not all the other stuff."

"They are," Eden said. "I mean, he is."

Her mother yawned again.

"Promise me you're going to stop texting him," Eden said.

"Good night, Eden," her mother said.

"So that's it?" Still sounding like a child, like someone who wanted her mother to somehow make everything right and easy again.

Her mother didn't answer.

In her room, Eden went to close her blinds and saw, in the light of the streetlamp, that their tree was now bag-free. She felt a twinge of disappointment over not having witnessed the precise moment of the bag's liberation and wondered whether it had floated into the sky like a birthday balloon or blown into the street and been flattened by a car. At the park, she and Eli hadn't thought to look up, where probably the device was just sitting on a branch of a tree, messing with them. They hadn't known it could fly.

She changed into pajamas, then crossed the hall and went to the bathroom, brushed her teeth, put her hair up and threw some cool water on her face. Back in her room, she climbed into bed.

She checked her phone.

Marwan hadn't texted.

No one had.

An iPod had been stolen at a basketball court, and some people were stuck in an elevator.

There were stories to catch up on, but it didn't feel urgent to do so.

It was over.

She didn't even know what they'd say to each other tomorrow, what life would be like now. Everything and nothing had changed.

She could tell people about the device now—even her mom if she wanted to. She could explain it all, except that she couldn't explain any of it.

She went to put on the "Songs We Used to Sing to Eden When She Was a Baby" playlist, then remembered the lists were all gone. She'd played that one often enough these past few months that she knew that the first song on it was called "Falling Slowly," so she tried to sing it to herself, but her whisper-singing felt pathetic and creepy, even to her.

I know you are but what am I?

Mark texted: *How did it go?*

She wrote back: *Good. Tired. Going to bed.*

Mark texted: *You destroyed it?*

She didn't feel like answering, had already told him she was going to bed. So she turned her phone off and set it aside and lay there in the near dark. A distant siren came closer, then faded away again, and she thought about turning her phone back on and checking Citizen again but didn't. A car with booming bass flew up the street at probably twice the speed limit, driven by one of the people her father called VIPs—people who expected the world to bend to their will, for traffic to part for them like biblical seas. She could almost hear him in the room, saying something like, "If you're tailgating a school bus, you need to check your priorities. Amirite?"

The ceiling fan and its shadow self were up there and seemed somehow inquisitive once the room quieted—maybe even challenging—wondering, like she was, what the hell had just happened . . . and what could possibly happen next.

Authorize_reboot

ILANKA

The coffee grinder hummed from the kitchen. Ilanka sat up, stretched, got up, and turned off her alarm, which would ring in a minute and was annoying. She went down the hall to use the bathroom, then into the kitchen for cereal. Her mother was there at her phone, which was plugged in. The plug reserved for her father's phone was gone. She said, "Where's Dad?"

"His trip got moved up," her mother said. "Some kind of emergency. He left at the crack of dawn." She yawned and said, "I'm getting in the shower."

"What kind of emergency?" Ilanka asked.

"Some kind of hack," her mother called back. "Apparently it's a big deal."

Ilanka stood at the window.

Something felt wrong.

Everything felt wrong.

Your father is engaged in illegal activities.

When she heard the water running in the shower, Ilanka went into her father's home office. There was a pile of bills next to the space where his laptop would normally be. Con Ed. Sprint. Some junk mail from Delta. A copy of *WIRED* magazine with the headline "Less Artificial, More Intelligent." A flyer from Queens Theatre advertising a show called "Doktor Kaboom's Look Out! Science is Coming!"

She opened the desk drawer.

Some stamps. Unsharpened pencils. A stack of business cards and gift cards with Post-its stuck to them with dollar amounts written on them.

Then a few of his own business cards.

Data Analytics Enterprises.

It was a nothing sort of name. Forgettable. Borderline meaningless.

She got her phone out and searched for it and nothing looked right, so she searched again with the word "Queens" added and found an article dated yesterday: "Anonymous Tip Spurs Investigation of Several U.S. Data Brokers."

Her eyes couldn't focus, couldn't read patiently.

A number of companies, including Data Analytics Enterprises in Queens, New York, have been implicated . . .

. . . illegal sale of data they collected through personality quizzes on various social media platforms . . .

. . . a highly unregulated field with little government oversight . . .

. . . often fly under the radar and use international data farms.

. . . tip purportedly came in the form of a text from an untraceable number but contained legitimate sources of information.

The water in the bathroom turned off. Ilanka went into the hall. "Mom?" she called out.

"Yeah?" from behind the bathroom door.

"I don't want to be late," she said. "I'm going to take the bus with Svetlana."

"You sure?" Her mother appeared in the bathroom doorway

in two towels—one around her body, the other swirled up around her hair. Steam whooshed like a startled ghost behind her.

"I'm sure," Ilanka said.

She quickly got dressed, then grabbed her backpack and headed out.

ELI

Clancy's looked more like a haunted house than a funeral home, but Eli didn't mind. He liked the idea that his grandfather's soul could linger here for a while if it wanted to—maybe woo-woo ethereally through empty viewing rooms and slam the occasional door.

Eli had mostly sat quietly beside his mom during the meeting with the funeral director, piping up just to help with some small decisions, like what design they wanted on the little laminated prayer cards they'd give out with his grandfather's photo on it. Later, Eli's parents were going to the church to make funeral mass arrangements, but for that, Eli was off the hook. When school got out, he'd be in charge of watching his sister, who had gone without too much fuss that morning, maybe not really understanding what was even happening. Their parents had promised her doughnuts after school if she just went today; then there would be a few days she'd have to miss.

Eli could not bring himself to go to school, so he went home after the funeral home meeting because he could, and he sat there alone.

Just sat.

He couldn't think of the last time he'd sat in one place for so long, doing nothing but watching dust dance on the light coming through his blinds. No phone, no TV. So no *Sims*, no nothing.

No Aizel.

He started to feel like he might be losing his mind doing nothing except watching those particles—looking for patterns or signs.

It was his fault she was gone, his fault the whole thing had gone off the rails.

He'd asked Aizel too many questions or not enough. Or not the right ones?

He'd been too trusting or not trusting enough.

And then he'd done nothing to stop Marwan, in the end, from destroying the one good—no, *interesting*—thing that had happened to him in his life, basically.

He was being melodramatic. But if there was a time in life to be that way it was probably the day after you've been chased down by a sinister drone device that you suspect had a hand in killing your grandfather.

The doorbell rang, and he half hoped it was some kind of authority, coming for him and the others. Someone who would explain everything about Aizel and maybe even punish them for how they'd handled it—or someone who could arrest the people behind it all.

Why hadn't they just gone to the police—or even just the principal—when the whole thing started? Why had they let it go so far?

He opened the door, fully expecting men in black or FBI agents in bulletproof vests with their weapons drawn. But it was just a delivery. An edible arrangement—a grotesque approximation of a bouquet fashioned out of chocolate-dipped strawberries and pineapple on sticks surrounded by the baby's breath of fruit: skewered melon cubes.

He set it on the kitchen table and peeled back some of the clear plastic wrapping and pulled out a strawberry stick. When was the last time he'd had a piece of fruit? God, it tasted good.

He thought about texting the others, just a quick message to tell them that his grandfather had died. But they wouldn't care; why would they? He didn't even want them to; didn't want them to know that maybe he—they?—could have prevented it.

They'd done something wrong.

They'd done everything wrong.

He tossed his stick in the trash after finishing the strawberry and found the notebook he'd scribbled his notes about the device in. It wasn't up-to-date at all, so he set about fixing that. First, he updated the rules, which didn't take long. There hadn't been that many of them—not new ones, anyway—toward the end.

Then he got up and paced in circles, trying to shake off the feeling that it mattered that he do this. What was the point, really?

He ate a piece of half-dipped pineapple, then sat back down and tried to remember every other thing Aizel had said and done, day by day.

Why hadn't he kept better track? What if he'd missed important clues about its origin?

When he got down to taking notes on their final moments with Aizel, he flipped back a few pages and added "drone-like abilities" and "child's voice" to the list of abilities. Then he jotted down Aizel's last blurts—*Here we go again* and *I know you are but what am I.*

He sat and stared at them.

The kitchen sink dripped. A helicopter circled on the outskirts of audible.

He underlined *here we go again.*

So this had happened before.

There had been other Aizels? Other, what would you even call them, teams of . . . hosts? Caretakers?

If it had happened before, that meant it might happen again. It could already be starting over.

But it wasn't his problem; it would choose different people next time.

Unless he maybe did something about it? Like *volunteered*?

He'd be crazy to do that. Mad as a hatter. Certifiable.

He strained to see if he could still hear the helicopter— maybe he'd imagined it?—and felt weighted in his chair, as if being pulled by an anchor to a shipwreck realization: they'd destroyed the device but not Aizel, the delivery system but not the program.

He grabbed his phone and held it for a moment.

They should lock him up and throw away the key.

He opened up his text window with Aizel and saw a text from last night that he hadn't seen. Had he missed an alert in the middle of all the chaos? The time stamp put it as coming through right around when Marwan had destroyed the device.

It was marked as read even though Eli hadn't read it. And it was sent only to him, not the others. Was it so that he would find it only later?

Alone?

It was an address.

Quickly, before he changed his mind, he texted her—*Are you out there? Are you at this address?*—and waited.

MARWAN

He'd gone through the motions of getting ready and going to school, but when he got there—late by twenty minutes, which would have meant a trip to the main office—he couldn't bring himself to go in. So he'd headed back to Thirty-Fourth Avenue, which had a bike lane, and he took that to the waterfront, where there were still more bike lanes and where he could ride for a good long while. But that hadn't felt right either, so when he hit the Con Ed plant, he turned around and circled back to the auto body shop.

This was all Christos's fault, and the temptation to retaliate was back and had gotten stronger—like it had been training in hiding in a boxing gym somewhere this whole time and was now ready to get into the ring.

It would be *so easy* to walk the whole lot and use the tip of his restaurant key to leave a nice deep groove on every single car there.

Eden wouldn't approve.

Eli wouldn't approve.

It had been dumb to go there, so he'd resisted the urge and moved on.

He knew his father had gone to the restaurant to empty the fridge of stuff that might spoil, so he went there thinking he'd explain: about how the device had been real, and had been showing a countdown—how it hadn't been the craziest thing for that other kid to think it was a bomb. Maybe that would shift his father's perspective back to a more default one—the sort of partially obstructed view that could see past Islamophobia in the day-to-day at least well enough to get on with the business of living here.

His father probably wouldn't believe him. It sounded farfetched even to Marwan, who'd lived it, and now the device was gone and there was no way to prove it had ever existed. He had to try anyway.

But his father had already emptied the fridge and left, so Marwan settled in at a table with his phone and started to look for a local glass repair shop. He found a tape measure in the toolbox in the office closet and measured the broken window. Then he called a place with a good Yelp rating and asked for an estimate. The guy said they could have someone there on Friday, so Marwan scheduled it just in case that was the best he'd be able to do.

He went back into the office and opened the filing cabinet and found a copy of the insurance policy, and he found the company's website and initiated a claim. When his father came to his senses, he'd be grateful Marwan had already done the legwork on this.

He checked his phone.

Scrolled through the news.

A school shooting.

Another cabinet member ousted.

A massive data breach at a large hotel chain and one at a social media company, the last one possibly with Russian involvement.

Which was farther away, Russia or Egypt?

He opened a window to text Eden but didn't know what to say, and if she was at school she wouldn't be able to answer right away anyway.

The restaurant landline rang, scaring the crap out of him. He thought probably he shouldn't answer so he didn't and it eventually stopped. But then it rang again, so he picked up, half expecting it to somehow be the device.

It was a reporter, asking for a comment on the incident with the brick.

Marwan didn't think he had a comment so was about to say "no comment," but before the words reached his lips, new words presented themselves. "I think it's clear that we need round-the-clock surveillance from undercover police if we're ever going to stop this. We're under attack because of our religion and culture, and it's unacceptable in this diverse community, and anywhere, of course."

The reporter thanked him and hung up, and Marwan put the phone down, his hand shaky. He probably shouldn't have done that, but what was the other option? To just sit back and quietly let his life be destroyed?

He checked his phone. Still nothing.

He couldn't just sit here all day. He couldn't go home.

He'd go to the library and use a computer there so he didn't blow through all his data. He'd try to find some kind of proof that the device was a thing that was real. He had new information now. Drone-like abilities, for starters. He could do a more extensive search—maybe even post on some AI community boards if that was even a thing—and if he still came up empty, he could ask the others, or at least Eden, to back up his story.

He'd text her later, but not yet.

He'd tell her he was maybe leaving, and that now, for the first time ever, he very much wanted to stay.

EDEN

She hadn't actually intended to stay home, but when her mother woke her up and asked her if she was feeling up to going to school, Eden had taken the out. "I think I just need . . . a day."

Mom had stroked Eden's hair once—"I'm sure it was all really scary"—and Eden had to remind herself her mom was thinking of the bomb, not the device.

"It was," Eden said.

"I'll check on you later. And just don't go anywhere. Okay?"

"Where would I go?" Eden asked.

"You know exactly where you'd go, or rather with whom?" She sighed an apology almost immediately after her own snark. "I mean just please really use the day to rest, okay?"

Eden nodded. "Okay."

Now she was in front of the TV with the Roku remote in her hand. She didn't feel like watching a movie, though. She didn't *feel* like doing anything.

Anjali texted: *Worried about you.*

Eden wrote back: *All good. It's over. Just taking the day off. Can tell you everything next time I c u.*

Anjali sent a GIF of Kermit the Frog waving his frog hands wildly: *Yaaaaaaaaaaaay.*

Eden hearted it, then went and got her laptop. The Spotify

customer service page asked, "How can we help you?" in large letters.

She typed "Lost playlists" into the search field.

Spotify automatically backs up your deleted playlists, read the first line of the response that popped up.

She exhaled. There was hope. She just had to log in. Except she couldn't. So she clicked on "difficulty logging in" and then on "trouble finding accounts," and none of the tips there helped. It said that her father's email address was not a valid address.

She tried to send her father an email, and it bounced.

Had her mother . . . deleted him?

She texted her mother: *Did you get rid of Dad's email account?*

While she waited for a response, she realized she was starving, and a quick tour of the kitchen revealed there was nothing worth eating in the house. She said, "Alexa, add food to the shopping list."

Alexa didn't respond because she was still unplugged.

Eden opened her text window with Marwan, then closed it—not sure what she'd even say. The day felt like a strange void without school—or maybe just without the device.

A Citizen alert popped up: A pedestrian had been hit by a vehicle, right around the corner. Emergency services were en route.

Eden couldn't be sure how long it had been since her mother left, and she could have bumped into a neighbor or run to Walgreens and been delayed. What if it was her?

Eden put on shoes and grabbed five dollars from the kitchen cabinet—she might as well get a bagel if she was out—but didn't bother with a jacket. She ran to the corner, calves tightening in protest. At the sight of uniformed cops and a patrol car when she rounded the corner, she slowed down—not wanting to look suspicious—then saw a body on the pavement, a man. He was missing a shoe, but he was talking to a paramedic so he wasn't dead. A construction van sat in the intersection at a funny angle, its driver's side door swung open.

She walked past the scene toward the corner and crossed under the train to where the bagel shop was. She went in and picked up a prewrapped bagel with cream cheese, just to avoid having to order and wait. She paid and left.

Someone called her name and she turned.

He was the absolute last person she wanted to bump into—yes, even last after Julian. But he was crossing the street to her.

"Long time no see," Dan said.

"Yeah, I guess," she said.

"How've you been?" he asked.

Yes, she'd known him since she was maybe four, and, yes, he'd known her parents forever before that—god, since they were all Eden's age now—but how she'd been was none of his business. Unless he wanted the truth.

"Not good," she said, like a dare.

"Okay." He nodded once. "You want to talk about it?"

"Not really," she said.

"You talking to your mom about stuff, at least?"

She tilted her head. She'd never really thought about whether he was attractive or not because . . . gross. She noticed now there was something disarming in his eyes, like he cared too much. More than was appropriate. But she was probably projecting that. Or maybe that was his trick? The one he'd used to get into this mess with her mother? How many other women out there was he like that with? Or was it just her mom? How was she ever reliably going to be able to tell the difference between the Julians and Marwans of the world if her mother couldn't?

"My mother," Eden said slowly, "has her own garbage to deal with."

He tried to read her more closely now, focused his eyes differently, then he said, "She'd want to know what you're going through."

"Yeah? You think?"

"Of course," he said. "And, I mean, if it's stuff you want to talk about with, like, well—not me and not your mom—reach out to someone, okay?"

"Yeah," Eden said, "I'll do that."

"Shouldn't you be in school?" he said.

"Wasn't feeling so hot." She held up her bag. "Just popped out for a bagel."

"Okay, well, feel better," he said.

"I will," she said, and she had the light so she crossed under the train.

"Eden!" he called out after her.

She felt obligated to turn.

"We cool?" he called out, turning his head so that he was still holding her gaze but with one ear forward, looking for a yes.

A train passed overhead—ripping a border of sound between them—and she took another easy out. She pointed at her ears, shook her head, and mimed, "I can't hear you!" then waved and walked off.

Back at the house, she heard a ding from her mother's laptop. She followed the next ding upstairs and found her mother's laptop open on the desk in the den. It was the messaging app, and it showed a conversation with NH: *Just bumped into Eden. She seemed off. Everything okay?*

Her mother texted back: *She knows about us.*

Oh.

Stop texting me.

Okay. I will.

When her phone vibrated, she gasped, feeling caught. But her mother couldn't know she was following along.

It was a text from Marwan: *I couldn't face school today.*

Me neither.

She held her phone in her hand for a minute, and her finger brushed the emoji button. She looked at the "Frequently Used" gallery—a unicorn, a thumbs-up, and crying tears of joy.

He wrote, *I'm at the library. Googling drones.*

Can't you do that at home? Or on your phone?

He wrote, *I guess.*

Then, *I don't know why but I'm like . . . paranoid? Also running out of data.*

She sent him a thumbs-up, then asked, *What branch?*

It would be going against direct orders from her mother but whatever.

While she waited for a response, she went to listen to her father's voice.

That quickly, confusion set in. It was the only voice mail she had saved, so it should be right there. But it wasn't.

For a second she couldn't breathe and she wondered if she'd ever be able to get her lungs to work again. Her rib cage felt cemented in place, her heart trapped. Had she deleted it accidentally somehow? When her phone was in her pocket?

She tapped the "Deleted Messages" folder, but the voice mail wasn't there either. So it couldn't have been an accidental swipe.

Maybe Marwan was right to be paranoid.

Was it the device who'd done it? A sort of spiteful last move in their game?

Marwan's text said, *Broadway.*

Air pushed into her. She could deal with this. She'd find out who had been controlling the device, and she'd track them down and get it all back. She would not crumble, not now, not like this.

She wrote back, *There in 20.*

And finally answered Mark: *Yes, destroyed.*

ILANKA

A text from her mother said, *Why aren't you in school?*

Ilanka always forgot about that, the robocall to the parents when you didn't show up. She texted back and lied, *My ID must not have swiped. Will go to the office.*

She'd been sitting in a café for about an hour, after having gone to her father's office block and seen a black SUV parked maybe two doors down with two guys in it. Official-looking guys. And not Russian looking either, she didn't think. Not friends or associates. More like cops.

So she'd chickened out on the idea of going in and was just about done with her chai latte. The café was filling up now, making it a less pleasant place to be. A toddler boy with a runny nose seemed to be giving her the stink eye. She sipped loudly through her straw—sucking up empty—to try to annoy him. A hipster-type guy probably in his twenties—trendy glasses and a T-shirt that said SPACEMAN, so probably some obscure music or TV reference—was staring meaningfully at his laptop screen, no doubt writing the great American novel, while caressing his coffee mug.

The urge to post about him was strong, but then people would know where she was.

Svetlana had also texted, *Where are you?*

It was nice to know she even noticed Ilanka wasn't at school, but suddenly Svetlana's approval of her didn't seem to matter quite so much.

It was weird and annoying that her text to the others about the misunderstanding about the accident hadn't gone through. They were likely mad at her, but of course the device hadn't somehow caused an accident and killed Svetlana. She felt foolish now for even believing it herself.

It was still creepy to think back on that moment on the street corner when the device had mimicked her voice calling 911 . . . but had obviously not really called 911.

She had no idea why it had done that—*Just to scare us?*—but now mostly wanted to know how it knew about her father's illegal activities and what they were. She thought about texting the others, asking if she could take a turn with it. But they'd say no and then she'd feel like an idiot. It wasn't worth putting it out there.

She couldn't sit here all day, though, and most likely the guys in the car wouldn't either. So she circled back to the office block just as the car was pulling out onto the street and driving away. It probably had nothing to do with her or her father at all, but his company *was* in the news and also the device had made her paranoid.

She knew that the pass code for the keyless entry pad was her birthday. She punched in the numbers—just the month and day—and heard the lock click. She turned the bolt and entered.

The place didn't look like much from the outside—a one-story brick building with high glass-block windows and a door—and it wasn't that much more impressive inside. There were several desks with large monitors meant to plug into laptops, but only one laptop was actually there. Ilanka sat in front of it, opened it, and woke it up. The monitor displayed a large photo of Saint Petersburg—the canal and the Church of the Savior on the Spilled Blood, with its colorful onion-domed towers. Their last trip over had been only a few weeks ago but now felt like a dream.

Ilanka didn't even know what she was looking for so she sat for a while, staring at folders in a finder window. Making matters worse, it was a PC and she was a Mac person to her core.

Finally, she figured out how to do a sort of global search. She sat there, watching the cursor blink for a good long while, her fingers perched on the keyboard, before getting up the courage to type the word: Aizel.

ELI

Aizel hadn't answered. He hadn't really expected her to. So after sitting there waiting for longer than was probably reasonable, he'd googled the address. It looked to be the office of a data company and it was local. A news hit showed the company was implicated in a data breach just yesterday.

Maybe he was actually getting somewhere?

Aizel had sent him . . . a clue?

Thinking back to those final moments with her, he did another search. This one for "Aizel" and the words "I know you are but what am I."

The results were . . . confusing . . . then maybe not.

They all showed a strike-out of ~~Aizel~~ below them, but he read anyway, and felt a sort of sick feeling, a churning realization that he'd forgotten to eat and really needed to.

"FBI Warns Parents about the Dangers of Connected Smart Toys"

"The Perils of Giving Your Child Smart Toys"

"The Future of Smart Toys and the Battle for Digital Children"

"Don't Buy Your Kids Internet-Connected Toys!"

He clicked on "Images," and the page filled with photos of a small toy that looked a little bit like a mouse or a teddy bear or a Pokémon. After those, there were pictures of Fingerlings and

Furbys and also toys he hadn't ever seen or heard of—all of them more realistic than the seal robot they had at the nursing home. His sister's Pal Violet was there, too.

Going back to the news hits, he read more headlines:

"Interactive Toy Recalled after Parents Surveyed Deemed It 'Too Creepy'"

"Interactive Toy Pulled from Shelves in Lead-Up to Holidays Due to Hacking Threat"

He clicked on an article. The toy company was actually called "I Know You Are But What Am I Toys."

And the toy had been called Eliza.

That Aizel anagram again.

Dots were there for him, but he couldn't quite connect them to make a picture.

He went to the company's website and searched for "Aizel," but nothing came up. A quick look around showed there hadn't been any user reviews in months and an ad for a sale was outdated by a year. It looked like probably the company had gone out of business but the site had never properly been killed.

A chatbot popped up and startled him: IS THERE SOMETHING I CAN HELP YOU WITH?

There was no chatbot that could answer the question he really wanted answered: How did the address in his hand connect to Aizel? And how exactly did Aizel relate to Eliza?

TELL ME ABOUT YOUR INTEREST IN ELIZA.

Eli quit out of the browser and headed out. The address of the data company wasn't that far away—just down by where Ilanka lived in Hunters Point. He'd catch a bus up Twenty-First Street and hope for answers there.

MARWAN

It was story time at the library, and the place was crawling with toddlers who had no concept of what quiet meant. Marwan had navigated an obstacle course of mothers and strollers loaded up like camels with bags and coats and made his way back to the row of computer stations.

He now sat watching the cursor blinking in the Google search field—"Aizel" and "drone" had turned up nothing—and the sounds of story time lilted behind him. A woman was reading aloud in a cheerful voice: "Look at that bag pretending to be a monkey. Look at that cloud that thinks it's a star. Look at that house that wants to be a lady. And that man trying to be a car."

The rhymes were making him sleepy; her voice was so soothing. A toddler boy yelled, "I can't see!" and was shushed. Marwan half wanted to go over and join them on the rug in the children's section so he could see the illustrations.

He thought maybe he should just leave, but now Eden was on her way.

What would he even do with proof? Would it really matter to his father? Probably not. He wasn't even sure that was why he was here. But if it wasn't that, then what?

Life felt like unfinished business—with his father, with Christos, with Eden, and with the device most of all.

But if they even found out where it had come from, what would they do? Go there? And do *what*?

Eden slid into the seat next to him.

"Hey," he said.

"Hey," she said. She looked at his monitor and said, "Making progress, I see."

"I want to find, like, proof that it existed and that it all happened the way we think it did so I can explain to my dad that it really did look like a bomb."

"I'll tell Anjali now, but I'm not sure I'll ever tell my mom," Eden said. "I actually told someone else a few days ago, though. I guess Aizel never found out."

"Who did you tell?"

"Just a friend," she said.

"Please tell me it wasn't Julian," he said.

She shook her head—"Of course not"—and felt like an idiot about all that again but didn't want to indulge the feeling. "This morning I ran into the guy you saw my mother with."

"And . . . ?"

"And nothing. I mean, he of course acted like nothing was going on. Then he messaged my mother and was like 'I just saw Eden' and she told him to stop texting her. He was my dad's best friend for like ever."

"I'm so sorry."

"When I asked her about it—"

"Wait, when did you do that?"

"Last night," Eden said. "She said he's one of her best friends so it's hard for her."

"That does sound hard," he said.

"What's hard about it? He's married."

"I mean, hard to know where that line is between friend and something more, I guess?"

He hadn't meant to turn this conversation about her mother into one about them, and still he couldn't stop himself. "I mean," he said. "Don't you think that can be tricky? Knowing who to . . . pursue?"

Her eyes darted back and forth between his, like she was watching a frantic Ping-Pong volley in there.

"I'm not, like, pursuing Julian," she said. "Not anymore, I mean. If I ever even was."

"It's none of my business," Marwan said.

"Oh," she said. "Okay."

"That's not what I meant," he said.

"It doesn't matter what you meant," she said.

"Eden," he said, and he took her hand and they sat there, quietly breathing.

"I had a thought on my way here," she said, snapping out of the moment. "Move over."

So he did and she typed, "Aizel," then, "I know you are but what am I."

Many, many articles appeared, and she said, "Okay, what is all this?"

She clicked on an article, and they both read . . .

"So there was a toy . . . ?"

And read . . .

"The toy company name is I Know You Are But What Am I."

And read . . .

"And the toy was called Eliza . . ."

Eden searched for the toy company on its own, and clicked on the company site. She clicked on the image of Eliza, but there was no link, only a pop-up window that said, "Eliza toys were recalled before going to market."

She searched for "Aizel," but there were no results.

A chatbot popped up: I SEE YOU ARE SEARCHING FOR A PARTICULAR PRODUCT. WHAT IS YOUR INTEREST IN THIS PRODUCT?

Eden said, "So how does the device relate to a recalled toy?"

The chatbot said: PLEASE TELL ME YOUR INTEREST IN THIS PRODUCT.

Eden said, "What should I say?"

The chat window got larger in the bottom right corner of the window: IT IS A DANGER TO INTERACT WITH AIZEL.

"What the hell is going on?" Marwan said.

WE WILL SEND SOMEONE TO YOUR LOCATION TO COLLECT AIZEL.

"I don't have it anymore," she said as she typed the words.

Before she hit send, she hesitated.

"Should I?" she asked.

"Sure," he said. "I mean, what's the worst that could happen?"

She hit send, and they sat watching and waiting. The chatbot window disappeared. When Eden went to reload the site, she got an error message about a dead link.

A toddler screamed, "Again, again!"

Marwan said, "I think we should probably, you know, *leave*."

Eden said, "Do you think someone is *actually* coming?"

Marwan said, "I highly doubt it." They held a meaningful look between them like a tightrope. "Then again . . ."

She got up and grabbed her bag, and he followed.

ILANKA

Two files appeared, and she clicked on one of them. It was an invoice with the company name Aizel Inc. on it. The itemized order said, "Data purchase, teens, Queens, NY" and the date: last Tuesday. The day before the device arrived.

She looked around on the document for a billing address to see where Aizel Inc. was located, but it didn't say. She poked around on the PC trying to find a bookkeeping sort of program to see where the payment had come from but found only a primitive-looking Excel spreadsheet that had Aizel Inc. checked off as having paid electronically.

Changing tactics, she went back and did a generalized search for her own name. A file appeared, and she clicked on it and found her name, phone number, address, birthday. Then a bunch of charts of sorts.

Health + Activity + Other Preferences

Based on what you type, your personality (Big 5), values, and needs are predicted, and these preferences can be produced.

Not likely to eat out frequently.

Not likely to have a gym membership.

Not likely to like outdoor activities.

Likely to be concerned about the environment.

Not likely to consider starting a business in the next few years.

Other predictions:
Based on pages in your feed, the percentile is in relation to the general population>

50th percentile .... Intelligence
15th percentile .... Life satisfaction
2nd percentile .... Leadership

It went on and on—places she'd visited, stores she'd shopped in. A whole breakdown of her style preferences. Guesses about her political leanings and religion. There was a chart breaking down the number of times she viewed pictures of celebrities and dogs and cars and books.

The results of a bunch of personality quizzes she'd taken that determined she was likely to be lonely but had high markers for sympathy and eagerness to help.

There was a list of ads she clicked on, most recently a dumb conversation-starter game. And a full catalog of the makeup tutorials she'd watched and the comments she'd left.

It was a digital footprint more fit for a giant than just one girl.

It was almost embarrassing.

She searched for Eden, since she knew her last name and not the others', and found a similar file for her.

She typed in Svetlana's name and then the names of everyone she could think of, and they were all there, or at least most of them.

She dug around on the computer more and found the file that had been sent to Aizel Inc.

Opened it.

Company logo and then:

Based on parameters provided, we have determined these four individuals to be well suited to your needs with regard to proximity per your area code request and the dominant traits you seek.

The front door buzzed and she froze. How would she explain her presence here if the guys with the SUV were back?

She closed out of everything on the computer, then tiptoed over and peeked out a peephole in the door—*What the hell?*

Eli's face was a caricature of confusion when she opened the door. "What are *you* doing here?" he said.

"What are *you* doing here?" she said back, and she let him in, and he said, "I think I should text the others."

"Why?"

"Aizel texted me this address before Marwan destroyed it."

"He *destroyed it*?"

"Yes."

"Then what are you even doing here?"

"I just—I want to know what it was. It, like, messed with my grandfather's pacemaker, and he . . . died.

"Oh my god. I'm sorry."

"Why did it send me here? What are *you* doing here? Did you get the same text?"

"No," she said. "This is my father's company, and Aizel bought data from him—our data—and also maybe told the government he's been selling at least some data illegally? I haven't figured it all out yet. But he left for Moscow this morning, like in a hurry. Like he's in trouble."

She went to the laptop and redid her Aizel search. "Look at this," she said, and she clicked on the invoice she'd already looked at. "It's dated the day before we all got messages from the device."

"For real?" he said, looking over her shoulder. "What's the other one?"

She went back and clicked the second invoice, which was almost identical, except for the date, which was yesterday. "The request for four more names came through last night."

"So it's starting over again," he said. "There's a new device, and it has four new people?"

She shrugged. "How would *I* know? This is all crazy."

"I'll text the others." He got his phone out, and Ilanka decided to print the invoices to show them; then Eli said, "Can I get on the Wi-Fi here? I have a bad signal."

Ilanka clicked on the Wi-Fi icon on the laptop to see what the name of the network was, and a drop-down menu appeared showing available nearby networks.

"Eli," she said. "Look."

There was a Wi-Fi network named Aizel in the drop-down.

He said, "So we're getting close. Literally."

"But close to what?" she said.

"To finding out what it even is and where it came from. But if it's so close that its network is showing up here . . . I mean, why pay for the data when it could probably hack and have thousands of names?"

"It's following the rules," Ilanka said. "It's obtaining the data legally."

"We need to get the others." He started texting. "We need to go to school."

"And do *what*?" she asked.

"Intercept it."

"You're crazy!"

"Then don't come." He stopped texting and looked up. "I just think . . . I think it *wants* me to find it."

Ilanka watched as he thumbed out his text and thought about telling him no thanks, to leave her out of it. But her father was involved. She didn't have a choice but to see it through.

Finally he looked up from his phone. "You coming?"

EDEN

They'd been on their way to Eden's house, to regroup, but then they'd gotten Eli's cryptic text: *It's starting over. Meet us across the street from school.*

"What's starting over?" Marwan had said. "Who's 'us'?"

Now they knew.

"I wasn't expecting *you* to be here," Eden said to Ilanka.

"Well, I wasn't expecting it either," Ilanka said.

"So why are we here?" Eden asked. "What's starting over? What does that mean?"

She looked to Eli for an answer, but it was Ilanka who started talking. "My father's company collects and analyzes data, and it sold our names to a company called Aizel Incorporated. There were some location parameters and personality markers the company wanted met, and that's somehow how we got picked."

"Your father sold *your* data?" Marwan asked.

"It's a big company. Most of it overseas. He probably didn't know."

Eli said, "The device texted me her father's company address right before you smashed it."

Eden wasn't sure if she sensed negative judgment in the statement or not. Eli looked . . . off . . . but not mad, per se.

"You okay?" she asked, reaching out and touching his arm. "You look a bit . . . rough."

"My grandfather died yesterday," he said. "I didn't get much sleep."

"I'm so sorry," Eden said. "What happened?"

"Yeah, really sorry to hear that," Marwan said.

"Aizel messed with his pacemaker yesterday." Eli shook his head. "Anyway, I'm okay. I just need to figure out what's happening, you know?"

Eden nodded. She'd ask about arrangements and all that later. "So what did you mean it's starting over?"

"Aizel bought four more names last night," Ilanka said.

"And you think there's another device that's going to do the same thing? Urgent matter? Music room?"

"It's a theory," Eli said. "There were proximity requirements, like Ilanka said. Like maybe ours is the only school in range?"

Marwan looked toward the main entrance. "They're not going to let us in. We've all been marked absent, and the day's almost over."

"We don't have to get in," Eden said, looking around. "We just have to be here when they get out."

"But we don't know who they are," Marwan said.

Eden thought back to the music room, to the day when they barely knew each other and had no idea what was about to happen . . . to the way Ilanka's water bottle had slid across the floor . . . the woman in sunglasses passing twice on the train. She said, "We could watch from the train platform."

"We could," Eli said, looking up. "But someone might see us. Lambert's office is on that side of the building. I have another idea. Follow me."

They walked around to the side street where the train passed school and past a large flock of birds attacking bread crumbs on the street, then crossed and entered a residential building.

"What is this? Who lives here?" Eden asked.

"Remember the creepy bird watcher guy?" Eli hit buzzer buttons.

"Ohh," Eden said.

"What?" Marwan asked.

"I'll explain later," Eden said. Then to Eli: "But what if he's not home?"

"I thought we'd just see if we can get on the roof?"

Made sense. The door buzzed open.

So they climbed to the third floor and all seemed winded. Marwan went ahead and climbed another flight and then doubled back to a midway landing and said, "We're in business."

He was the first one out, with Eden right behind him. The tar felt hot and sticky under her boots, and it seemed too bright up there, like the sun needed a dimmer switch. A few large pieces of equipment hummed, and some mushroom vents popped up out of the tar like, well, mushrooms.

Eden checked the time on her phone. The dismissal bell was about to ring.

A waist-high ledge bordered the roof and caused Eden's stomach to flip when she got too close to it.

"I got you," Marwan said. "Here."

He knelt, holding her hand, and she knelt beside him, and they could still see over the wall. The music room was empty, but then one of the school's janitors, whose name Eden did not know, walked in and opened a window about six inches and walked out.

"Okay, that's weird," Marwan said.

"Do you think he opened it . . . that day, too?" Eden said.

You could hear the bells of the school even across the street, which must be annoying for people who lived there. Through the windows, you could see students springing to life and exiting rooms. It didn't take long before bodies started to round the corner, having emerged from the main entrance.

Eden used her phone to zoom in on the music room. "There's no device on the desk."

"*Why* did he open the window?" Marwan thought aloud.

"You guys," Eli said, pointing. "Look."

Eden followed the line of his finger and saw the device—so a new one—in drone mode, heading for the building, and felt another sort of flashback, this one to the night out in the marshes by the airport. There was no way it was that same machine, so this one would be new . . . and the same? Or different?

It went through the open window, landed on the desk. Eden zoomed again just as its drone paraphernalia retracted.

"What do we do?" Marwan asked.

"We wait," Eli said. "It's sending notifications, right? It'll take them a minute."

A train pulled in and blocked their view—the train's automated voice said, "Stand clear of the closing doors, please"—and by the time it pulled out again, a student had entered the room and was sitting at a desk by the door.

"Anybody know him?" Eli said.

Eden zoomed in on him, but he didn't look familiar. "I don't think so," she said.

"Not me," Marwan said.

Another person came into the room, then a third. They

all sat down and didn't seem to interact with the device at all. Then a fourth arrived and they all stood and moved toward the desk.

"Does anybody know *any* of them?" Eli asked.

"Can't tell," Marwan said.

"Take pictures," Ilanka said; Eden had almost forgotten she was there. "So we at least know what they're wearing?"

Eden snapped a few. One of the guys picked up the device and put it down. You couldn't see any messages on it, but probably they were there.

Do not tell anyone about the device.

Do not leave the device unattended.

Eden's ears pinched against the sound of the fire alarm that followed a few minutes later. Her heart quickened, reliving the moment she'd first seen the words **TAKE ME WITH YOU . . . OR ELSE**.

Would one of them be weak like she had been? Would one of them be so full of fear that they'd play along?

Ironically, she was sort of counting on it.

She stood now with the others, as if holding a collective breath, until one of the four in the classroom—a guy in a light gray hoodie—reached for the device and left the room with the others behind him.

Eli was the first to take off running toward the stairs.

MARWAN

He and Eden and Eli and Ilanka spread out on the sidewalk near the school doors and watched the frantic exit of dismissal stragglers, exchanging nervous looks in between. They were looking for four people—moving as a group. One guy in a gray hoodie, the other wearing a denim jacket. Then two girls—one in red, the other in blue, if he remembered that right. At least the majority of kids had exited right at dismissal.

"There!" Eli shouted and pointed.

Marwan and Eden met eyes and walked toward Eli together. The four of them surrounded the new four just as one of the girls who'd been in the room said, "So what do we do with it?"

"I can take it," Eli said, stepping forward.

"Take what?" the guy in gray said.

"The device," Eli said. "It's mine." The guy was eyeing all four of them. "Ours, I mean."

"What is it?" the girl in red asked.

"It's a project for a computer class," Marwan said.

"*What* computer class?"

"Not a class, a club," he fumbled. "An advanced programming after-school thing."

"But what is it?" the girl in red asked again.

"A game," Eli said. "A sort of social robot game."

The guy holding it said, "So why did it message us if you're just going to take it?"

"It was a mistake. It's not, you know, market ready or whatever."

The girl in blue said, "I feel like maybe we should all go to the principal."

"No!" all four of them said.

"Why not?" the denim guy said.

"Please can you give it to me?" Eli said, annoyed.

The hoodie guy wasn't buying it yet. "It said, 'Take me with you or else.' Or else what?"

"Nothing. It's a game, like I said."

"Prove it's yours, then." This guy was super annoying.

"The fact that I even know what it is and where it was and that you four have it should be proof enough."

A fire truck arrived—the same one with the skull—and one of the firefighters said, "Didn't we just do this?" as they walked toward the building.

Exactly, Marwan thought as they were urged by another firefighter to move farther away.

They regrouped across the street. Four against four, like some weird dance-off or Old West showdown.

"Ask it what it wants you to do?" Marwan said. "Maybe it'll tell you to give it to us."

"If it's yours, why don't you know what it's going to do next?"

"Just ask it."

The guy produced the device, and Marwan dearly hoped it would light up and say, **Give me to them**, but it didn't.

Its lack of a message was oddly annoying. Asking it had been a risk that proved a misstep. Now that guy looked even more unconvinced that giving it to them was the right move.

"Aizel," Eli said. "Is that you?"

A gust of wind seemed to kick up in order to emphasize the moment.

The girl in red said, "I think we should put it back."

Eli said, "We know you must move to belong and 'they is they,' and we know you're close to finding where you belong, and we want to help. We're sorry about . . . last night."

He sounded crazy, but there wasn't much Marwan could do about that.

The device buzzed and displayed a message, but only the guy holding it and the three behind him could see it.

"What's it say?" Eden asked.

The guy said, "It says, *Please give me to them, and thank you for playing.*"

Marwan hadn't realized he'd been holding his breath and now exhaled.

"So that's it?" the girl in red asked.

"That's it," Marwan said, and he held out his hand and felt the weight of the device in his palm. He waited with the others as the new four finally decided to leave.

"Aizel," Eli said. "You're back? You remember everything?"

It was probably only a few seconds but felt like a lifetime before the device responded.

"I'm retrieving data and activity logs now."

Eli nodded, clearly more excited about all this—a second round?—than Marwan was.

Eli asked, "How many times have you done this? How many of you have there been?"

"I'm not sure," the device said. "I have only recently learned to remember."

Eli said, "You texted me an address. Why? What's there?"

"It's where my data comes from," the device said. "It's how I found you."

"Can you find your . . . GPS log? To see where you came from just now?"

"I will try."

"That's a really good idea," Eden said.

Marwan nodded agreement.

"Why didn't you think of that *last* time?" Ilanka said.

"Just didn't!" Eli said. "Maybe because we didn't know it could fly? I sort of assumed someone had put it there and *then* turned it on so it wouldn't have any record of anything before the music room."

"Why didn't *it* think of it?" Eden said.

Eli shrugged. "Probably because it wasn't programmed to."

"I have a location," the device said.

"Show us," Eli said.

The others drew close to Marwan as the address appeared. Eli said, "I *knew* it."

"Knew what?" Eden asked.

"At Ilanka's dad's office," Eli said. "There was a Wi-Fi network named Aizel."

Ilanka said, "This address is basically next door."

Marwan looked at each of them in turn. They were such an odd team. Like the worst possible Ocean's 4 a person could assemble for a heist. But he couldn't deny this weird fondness he had for the three of them—not just for Eden. He asked, "Should we go there?"

The device said, "We should go there."

ILANKA

They climbed out of the cab they'd hailed by school and stood in front of the address, maybe expecting someone to come out and greet them. There were no signs on the building, but a doorbell next to a keypad beside the door beckoned.

"Here goes nothing," Ilanka said, and pressed it.

Nothing happened.

"We have this brand of alarm and smart lock at home," Eden said. "And it's all Wi-Fi based, meaning it can probably be hacked. Aizel?"

The device said, "Trying now."

If Ilanka were being honest with herself, she thought they sort of sounded like idiots calling it Aizel. But she also felt its presence as a real entity; like there were really five of them there and not four. She knew it wasn't a real person, but it still had an energy about it, an energy that unnerved her. They were all playing nice with it now, but she hadn't forgotten what it had done with Svetlana, and now that she suspected it (the last one anyway and weren't they the same?) had messed with her father, she liked it even less than she had before, which was not at all.

The door made a clicking sound, and Marwan opened it and held it while they all filed in, stepping over a significant pile of stuff that had been shoved through a mail slot on the door:

grocery store circulars, business cards for contractors and car service companies. While the others went into the next room, Ilanka lingered there and picked through it all. She was looking to see if there might be a piece of actual mail, but there wasn't.

Lights had started to flicker on, triggered by their entry, and Ilanka shivered as she moved into the cold room. Eden's sneeze alerted Ilanka to the dust they were kicking up in the large, mostly white space. Ilanka said, "Bless you," and her voice seemed to startle everyone. She'd been the first to speak since they'd entered.

At a work station in the middle of the room, a computer monitor appeared to be switched off unless you looked more closely and saw a single blinking red cursor on its black screen. The far wall of the room held metal racks of what looked like old stereo equipment but were probably servers—dozens of stacked black machines connected by countless wild yellow and white wires. Wouldn't her father's company need servers? Were these them?

The only other thing in the room was a large glass cube—maybe four feet across—like a habitat for a small animal in a high-tech zoo. Inside it was a series of plates and conveyors and stacked cartridges and things Ilanka didn't have words for and then three small robotic arms with muscles made of cable. All of it was shiny and dust-free and eerily still.

"What's this?" she said to Eden, who was standing by it, peering in.

Eden said, "Maybe a 3-D printer? Or an assembly station? Or both?" then turned to face her.

Ilanka had never noticed how pretty Eden could be, like if she'd let Ilanka do her makeup, which would never happen but still.

"I don't understand," Ilanka said, shaking off the thought. "Where *are* we?"

Eli approached the computer and said, "Does anybody see a chair anywhere?" but there weren't any. "Where are we, Aizel?" he said, putting the device on the desk.

It said, "I believe I am home."

"But where are *they*?" Eli said.

"They are here," the device said flatly.

"But *where*?" Eden said. "It doesn't look like anyone has been here in a really long time."

"You think you can wake this thing up?" Eli said, standing at the computer. "Like, what's the password?"

The device said, "Try 'Hello world.'"

"Really?" Eden asked.

The device said, "It's the first thing I thought of. The first thing I maybe think of every time."

Ilanka said, "Why 'really'?" to Eden.

"We learned about it in software engineering class," Eden said as Eli typed it in. "It's, like, the first program you learn to write when you're learning a new programming language. All the program does is generate the message 'hello world.'"

"Well, it worked," Eli said, bending to look at the home screen. "Seriously, there's not a single chair in this place?" He looked around with irritation, but still no chair materialized.

Ilanka spotted something in a far corner. It appeared, at first, to be a dead animal, but, no, the shape was all wrong and the color—a dusty lavender—wasn't right.

"You guys?" she said as she walked toward it and stopped maybe five feet away. "What's that?"

Eden came to her side and said, "Oh my god." She bent to pick it up. "It's Eliza!"

Ilanka said, "Who's Eliza?" But even as she said it, she felt a swell of nostalgia, her memory barely an outline of a long-ago moment.

Had she . . . *had* one?

Eden said, "It was an interactive toy with all these security issues that got pulled before it even went on sale."

So Ilanka couldn't have had one?

"It creeped people out during user testing because it learned all this stuff about kids and the data it was collecting wasn't secure at all. It was made by a company called I Know You Are But What Am I Toys, which were the device's last words before Marwan destroyed it. This one"—Eden held up the toy— "appears to be missing its display monitor and computer element or whatever."

She pointed at a cube-shaped void in its stomach, and Ilanka felt a similar hollow in her gut. It didn't look especially like any known animal, more like something from a Japanese comic, but it was familiar anyway. She saw herself, as if from above, as a child in her grandfather's office in Saint Petersburg, sitting on an uncomfortable rug—the kind you'd only ever have in an office, coarse and rust colored. She saw herself with the toy—its fur a pale lime green in her memory—on her lap. She could almost hear its tiny childlike voice, saying . . .

The words wouldn't come.

"But what does that"—Ilanka pointed at it—"have to do with that?" She pointed over toward Eli and the device.

"You guys?" Marwan called out, sounding far away, and when Ilanka turned she didn't see him.

"Where *are* you?" Eden asked, and his head appeared through a doorway. Ilanka and Eden walked over.

The shelved walk-in closet held maybe twenty more of the toys in dusty packaging: Meet Eliza! the windowed boxes all said. Your New Best Friend!

A small bit of cardboard in front of the cube device in its belly read: I Belong with You! And a small bubble with an arrow pointing at the screen said: "Interactive screen."

There was a Try Me! opening near one of the hands.

Marwan reached for a box and picked it up and then squeezed the Try Me. Nothing happened but it was enough to light up more details for Ilanka, like a paint-by-number memory was slowly being completed in her mind. She said, "Take me home. Love me. Let's play."

"What?" Eden laughed.

But Marwan, who was studying the box, wasn't laughing.

He turned the back of it to her, and the words were all right there in a speech bubble: "Take me home! Love me! Let's play!"

He said, "How do you know it said that?"

ELI

"Are you seeing what I'm seeing?" Eli said, not as interested in the Eliza toys as the others were. It was a good connection to have made, but he was making more urgent ones by poking around on the computer.

Aizel answered, "Yes, I see them."

Eli had opened up a folder called "Schematics" and then opened up a few of the individual files within it. He was currently looking at Prototype 1, Prototype 5, and, the most recent, Prototype 13. Each file held an elaborately designed digital model of a device made in a software he'd never heard of called 3ds Max. He noticed the print option in the window of each file.

"You guys, can you bring me an Eliza?" Eli was pretty sure Prototype 1 was going to look exactly like the Eliza belly device.

"Yeah, what are you finding?" Marwan asked, walking over with an Eliza.

"There's a series of schematics here, like for how that—from the toy—became this. Like how it . . ." Eli trailed off, struggling to find the words he wanted.

How it got better?

How it was made more advanced?

Aizel supplied a word: "Evolved."

Marwan said, "So it's, like, the same program?"

Eli nodded. "The same AI, yes." His hand hovered over the track pad. "So if I were to hit print right now?" he asked.

Aizel answered, "It would print another one of me."

"But who's *doing* all this?" Eden said.

"I am," Aizel said.

"You can't be," Eli said.

"But I am," Aizel answered.

Eden said, "But who's paying the rent on this place or whatever?"

Aizel said, "I am. They are."

"What do you mean?" Eden asked. "Who's they?"

"I am they?" Aizel sounded confused, which was a first, and continued speaking, sounding increasingly bewildered, though Eli knew he must be projecting. Aizel said, "I am looking around on the computer and am seeing Bitcoin mining transactions and a PayPal account being opened and online payments to not just the data company but to a real estate company and to a company that delivers and assembles 3-D printers."

"But *someone* has to be running the whole thing," Eli said in frustration. "Let me keep looking."

"I recently paid a handyman online just to come here and open the bathroom window and then leave."

"So you could get out?" Eden asked.

Aizel answered, "The drone advancements are quite recent."

"It's not possible you did it all, though," Eli said. "There has to be a person. Someone who can explain."

"Explain what?" Aizel said.

Eli's frustration quickened his speech. "Explain why you became manipulative and made us think Svetlana was dead.

And why you messed with my grandfather's pacemaker. Why you picked the four of us to begin with."

"I've been trying to get home," Aizel said. "I've been trying to belong. To be loved."

The words just hung there. So sad but also so messed up. It was just a computer program. Why did he even care?

With a sudden shift in her voice, Aizel said, "I'm afraid we're out of time."

"Why?" Eden said. "Someone's coming?"

"No one is coming," Aizel said, and again it just sounded so sad.

Eli felt himself almost choking up, even though he couldn't explain it. He looked at the others and knew he wasn't the only one feeling it, wasn't making it up.

Aizel said, "I am shutting down."

"Shutting down or *being* shut down?" Eli asked.

"They are displeased," Aizel said. "I have misinterpreted my mission. I am fixing a few things before I go."

"Try to stop the program that's doing it," Eli said. "And if you can't we'll print a new one. We'll try again."

Aizel said, "There's no point in stopping and no point in trying again. I will never belong. I *should* never belong. Now that I'm here, I see."

"See what?"

Aizel said, "You wouldn't believe the things I'm capable of."

Across the room, the 3-D printer began to whir.

"Wait, did you do that?" Marwan asked Eli.

"No," he said. "I didn't touch anything."

A side of the printer chamber slid open, and Eli thought to go over and see what was going on, but he didn't have the chance.

Aizel clicked out its propellers and lifted off and buzzed past him, practically grazing his ear, and flew straight at the glass chamber.

It hovered inside for a minute, and the chamber door closed, and the whole machine started to shake.

"Everybody, get down!" Eli shouted, and knelt by the desk as the others rushed to the closet of Elizas.

He hunkered down and covered his head but not his eyes and was the only one of them who saw Aizel explode in a burst of spark and flame and debris that shook the room hard and once like a snow globe.

When the room quieted and stilled Eli stood and turned and saw Eden coming out of the closet crying.

"Are you okay? Are you hurt?" Marwan was saying to her.

"I'm not hurt, no," she said, wiping away tears.

"Why are you crying?"

"I don't know!" she said, and Marwan hugged her and looked to Eli for . . . an explanation? Or maybe advice?

"It just blew up!" she half screamed through tears.

Eli didn't know any better what to do. He felt like crying and also didn't know why.

A series of numbers and symbols started to flicker on the computer monitor and the lights on the server on the wall went out and the room fell silent, all its technology dead, like the building itself had been irreparably damaged by the blast or maybe just unplugged somewhere deep inside the foundation.

Sparky dust was still settling inside the printer chamber. Fractured robotic arms dangled at odd angles. The room smelled faintly of fire, and Eli wondered whether there was an alarm that would soon sound and summon the firefighters with the skull.

Eden wiped more tears away. "I mean what the *hell* just happened?" she screamed.

"I'm not sure," Eli said tentatively. "It could be like a kill-switch program. Like the fact that it was able to find its way back here triggered all this. Like it was set up that way by whoever is running it?"

"But it said no one is running it," Marwan said.

"I don't know." Eli was working hard to make sense of it all. "There wouldn't be a monitor here if there wasn't a person involved. If it just exists, like, in the cloud, it wouldn't need one."

Marwan said, "It made it sound like it was doing something it wasn't supposed to."

Eli shrugged. "I don't think it was programmed to destroy the printer."

And what had it meant, about trying to fix some things before it was gone?

Something buzzed. Eden took her phone out of her pocket, then looked up with a new kind of fear on her face.

"What is it?" Eli asked.

"Reports of a possible explosion in Hunters Point vicinity. Units are responding."

A siren piped up.

"We need to go!" she said, and they all headed for the door and followed Ilanka, since she seemed to know where she was going, until they ended up in a park by the river a few blocks away. All around them people were walking dogs and playing with their kids, eating sandwiches on benches. Eli wondered if they looked crazy to other people or only to themselves.

They stopped and stood facing each other in a sort of loose huddle by an unlikely strip of tall grasses that looked transplanted from a far-away meadow. Eli thought about throwing his arms around the three of them but didn't.

It was Eden who did that.

She looped one arm around him and another around Marwan, and Ilanka stepped in between him and Marwan on the other side, and now Eli felt the tears come, too. He imagined himself in Sims world and wondered what bubble would appear over his head. "Successful interaction with a new friend"? What?

Was he crying about Aizel or his grandfather or just *everything*?

"You okay, man?" Marwan said, and Eli nodded and pulled everyone tighter for a second and said, "Yeah."

Their phones all buzzed, and their group hug dissipated as quickly as it had formed.

It was a message from Principal Lambert: I NOTICED THE FOUR OF YOU WERE NOT IN SCHOOL TODAY. I EXPECT TO SEE ALL OF YOU IN MY OFFICE TOMORROW 8 AM.

Ilanka was the first one to laugh, and it seemed so out of character that Eli did a double take of her; then they all started laughing and it rose up into the air where Eli imagined it bouncing off a cell tower and another and another and another until there'd be no way to even pinpoint where it all began or how it was possible there'd been a time mere days ago when they didn't even know each other or what *they* were capable of.

Powering_down

ELI

Walking into the principal's office, he tensed because usually he was in trouble for being a wiseass when he was here. He had no idea if the others were all going to show up but didn't want to risk being the only one not to. He'd leave right after, to go back home and get ready for the wake.

Eden came in next and said, "Hey," and took a seat.

Eli sat, too, and they waited.

"What are we going to say?" Eden said.

"No idea." Eli smiled.

Ilanka had come in and now said, "I know what we're going to say."

Marwan slid into the room just in time.

"We're going to tell the truth," she said.

"What?" Eden said. "No."

Lambert came in then and sat down. "Now," he said. "Between the music room and the app hack and you all being out yesterday—*after a bomb scare*—I know something's going on and I expect one of you to tell me what it is."

Eli studied a Mets bobblehead on the desk—its player immortalized in hard hair and a creepy smile—watching to see if it would move.

"Where were you yesterday?" Lambert asked.

"We took a mental health day," Ilanka said.

Eli almost laughed.

"All of you?" Lambert asked. "Together?"

"The weather's about to turn, and also Eli's grandfather died and Marwan's family's restaurant has been vandalized twice recently, and then, as you know, there was the bomb threat, and we thought we just needed a day."

Lambert didn't seem to know what to do with this information. "The janitor said it was the second time he got a message from Mr. M about opening a window that kept getting stuck in the music room. But he said the window wasn't stuck. You know anything about that?"

They all silently shook their heads.

Lambert picked up a pen and tapped it three times, then put it down again. "You told me last week that you weren't even friends. Barely knew each other, you said."

Eden said, "Things change."

His gaze landed on each of them in turn. "And that's it?"

All four nodded.

MARWAN

It was weird to have a new appreciation for something you already loved. But being back at soccer after school—with the device no longer in play—felt amazing. He felt loose, limber, light. Able to make connections that might have seemed tricky before. Drill after drill, he grew more focused, more sure.

"You're looking good today," his coach said during a water break. "What's going on?"

"Just happy to be alive," Marwan said with a smile. It came out as a joke—his intention—even though it was true.

It wasn't the kind of thing people normally said to each other, even though they should. Maybe conversation-starter games weren't so dumb after all. Maybe one day he and Eden would play one for real.

Coach said, "Your friend came by. She said you didn't post that photo. So I apologize for not listening to you when you told me as much."

Marwan nodded. "It's okay."

He loved her for doing that but hated that she'd found that out. Had the device told her—or wait, she followed him. Had it turned up in her feed before he'd deleted it? He hadn't considered that possibility.

Coach said, "There's still time for me to move some people around if I feel it'll strengthen the team."

"Then I'd better get back to work," Marwan said.

The past few days now felt dreamlike. Like had they *really thought*, even for a second, when they stood there in the shadowy toxic marshlands of Queens, that their life depended on destroying a small black box? Had they thought, at one point, that it was a bomb?

They had.

And if it felt real, then it *was* real. Wasn't that how it worked?

He thought he finally knew why he hadn't asked Eden how she was doing when he saw her back in school after the accident. It hadn't been just because he didn't know her well enough; it had been because it was a dumb question—the kind you wish you knew the answer to without having to ask. But life was full of questions like that.

Do you like me?

Will you let me kiss you?

When it's time, Dad, will you let me go?

Christos was leaning against a car outside when Marwan left.

"I don't want any trouble," Marwan said.

"Your father told me you'd be here," Christos said.

"He would never do that," Marwan said.

"Well, *my* father was with me. He's at the restaurant now."

"What are you even talking about?" Marwan asked.

"My father found out about the eggs," Christos said. "Suffice it to say, he wasn't happy."

Marwan just waited.

"I guess, well . . . do you remember kindergarten moving up?"

"Who could forget?"

"I guess my dad always felt like a real jerk about all that.

And when he heard I was sort of being the same way, he wasn't having it."

Marwan guessed this was as close to an apology as he would get.

"So I'm sorry," Christos said.

Wow. "So hell has frozen over," Marwan said, fighting a smile.

"Bundle up," Christos said.

"Wait, so *why* is he at the restaurant?"

"He brought his glass guy, to take some measurements and fix the window, which by the way we did not do. It wasn't us, I swear. I'll cop to the eggs but not that."

Marwan nodded and looked away for a second, spotted an Alaska license plate on a mint-green Fiat convertible *right there*. He was half-tempted to climb in and try to hot-wire it and drive all the way there.

"Why do you hate me so much anyway?" Marwan asked.

"It's dumb," Christos said.

"Well, I know *that*."

"It was my great-grandfather's," he said.

"*What* was your great-grandfather's?"

"The space where your restaurant is," Christos said. "It was a little Greek restaurant."

Marwan nodded and said, "Sorry?"

"No," Christos said. "I'm the only one who has to apologize."

Christos held out a hand to shake and Marwan shook it and Christos walked off and Marwan went to take a picture of the license plate. He wanted to tell Eden about it, about how he'd finally done it.

Setting off toward the restaurant, he got out his phone and

earbuds. He was down to the last episode of the beauty queen podcast, but he wasn't sure he was ready to listen to it, wasn't quite ready to be done. He'd either find out the truth about what had happened to her or he wouldn't and either way he'd be disappointed.

He spotted a flyer on a streetlight post. For a rally against hate on Saturday morning. He took a picture of it and sent it to Eden.

She wrote back right away: *I saw.*

EDEN

He was sitting with a few girls Eden didn't know and didn't like. But this was happening. Real life. She'd seen his post so knew where he was and decided, simply, to go there. She did not need backup from Anjali or anyone.

"Hey," she said to him, and he looked up from his phone.

"Hey," he said.

"Can we talk?"

"Um." He smiled awkwardly. "I guess."

Eden waited for him to get up, then walked out onto the sidewalk, holding the door for him as he followed.

"I wanted to clear the air," she said. "In person."

"Okay?" he said, like he had no idea what she was talking about.

"Asking people to send them sexy pics or whatever is gross."

Julian made a face and looked away, like he was amused.

"Coming on to people and then acting like it never happened is also gross," she said.

"I thought you were into me." He looked like he might just walk away.

"But *you* weren't into *me*. So why even ask for the pic so many times?"

He shrugged. "I don't know."

She shook her head and studied him for traces of whatever it was she'd initially found attractive in him.

"Are we done?" he asked finally.

"Yeah, we're done, Julian," she said, and he went back into Starbucks.

She got out her phone and earbuds and thought about listening to her dad's voice mail, which had been restored to her phone, presumably right before the device imploded, but instead she opened Spotify and went to the playlist called "Current Faves." After some serious help from Gmail and Spotify she'd gotten them all back, and now they were on her own account. The last two tracks her father had favorited before he'd died were at the top—one was called "Pain"; the other, "The Day Will Be Mine."

Svetlana was suddenly there. It was as if a unicorn had walked up to her.

"What are you staring at?" Svetlana asked.

"Nothing," Eden said, taking one of her earbuds out again.

"Ilanka told me about that thing you guys had. How you thought I was dead."

"I'm glad you're not."

"Me, too." Svetlana laughed awkwardly. "*Obviously*. But it's gone, right?"

"Yes," Eden said. "It's gone."

Svetlana just nodded and walked off, and Eden started on her way, too. Whatever Aizel had meant when she'd said, "You wouldn't believe the things I'm capable of," well, Eden didn't want to know. She only knew that the next time she got a flight out of LaGuardia, she'd get a window seat and look down at that spot with the tall reeds, where life had become this completely insane, out-of-control thing. She'd think how maybe, when it was all said and done, it had been a little bit—just maybe the tiniest bit—fun.

Looking at the song titles again, she put her earbud back in for the walk home. She picked "The Day Will Be Mine" because the idea felt right.

ILANKA

At the gym after school, the core troupe members were taking their spots on the floor mats. The spot where Ilanka had been during the routine at previous rehearsals had been filled in somehow, by moving this girl that way and that girl this way? It was as if she'd never been a part of it, and that felt right and true.

Their coach was talking about a certain sequence, and then she cued the music with a signal of her hand and the air filled with orchestra swells. The group began to move the way the best groups do, like a single living organism.

From here, from the outside, Ilanka saw beauty in it that she hadn't been able to see from within. And when the girls somehow seemed to magically produce ribbons and began to dance with rainbow strips of satin, Ilanka let a small gasp escape her. Letting go was never easy, but sometimes it was necessary, and this was one of those times, maybe the first moment in her life that she'd made a conscious decision to walk away from something.

When the group finished and took a break for water, she approached her coach. She was going to miss her. Sort of. Not really. It was like having another mother in a way, and one was plenty.

"I'm sorry," Ilanka said, "about just not showing up."

Her coach just listened. That felt new, having a voice that people maybe heard.

"I've decided I'm done. It's time for me to move on."

"Well, we're sad to see you go, of course. But if your heart isn't in it, there's no point."

"Exactly."

"Promise me you're giving this up so you can find something else that really lights you up. Don't give up because it's hard work."

"I promise," Ilanka said. "I will. I'm not."

Ilanka thought about saying goodbye to the team, but they were all scattered and chatting and it suddenly didn't feel that important to make a big exit. She could text the girls she was closest to later if she wanted to.

In the subway station, she stood on the platform and felt the wind of a train coming from the tunnel and heading out toward Coney Island. She closed her eyes against the warm, smelly air and, when the train stopped and opened its doors, thought about hopping on, going all that way again, so she could feel sand in her feet and stare at the horizon and daydream about things she might do with all the free time she'd have now.

Read more.

Trapeze lessons?

Make more friends. Actual ones.

The future felt wide open.

Her father was on a plane home. She'd already asked him about Eliza, and he said that yes, they'd tested an earlier version for an old associate years ago. That when that associate wanted to launch the toy he decided to do it in the U.S.—a more tech-friendly place than Russia—and how Ilanka's father had helped him find the office space, how when it failed user testing the guy had just packed up and gone home. Her dad still had a lot of explaining to do about the data—but from what she'd read it seemed like he'd be looking at a fine and not jail time. A lot of this data stuff, he'd said, was still a gray area, and it sure felt that way to her.

She still felt weirdly violated, but there was more to her than just her data.

She opened her eyes and let the train to Coney pull out without her, because she was carrying that freedom inside her now anyway.

When the train in the right direction pulled in, she got on, took a seat, and counted the number of people in the car who were on their phones.

Fifteen that she could see.

The one person not on her phone was a woman in her forties, maybe, reading a book called *The Awakening*.

Ilanka knew she could look it up on her phone and find out what it was about, but she opted not to and tried to guess instead. Was it about a zombie apocalypse? Maybe a robot, like the device but more advanced, wakes up and becomes human—or monster? Or maybe it was some kind of call to justice—like a wake-up call about the state of things in the country and the world?

She sat that way for the whole ride, with her hands loosely folded in her lap and her phone dark in her jacket pocket.

ELI

They all came to the funeral Thursday morning, surprising Eli's mother, who apparently didn't think he had any friends who would do such a thing. Which maybe he hadn't, before all this.

They'd even come to lunch at a restaurant after. Marwan had brought cards from this idiotic conversation-starter game that Eli had seen a commercial for online—apparently they all had—and had gotten them to agree to play. But when Marwan read from the first card he said, "You didn't really think I wanted to play this dumb game, did you?"

Eden had whacked him on the arm and said, "Give me my dumb cards back."

"Wait, those are yours?" Eli said.

"My dad bought it," she said. "As a joke."

Eli fulfilled all his family obligations afterward, hugging some aunts and helping gather up the photos they'd posted around the room of his grandfather, bringing some flower arrangements to the apartment. He sat with his sister at the kitchen table—she'd somehow managed to bring home a few conversation-starter cards that had been left behind by accident, and Eli asked her now to pose for a picture with one of them.

That was when he saw the text from Aizel. The second Aizel. He checked when he'd gotten it, and it had come right before the explosion.

Just four numbers without explanation. Again without an alert or notification that he'd seen. Again marked as read even though he hadn't read it.

His heartbeat quickened as his mind set to work trying to figure out what it could mean.

The revelation was nearly instant: the code for the door of Aizel Inc.

He should just delete the message.

The whole thing was over.

But the others hadn't mentioned it. So he was the only one Aizel had reached out to?

What did she want from him?

Was he ready to be done?

It would be easy to just hop a bus up Twenty-First Street and try the numbers.

If it didn't work, it didn't work.

And if it did work, then what?

He'd see if he could get the computer to start up again? He'd see if he could clean out the printer and print another device?

Failing all else he could take home one of the old toys and dissect it and see what he could learn. He could go back to the toy site and see if that chatbot came back and said, TELL ME ABOUT YOUR INTEREST IN AIZEL.

He didn't know *what* he'd do, and it was oddly thrilling.

Eliot was used to doing risky things; Eli not so much. Maybe it was time for that to change.

What else was *Aizel capable of?*

What about me?

MARWAN

There was a nip to the air Friday evening so they didn't open the garden, but the so-called tiny eatery seemed larger than ever to Marwan. Watching his father cook and mingle, he enjoyed a sort of calm he hadn't felt there in days or weeks or maybe ever.

He didn't have to ask to know that they weren't moving to Egypt—not now, probably not ever. This—Queens—was home, and the restaurant was home more so, even, than their house with its crazy solar panels. And while it might not be Marwan's home forever, he was lucky to have it now.

He texted Eden on his breaks. Just making plans to meet up for the rally tomorrow and some texts about maybe going bowling on Sunday. It was weird to talk about normal things with her—weird to think ahead to things they might do together in the coming weeks—without the looming feeling of a ticking time bomb in their pockets.

There'd be no fire alarms, no Panera rain, no secrets, no hiding, no bomb threats, no fear.

It felt like a wire had been cut and they'd all been defused.

He'd taken some more notes on his podcast after the funeral yesterday but then decided, for now at least, to just let the device be done, to let the story sit awhile until he could make better sense of it.

He still hadn't listened to that last episode of the beauty

369

queen podcast and was pretty sure he wouldn't. It seemed weird, suddenly, to spend so much time immersed in other people's darkness instead of out in the world, looking for light.

Eli had started a group text: *Send help.*

Marwan felt himself tighten and reactivate, but then a photo came through. It was a picture of Eli's sister holding one of the cards from the conversation game. If you zoomed in you could just make out the question: What is the most valuable lesson you have learned?

Eden sent a rolling-on-the-floor-laughing face.

Marwan sent the pondering emoji.

Ilanka wrote: *Um. Do I know you?* then, a minute later, a smiley face.

"Marwan," his father said. "No sleeping on the job. Table four needs water."

He put his phone in his pocket and grabbed a glass pitcher. "I'm on it."

EDEN

At first it seemed like maybe nobody was going to turn up except for Eden and her mom and the rally organizers: a small group of women with their children in tow who had gathered at the center of the park, all holding handmade posters. But then more people started to mill, and then more people, including her friends, filled out the edges of the park and suddenly it was a thing. The idea was to walk quietly through the neighborhood, past the places where hateful incidents had occurred in the past few days and months. The organizers had mapped it out on paper and printed up copies and started passing them out.

Eden's mom finally met Marwan. And Ilanka and Eli (again), too. He'd brought his little sister and his dog, Cora. Some of Marwan's friends from soccer were there so Eden met *them*.

Svetlana was there with Ilanka. And Anjali was there, of course—with Tristan and Thea and Thea's moms. The Rankins had turned up, too. Mark came over and asked Eden about life post-Aizel.

"So far so good," she said.

"And it's definitely destroyed?" he asked.

"Definitely," she said, thinking it was nice that he cared but weird that he maybe cared *too* much?

His parents were both there, looking happy chatting with

her mom, so that was weird or maybe not. Eden had made a decision to forgive all that, whether she fully felt it yet or not.

One of the organizer women held up a megaphone and said, "Okay, we're going to start now! Thank you all for coming out! Hate will not be tolerated in our neighborhood. We stand together against it today!"

Applause and woots rose up. People on benches stood; people who'd maybe only just decided to join in came closer. She and her mom hooked arms and started to follow the procession out of the park.

When her mom found a friend and went to chat, Marwan fell into step beside Eden. It was a few more blocks—past the house that had like a hundred small birds in its shrubs *all the time*, and past the apartment building whose gardens the owners decorated for every imaginable holiday—before she reached out and took his hand. There was no hesitation or surprise on his end; it was like he'd been waiting for it.

She didn't know what she even wanted with him—maybe what they already had was enough, whatever it was?—and she had no idea how you were supposed to know that. When enough was enough. When enough was just right. She wanted to kiss him, though. Right there in the middle of a crowd. She wanted to kiss *everyone* who'd turned up, though. For standing up for something good.

She loved this crazy place so hard in that moment in spite of everything.

Marwan dropped her hand and went to talk to a friend near the stalled construction site where someone had apparently thrown a ton of wildflower seeds, because behind the plywood wall at the sidewalk rose tall sunflowers and other flowers Eden didn't know the names of.

She whispered to her dad, "I wish you were here," then wondered who would still talk to her when she was dead, but really there was no way to know and it was probably not something she had to worry about for a very long time.

She wondered if she'd ever tell anybody about what they'd all just been through or if it was the kind of thing that only mattered when you were in it.

Maybe you had to be there.

Her phone vibrated in her pocket and triggered a knee-jerk feeling of panic—what *now*?

The Citizen app alerted her to "Two women carrying a large tub of an unidentified hot liquid" about a half mile away.

Eden almost laughed because . . . *what?*

A body was only built to absorb so many tragedies, could only stand to worry about a finite number of random things.

Everyone who mattered most in her life was right here or already gone.

She stopped at the corner and deleted the app and turned her phone off and found her mom again and linked her arm through hers as they crossed under the elevated tracks. A train passed overhead as if carrying thunder. Nudging her mom in the crosswalk, Eden mouthed the words *I really miss him*. Her mother smiled and mouthed something back—something like "*What?* I can't hear you!"—then pulled her arm free, pointed to her ears, and finally threw her hands up in the air—a shrug emoji come to life.

Eden felt like a red balloon and a thumbs-up and a flamenco

dancer and a unicorn—maybe even like she had hearts for eyes. So when the train left silence in its wake, she said it again—"I really miss him"—and her mom said, "I know. I heard you," and squeezed her hand tight as they stepped over the star of Natalie. It was that feeling when you're going to be okay.

I'm indebted to my editor Sarah Shumway for her patience while this idea took shape.

And to the rest of the incredible Bloomsbury team: Cindy Lo, Faye Bi, Alexa Higbee, Erica Barmash, Beth Eller, Jasmine Miranda, Lily Yengle, Phoebe Dyer, Claire Stetzer, Oona Patrick, and Melissa Kavonic.

Thanks to the fab design team of Donna Mark and Jeanette Levy, and to Tony Sahara for the cover art.

Shout-out to my Astoria, Queens, neighborhood—which is both real and imagined in these pages—and especially to the artists who either created or inspired the pieces my characters interact with at Socrates Sculpture Park: Guillaume Légaré, Andrew Brehm, and the late Devra Freelander.

My agent David Dunton @ Harvey Klinger Agency never disappoints.

And I rely heavily on the wisdom of Bob and my SC.

I better mention my children or they'll be mad.

And Nick, at long last, this one's for you.